COOPER'S CORNER CHRONICLE

Famous Faces on Main Street

Our town may be small, but it's never short of celebrities. Travel writer William Byrd paid us a visit in the summer, and New York columnist Jaron Darke will make his home here for part of the year now that he and Bonnie Cooper are an item. We have our barber, Rowena Dahl, a former star of daytime TV, and recently, New York's talk radio host Emma Hart has been a regular visitor.

Emma often pops in to spend time with her grandparents, Dr. Felix and Martha Dorn, who couldn't be prouder of their granddaughter. Emma's call-in show has been a hit from the start, and its popularity is growing. The Dorns say that Emma loves the change of pace our small town offers, and the friendliness of the people here.

Like so many other New Yorkers, she's also discovered the warm hospitality of Twin Oaks Bed and Breakfast.

With the holiday season fast approaching and our Berkshire hills soon to be overrun with skiers, Cooper's Corner will have an increase in visitors both famous and not so famous. And, of course, we welcome them all!

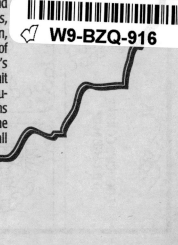

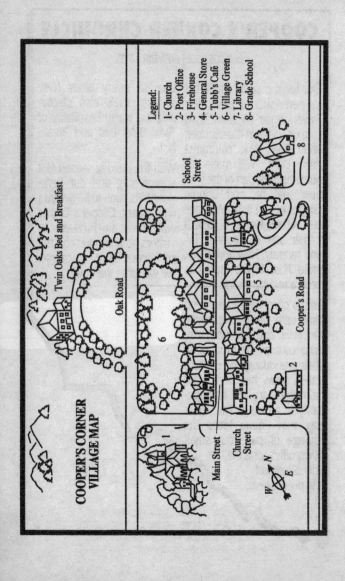

COOPER'S CORNER
VILLAGE MAP

Twin Oaks Bed and Breakfast

Oak Road

Main Street

Church Street

Cooper's Road

School Street

Legend:
1- Church
2- Post Office
3- Firehouse
4- General Store
5- Tubb's Café
6- Village Green
7- Library
8- Grade School

N
W   E
S

COOPER'S CORNER

MARISA CARROLL

Strangers When We Meet

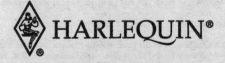

HARLEQUIN®

TORONTO • NEW YORK • LONDON
AMSTERDAM • PARIS • SYDNEY • HAMBURG
STOCKHOLM • ATHENS • TOKYO • MILAN • MADRID
PRAGUE • WARSAW • BUDAPEST • AUCKLAND

HARLEQUIN BOOKS
225 Duncan Mill Road, Don Mills,
Ontario, Canada M3B 3K9

ISBN 0-373-61254-0

STRANGERS WHEN WE MEET

Marisa Carroll is acknowledged as the author of this work.

Visit us at www.eHarlequin.com

Printed in U.S.A.

Dear Reader,

There can be few places more romantic to meet and fall in love than a century-old farmhouse in the beautiful Berkshire Mountains of Massachusetts.

That's what happens to our characters, financier Blake Weston and late-night talk radio host Emma Hart. In STRANGERS WHEN WE MEET, their paths cross and their destinies merge at Twin Oaks Bed and Breakfast. But there are complications. Emma is all but engaged to local Realtor Daryl Tubb, and just days before arriving at the B and B, Blake finds the woman he planned to marry in bed with the two-timing Daryl. Should Blake tell Emma the truth about her faithless fiancé? Or should he be a knight in shining armor and give the other man a chance to prove his one-night fling was a once-in-a-lifetime mistake?

Love at first sight can sometimes be a very complicated affair.

We hope you enjoy reading Blake and Emma's story as much as we enjoyed writing it. Someday we hope to make our own journey to the Berkshires, and over a hill or around a bend we're sure to come upon the real-life version of Cooper's Corner and Twin Oaks Bed and Breakfast and feel right at home.

God bless,

Carol and Marian
(Marisa Carroll)

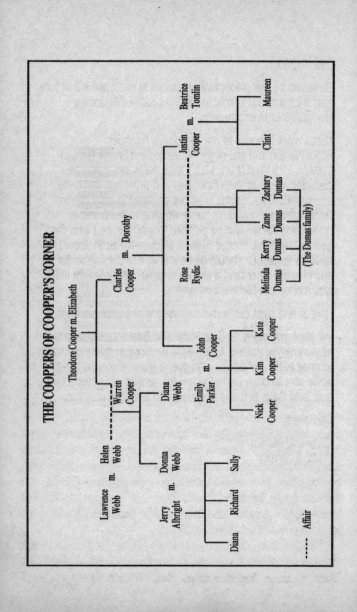

THE COOPERS OF COOPER'S CORNER

Theodore Cooper m. Elizabeth

Lawrence Webb m. Helen Webb

Warren Cooper

Charles Cooper m. Dorothy

Justin Cooper m. Beatrice Tomlin

Clint   Maureen

Rose Rydic ---- Justin Cooper

Melinda Dumas   Kerry Dumas   Zane Dumas   Zachary Dumas
(The Dumas family)

Diana Webb

Donna Webb

Jerry Albright m. Donna Webb

Diana   Richard   Sally

John Cooper

Emily Parker m. John Cooper

Nick Cooper   Kim Cooper   Kate Cooper

---- Affair

CHAPTER ONE

"MICHAEL FROM Manhattan's up next. Seems like Michael's got a problem most guys only dream of. His girlfriend wants a ménage à trois. And get this. He's got second thoughts! You're listening to seven-eighty, radio WTKX, the voice of Extreme Talk Radio in the Big Apple. This is your host, Emma Hart. It's ten fifty-five p.m. Time for adult radio. So don't be shocked at the subjects, and don't call the station complaining your kids are listening. They shouldn't be up at this time of night, anyway."

Blake Weston punched the button on the dashboard console to bring up the volume another notch. Not because he didn't want to miss a word about the guy with too many oversexed ladies in his life, but just to hear Emma Hart speak. There was unadulterated sex in the whiskey smooth voice coming over the car radio, just as there was every night he listened. He sometimes wondered what the woman behind the microphone looked like. But he wasn't a fanciful man, and he knew there was no way her face could match that come-hither voice. To tell the truth, he didn't want it to. He was involved with a beautiful woman, and beauty like that demanded a lot of a guy. At least Heather did.

"We're here tonight and every night to discuss what matters to those of you out there who make this city hum. Men. Women. Relationships. Sex. What's your problem?

Too much love? Not enough? Tired of looking for Mr. Right in all the wrong places? Give me a call at one-eight-hundred five-five-five WTKX. For those of you who've had too long a day, that's one-eight-hundred five-five-five-nine-eight-five-nine. Michael's up next on *'Night Talk with Emma Hart'* after our commercial break. Stick around, folks. This one ought to be good.''

Blake's mouth twisted into a mirthless grin as he glanced at the dashboard clock. Nearly eleven. He'd had a long day. A long week. A long year. In fact, five long years. But tomorrow he was leaving the city and his responsibilities at Braxton, Cartright and Wheeler Investments, Inc., behind for a week in the Berkshires. It was a little past prime color season, and that suited him just fine. It meant the leaf peepers would be gone for another year, and Cooper's Corner, Massachusetts, would have returned to the sleepy little village he'd first come across last spring.

The light turned yellow, and he gunned the Dakota through the intersection, wondering for the thousandth time why he continued to drive in the city, and a truck at that. The parking fees alone would keep his parents in tofu and bean sprouts for a year. He ought to sign up for a driving service like any sane man, but so far he'd resisted. You could take the Indiana farm boy out of the country, but you couldn't take the country out of the farm boy. At least not where his pickup was concerned.

The break ended, and her voice filled the night once more, making him forget about parking fees and beating the lights.

''Hi, Michael, are you still there?''

''I'm here.''

''From what it says on my screen, you've got the kind

of trouble most guys only dream about. What's the matter? Afraid you're not up to it?''

"Well…" The guy named Michael cleared his throat. "Not really. Well, yeah," he finally muttered.

"Hey, I imagine deep down a lot of guys feel just like you do," Emma Hart responded. The husky voice was teasing, but with an underlying warmth that took the sting from the words. Blake tipped his head toward the radio, anticipating what she'd say next.

"No kidding?" Michael sounded dumbfounded, too.

"Sure. Sex is the most intimate act we share with another human being. It makes us vulnerable. Men and women both. Being in the right place in your head is important. Especially if this is really making love, not just some kind of recreational roll in the hay. Am I right, Mike?"

"It's not. I mean, it is love. At least for me." Michael was, sounding a little more sure of himself. "I love, her, but— Well, things haven't been quite as good between us lately. Maybe I haven't been, you know, paying as much attention to her as I should. I work sixty, seventy hours a week. So does she. Hell," he blurted out. "That's not the reason. I'm not James Bond. I don't want to get naked with her girlfriend. And what if—well, even if I do, and then…you know…nothing happens…"

"Have you told her you're not comfortable with this?" The teasing note was gone from Emma Hart's voice. Her program was cutting edge, and she didn't pull any punches when it came to sex in the city, but if you stripped away the titillating double entendres and shock-value lead-ins, her advice was pretty straightforward.

"No. She thinks I want to. Like you said, man, it's every guy's dream, right?"

"Every adolescent's dream, maybe. But what about a

grown man who wants to make a commitment? And yeah, ladies, there are such animals among us. Pretty rare, I admit, but out there all the same if you're willing to track one down. Or is Michael just being stodgy and uptight? It's the twenty-first century, after all. Use a little caution, practice safe sex and why not take a bite or two of forbidden fruit? Stay on the line, Michael. Let's get some other opinions here. This is Emma Hart on Extreme Talk Radio seven-eighty. The number is one-eight-hundred five-five-five nine-eight-five-nine. Get on the phone and let Michael know what you think of his dilemma. He says he loves his lady. She wants to try something a little bit kinky, a little naughty, but Michael's an old-fashioned kind of guy. And come on, listeners, let's face it. That's a lot of body parts to keep track of. Anyone could get...cold feet.'' Her laugh was every bit as sexy and appealing as her voice.

"Hey, this one's lighting up the lines like Fourth of July fireworks. We've got two guys, Hank and Antoine, saying go for it. And three ladies with other suggestions. Let's take Diane from Queens first. Diane you're on *'Night Talk.'* What advice do you have for our shy guy?''

"Hi, Emma. I've listened to you every night for almost two years.''

"Thanks, Diane, that's what I like to hear.''

"Tell him he can call me any time he wants. I've been dating losers in this town for ten years who couldn't get their pants off fast enough if someone made them an offer like that. I'd give my right arm for a nice, old-fashioned kind of guy like Michael who's only interested in one woman at a time. Believe me, he won't need an extra body around if I'm in bed with him. Hey, Michael, are you listening? She's a pervert. Dump her. Call me. My number's—''

There was a click, and Emma Hart's voice reached out to him once more with laughter. "No can do, Diane. This isn't a dating service. We're just here to talk about the things that are important to us Gen X-ers. And sex is sure one of them. We're coming up on the top of the hour. I have to go to the news. Michael, can you hang on until after the break?"

"I'll wait."

"Great. When we return, we'll see if we can't come up with a solution to your problem that will make you both happy. And maybe all three of you."

With that provocative tag line, the show's theme music came up and Blake switched off the radio. He pulled the Dakota into his parking bay in the garage beneath his co-op building and switched off the engine. The last caller had said she'd been dating in the city for ten years. That was a long time to be in the game. She sounded tired of the whole scene. He was, too. Maybe that's why he tried so hard with Heather, despite their differences. Was he sticking with her because he couldn't live without her, or simply because he was tired of living alone?

He sure as hell was too tired for one-sided self-awareness sessions this late at night. He didn't believe in love at first sight. Love was something you worked at, invested in, kept a close eye on, just like the stock market. It wasn't romantic, it was damned hard work, but it was a good formula for success. Hard work was the name of the game in managing a multibillion-dollar investment fund *and* in life. So he was going to keep working on his relationship with Heather, and sooner or later it would turn into love.

Blake grabbed his briefcase and laptop and opened the door. When he did, a brochure sailed out onto the concrete. He picked it up and studied the century-old farmhouse pictured beneath a wrought-iron sign. Twin Oaks

B & B. It looked peaceful and welcoming sitting among the big oaks and maples surrounding it. He couldn't wait to get there. He wondered if he could talk Heather into leaving a day early? He doubted it. She hadn't wanted to make reservations there to begin with. Too quiet and off the beaten track to suit her. An early morning start and Heather Markham were mutually exclusive terms—unless, of course, he caught her just coming in from a night on the town.

Heather had more friends than he could count, and they all partied as hard as she did. She might not even be in the apartment now. She'd said something about attending the opening of a new club in Harlem. She'd wanted him to join her there when his dinner meeting was finished, but he'd begged off.

He hadn't expected his meeting with one of the firm's biggest out-of-town investors to be over until after midnight. But D. Miles Rutter had gotten a call from his wife earlier in the evening that one of their grandchildren had appendicitis and was undergoing emergency surgery in the morning. He'd cut the meeting short to fly back to Florida on his private jet. "Twenty years ago, if this had been one of my kids," he told Blake, "I would have let my wife handle it and I'd stay here with you and make damned sure you weren't doing anything stupid with my money. But two heart-attacks and coming this close—" he touched his thumb to his index finger "—to being divorced by the woman I've loved since high school changed my outlook big time. Money's great to have and I've worked hard to get mine. But there are other people just as good at making it as I am. You're one of them, Weston, so I'm going to let you do what you do, and head home. There's a hell of a lot more important things in life than money, and family's one of them, remember that."

Blake couldn't attest to the family closeness part of it. He seldom saw his parents since they'd moved to Florida five years earlier to join a gaggle of other aging sixties flower children in a commune near Kissimmee. His brother, Ash, a biotechnical engineer, was working as hard as he was, and his sister, Summer, was completing her residency in pediatrics at a hospital in Cincinnati. He'd been on his own since the day he graduated from high school, and so had his brother and sister. Still, he knew they'd be there for him if he needed them.

He leaned against the brass railing along the back wall of the elevator and stared at his dull reflection in the doors. He might as well stop trying to turn his mind in other directions. Like Michael from Manhattan, he worked a great many seventy-hour weeks, and even longer. Heather had a right to question his commitment to their relationship. They had a lot to work out, and he hoped the coming stay in the Berkshires would give them the quality time they needed to plan their future together.

The elevator doors slid open, and he fumbled in his pocket for his key as he walked the short distance to his corner unit. He'd been lucky to get this place. The apartments were from the twenties, big and high-ceilinged, and most of the other owners were young professionals like himself, a few with babies and toddlers. When he and Heather decided to start a family, they wouldn't have to look for someplace that welcomed children.

And they'd have the place in the country—the-hundred-and-fifty-year-old homestead he'd finally made up his mind to buy. Heather would get used to the idea of living part of the year in the country once he got the place fixed up. He'd call the Realtor in Williamstown first thing after they got to Cooper's Corner and tell him to go ahead and close the deal. What was the guy's name? Tubb, that was it. Devin? Darwin? Something like that.

He opened the apartment door and found the man whose name he couldn't quite recall standing in the middle of his living room floor, shrugging into—or out of—his coat.

Blake might have bought the real estate agent's stammered explanation that he'd had business in the city and had stopped by to tell Blake there was another offer on the farm and that Heather had kindly invited him to stay for drinks. After all, that's what Blake wanted to believe—and it was just plausible enough to be true. If, that is, the woman he'd just been planning to ask to be his wife hadn't chosen that moment to walk into the room wearing nothing but her pearls.

"ARI, HERE'S WHAT I think you should do. Try taping a performance of your amorous next-door neighbors the next time they wake you up at three a.m. with their marital gymnastics, and leave it in their mailbox along with a note suggesting they at least move their bed away from the wall and tone it down a notch or two or you'll send the a copy to the tenants' grievance committee. Bet ya a nickel that gets you a good night's sleep. That's all the calls we have time for tonight, folks. Stay tuned for Rob McKee from now till six, and Julie Reimund bright and early tomorrow morning with all the news and traffic reports you'll need to maneuver through the gridlock out there. You'll be getting the best of some of our past *'Night Talk'* shows hosted by my producer, the talented and lovely Armand Williams." She grinned back as the burly six-footer gave her a sour smile while he counted down the last ten seconds of the show with hand signals. "Be sure and join him at our usual time Monday night. This is Emma Hart. You've been listening to *'Night Talk'* on WTKX Extreme Talk Radio. Now, go take on the night.''

Emma pushed the button that cut off her mike while Armand gave her an all-clear thumbs-up as he loaded the last cart of commercials and the hourly news report that would follow her theme music on the air. She took off her headphones and leaned back in her chair, taking a long drink of water from the bottle she always kept on a table behind her console.

"Good show," Armand said, coming into her studio. He would have already made sure that Rob and his producer, Becca, were set to take over the air when the break ended. "Are you all packed and ready to head for the hills?" he asked, grabbing a bottle of water from the little fridge along the back wall—one of the perks she'd requested when she negotiated her contract the year before.

"All packed."

Armand settled his bulk on the edge of her console. "He called three times tonight. I didn't put him through." He took a long swallow of water, giving her a moment to answer.

He was Daryl Tubb, the man Emma was thinking seriously of marrying. Or more precisely *had* been thinking of marrying. Lately she wasn't so sure. "Thanks for holding him off. He knows I don't have time to talk to him during the show."

"You're going to have to talk to him sooner or later. You're supposed to be announcing your engagement to the whole town of Cooper's Corner this week, remember?" Armand was a big man with a face scarred from youthful gang battles but a gentle, deep voice that appealed to female callers and kept the powers-that-be happy with the numbers when Emma was out of town.

"That plan has been changed." Emma got up and went

to look out the window at the blank face of the warehouse across the street. The rain-slicked side street below her was nearly devoid of traffic at this hour of the night. WTKX boasted they were the voice of the Big Apple, but the truth of the matter was that the studio was in a not-so-fashionable neighborhood a long way from midtown, and their transmitter towered over the wilds of New Jersey.

"I hope that means what I think it means. Are you going to give the two-timer the boot?"

"He's not a two-timer." She'd only found him holding hands with a client in their favorite restaurant one evening when technical difficulties had forced the station to run a repeat of one of her shows. She'd been at loose ends and stopped in for a bite to eat. It was the last place in the world Daryl would have expected her to be that night.

It was certainly the last place she'd expected to see him, and she'd quickly left. He'd denied he was even in the city until she told him point-blank she'd seen him with her own eyes. But he'd insisted it was a business meeting, nothing more sinister than that. It was her own fault she felt as betrayed as if she'd found him in bed with the woman.

"Have you told your grandparents the announcement's on hold?"

Emma sighed. "No."

"They aren't going to be happy about it."

"I know. They like Daryl. But—"

"But it's hard to come up with an excuse for things going sour between you."

Emma turned slowly to face her friend. "Do you think I'm overreacting?"

"It doesn't matter what I think, you know that. It's how you feel."

"He said he didn't tell me he was coming into the city because he knew he didn't have time to see me."

"And you believe him?" Silence followed the question, stretching out into the almost deserted station, begging for words to fill the void. Armand was almost as good at getting a reluctant caller to tell the truth as she was.

Emma shrugged. When she'd confronted Daryl about the meeting, his explanation had sounded sincere enough. She was a client, a very wealthy woman whose fiancé was on the verge of buying a large property for a summer home. It was an important sale. The woman was wavering and wanted reassurance... And the clincher... "If I was cheating on you, would I risk meeting her in our favorite restaurant?"

Armand knew her well enough to accurately guess her line of thought. "C'mon, Emma. Meeting a business client is the oldest excuse in the book, and the reason he gave you for it doesn't sound all that ethical in the first place." They'd been over this before. Armand wasn't going to come up with a magic solution to banish all her doubts, and they both knew it. He was a friend, a sounding board and a shoulder to cry on if she needed it. But she didn't. She would resolve this problem on her own.

"I know. But—it's too late now. I promised him I'll spend the week in Cooper's Corner the way we'd planned." Why? she asked herself for about the millionth time. Because she really loved him? He was a good man at heart, just ambitious and perhaps a little weak. She believed that—or told herself she did. Or was it because she was staring thirty in the face, and in the last two and a half years she'd heard thousands of sad stories on the air to know that finding Mr. Right was hard enough out there on the busy streets of Manhattan. Finding Mr. Perfect was damned near impossible. If she wanted a home and family and children somewhere down the line, she'd better quit being so hung up over one misstep, one less than candid explanation of a business meeting with a beautiful woman. It was the kind of advice she gave out over the air. Why was it so hard to apply to her own life?

If it was just one misstep, and not a pattern.

How well did she truly know Daryl, after all? Their love affair had been the whirlwind kind. Sparks had flown from when they first met at her grandparents' Super Bowl party at their home in the quaint Berkshire village of Cooper's Corner. Love at first sight. It ran in the family, if the courtship stories of her parents and grandparents were true. But the truth of the situation was she didn't know if her initial attraction to him had blossomed naturally into love or was only wishful thinking on her part.

She'd noticed so many of her callers seemed to doubt their feelings these days. She suspected it had something to do with the awful events of September 11, which had altered all their lives. She sometimes wondered if an echo of that trauma wasn't in part fueling her need to connect in the most intimate way possible with another human being.

After all, she and Daryl were apart most of the time. His successful real estate business was centered around Cooper's Corner and its larger neighbor, Williamstown, almost a hundred and fifty miles west of where she was standing at the moment. They only saw each other when she could get a weekend free from promotional duties for the station or he drove into the city to meet a client...

"I'm just saying don't end up like the women who call the show and cry on your shoulder." Armand's rich baritone interrupted her reverie.

"Don't worry. I've heard enough sad stories from

women who let their hearts rule their heads. I promise I won't be one of them. Now, I've got to get out of here before Carmen shows up and tries to talk me out of taking the week off again.'' Carmen Quiroga was the station manager and none too happy that Emma was taking time off so close to the next ratings sweep. She didn't want any of Emma's audience losing interest and drifting away just before the evaluation that would determine the station's standing and—more importantly—the rates they could charge for advertising.

"I'll keep 'em listening while you're gone.'' In talk radio it wasn't the number of callers a show engendered that mattered to the powers that be. It was the listeners who counted. A show could seem successful with just a few dozen regular callers. It was the first-time caller, long-time listener on the line that made the owners' faces light up in a smile. People like Diane, who listened night after night, then kept their radio tuned to the station during the day—and bought the advertisers' products.

"Just don't get so good at it you take my job,'' she warned, letting Armand know she was teasing with a smile.

"No way. I'm not interested in your job. We're going to the top together, remember? Nationally syndicated. Close to a million top-end demographic listeners in the top hundred urban markets across the country. Chicago. Atlanta. San Francisco. Producer for the Queen of Late-Night Talk. That's what I want to see on my résumé.''

"It's not a done deal yet, Armand,'' she reminded him.

"It will be if you want it to be.''

"I do want it,'' Emma assured her friend. But deep down she wasn't as certain of that as she'd been three weeks ago. Back then she had thought she could have it all—marriage, career, a family. But Daryl had damaged

the trust she'd placed in his love, and in doing so he'd
made her doubt her commitment to their relationship. And
to the future. She'd begun to question herself—and her
work—in all kinds of ways. If she could be this conflicted
about what to do in her relationship, how could she counsel others with their problems? And she did think of her
show as a kind of counseling session. It was what she'd
trained to do, just not exactly this way. She was almost
more angry with Daryl for planting that seed of doubt
about her career than she was for the blow to her heart.

CHAPTER TWO

THE MOMENT Emma walked through the front door of Twin Oaks Bed and Breakfast she felt her stomach knot in sheer anticipation of sitting down to a plate of Clint Cooper's incredible walnut griddle cakes. She took a deep appreciative breath. Cinnamon. Spices. Toast. Bacon. Coffee. A whole panoply of wonderful smells swirled around her.

She was starving, and it looked as if she'd arrived in time to have breakfast. She smiled. Despite her reluctance to face her grandparents and her acquaintances in Cooper's Corner with the news that she and Daryl were no longer a couple on track for a summer wedding, she was glad she hadn't opted out of coming to the inn.

"Emma, we didn't expect you until this afternoon." A voice with a definite New York accent greeted her. "I'm afraid your room's not ready." Maureen Cooper, Clint's sister, appeared in the wide entry hall with a welcoming smile and outstretched hands. She was a few years older than Emma, tall and statuesque, with thick, rich, chestnut hair and jade green eyes. Her grandmother had commented more than once that Emma and Maureen looked enough alike to be sisters, Emma thought, though Martha Dorn was being generous in comparing Emma's subdued auburn highlights and brown eyes to Maureen's striking good looks.

"I couldn't sleep so I got an early start." She ordinarily

slept in, especially on weekend mornings, but last night she'd lain awake tossing and turning. As dawn lightened the Manhattan skyline she'd given up trying to sleep. She was out of the city and on her way to Cooper's Corner before the sun was barely over the horizon. "I didn't expect my room to be ready. But please, don't tell me I'm too late for a plate of Clint's griddle cakes."

"We never run out of griddle cakes." Maureen glanced through the wide archway into the sunnily decorated dining room. "But I'm afraid you'll have to share a table. Is that all right?"

"I'd sit with the devil himself to get at Clint's griddle cakes," Emma assured her.

"I just might be able to oblige," Maureen responded under her breath.

"I'm sorry, I didn't quite hear what you said," Emma replied as she hung her jacket and carryall on a hall tree just inside the gathering room, which mirrored the dining room on the other side of the wide hallway.

"Nothing, just talking to myself. Is Daryl joining you?"

She'd have to tell Maureen something of what had happened between her and Daryl sooner or later. She considered Maureen a friend, if a new one, and the innkeeper would find it odd if Daryl didn't join her in one of the cozy upstairs bedrooms. They'd stayed here twice before. Daryl's apartment in Williamstown was inconvenient for Emma to visit her grandparents, and not nearly romantic enough, he'd coaxed with his winning smile. Besides, they both wanted to help Maureen and Clint get their bed and breakfast off the ground. That was the excuse Emma had given her grandparents for not staying with them these past few visits. They had accepted Emma's decision, because they were fond of Maureen and Clint and wished them well, but they didn't like it. It made Emma feel torn and took a bit of pleasure away from her stay in Cooper's Corner.

Now she began to wonder if there were other reasons Daryl didn't want her visiting him in Williamstown. Other women she might chance upon him with, or who might see them together? Mistrust had reared its ugly head again. She sighed. Her good mood was gone. "He's tied up for the day—I'm on my own," she explained hastily, realizing the silence had stretched out a little too long.

Maureen led the way into the dining room, with its chintz-covered chairs and huge mahogany table. Large vases of late season mums in a riot of fall colors crowded the wide windowsills, and smaller arrangements graced the table. The bright, warm space with its wide-planked pine floors was filled with guests enjoying Clint's cooking, and the big dining table didn't have an empty seat. Although Clint and Maureen served breakfast for guests only, their wonderful afternoon teas were often attended by local residents. At the thought of all that home baking, Emma's stomach growled again.

"I'm afraid the only available seat is at the little side table we had to set up for Mr. Weston. I'll introduce you."

"You're sure he won't mind?"

"Rules of the house." Maureen smiled. "Open seating at breakfast. Good morning, Mr. Weston."

The man she addressed hadn't noticed their approach as he sat staring at his coffee cup. He looked up, blinked as though bringing them into focus, then rose to his feet, a little unsteadily, Emma noted. He was an inch or two over six feet, just enough taller than her own five feet ten that she didn't feel as though she had to slouch, a habit

left over from her high school and college days that had
proved hard to break.

"Emma, this is Blake Weston. I hope you don't mind
Emma joining you for breakfast, Mr. Weston. She's had
a long drive out from the city and she's famished."

He opened his mouth to protest, Emma was certain, but
remembered his manners. Or, at least, the rules of the
house. "No, of course not," he said. "Please, join me."

"Thank you." Emma slid onto her chair so he could
resume his seat.

"Are you having the buffet, Emma, or would you just
like Clint's griddle cakes?" Maureen asked with a smile
that told Emma she already knew the answer.

"What do you think?" Emma grinned at her.

"One order of walnut griddle cakes coming up."

Maureen nodded at Blake Weston and turned away.
Emma folded her hands in her lap and found herself staring at the top of the man's head as he went back to contemplating the coffee in his cup. He had a thick head of
dark brown hair cut a little shorter than was fashionable
at the moment, and nice ears that lay flat against his head.
He hadn't shaved yet, and a shadow of dark beard rough-
ened the uncompromising line of his jaw.

"Thank you for letting me share your table," Emma
said, as mindful of her manners as he was.

"What?" He looked up at her words. His eyes were
gorgeous—hazel, her grandmother would call them—a
mix of green and gold and brown...and red. Gorgeous
bloodshot eyes. And his hands trembled slightly when he
lifted the coffee mug to his mouth.

Good Lord, he's hung over.

After one more frowning look at his coffee cup, he met
her gaze with a rueful, almost embarrassed expression.

"I'm afraid I'm not good company this morning. I…I had a rough night."

"You don't owe me any explanation," Emma said hurriedly, mortified she'd been so transparent as to let her thoughts show on her face. One of the drawbacks of working alone in a sound studio, isolated from audience and co-workers, was that she sometimes forgot herself in public.

"I have no head for champagne," he said, closing his eyes as though to shut out the brilliant morning light pouring in through the window.

"Excuse me?" Emma glanced over his shoulder, hoping to see Maureen.

"I drank an entire magnum of Dom Perignon last night. I hate champagne, and it doesn't much like me. But what else do you use to toast an engagement?" He took a swallow of coffee and grimaced. "I feel like hell."

He certainly didn't look like a man who had just popped the question to the girl of his dreams and been accepted. Especially since there was no girl of his dreams in sight. "If you drank all that, I don't doubt you're miserable. But if it was for your engagement, let me offer my congrat—"

"I couldn't let it go to waste, now could I?" he said flatly, cutting her off in mid-sentence. "Even if it turned out to be a celebration for one."

Emma's advice-giver instincts were on full alert. She forced herself not to succumb to the urge to elicit his story. An unhappy man, sitting alone… It had all the earmarks of a love affair gone bad. She ought to know. Except for the hangover, she was in the same situation. "I…maybe I should go."

"No. Look. I'm the one who should go. I'm making

an a—an idiot of myself, and all you're wanting is your breakfast. I'm sorry, Miss—" He stood up.

"Emma," she said. "Emma is fine."

"Emma. Please forgive my bad manners and my rudeness. I'll leave now so you can—"

"No…please," Emma interrupted. "That's not necessary. You don't have to go. I'm the one who invaded your space, you know—"

"I don't have much of an appetite anyway. Good morning." Before Emma could respond in kind, he left the dining room abruptly and mounted the stairs.

Just then Maureen appeared with a tray on which sat a steaming plate of griddle cakes, a pitcher of maple syrup, a carafe of coffee and a glass of orange juice. Emma's stomach growled so loudly she was certain the whole room could hear.

"Mr. Weston left you?" Maureen asked, setting the food in front of Emma.

She nodded, concentrating on pouring the thick syrup over the pancakes just so.

"He said he wasn't hungry."

"Perhaps he'll be…feeling better by teatime."

"Probably," Emma answered in what she hoped was a neutral tone. With a hangover like his, it might take longer than a few hours to regain his appetite. She would have liked to ask her hostess more about Blake Weston but she didn't want to put Maureen on the spot. And what would she ask, anyway? Had he made reservations for two and then shown up alone—like she had?

"What are your plans for the day?" Maureen asked, changing the subject with all the aplomb of Emma's diplomat father.

"I think I'll walk into the village and visit my grandparents."

"It's a beautiful day for a walk, although I'm afraid the long-range weather forecasts are calling for rain and even the possibility of snow later in the week."

"Then I'd better enjoy it while I can." Emma took a bite of griddle cake swimming in syrup and closed her eyes in ecstasy. "My compliments to the chef," she said. "I've been thinking of nothing but this moment for weeks. It's my main reason for coming back to Cooper's Corner over and over."

Maureen laughed. "Don't let Daryl hear you say that. You'll break his heart."

If Emma's mouth hadn't been full of another bite of griddle cake, she might have let slip the fact that the shoe was on the other foot. It was Daryl who had broken her heart, not the other way around.

HAD HE REALLY made as big a jackass of himself as he feared back there in the dining room? Blake leaned his weight on his hands and felt the rough stone of the bridge parapet bite into his palms. He stared into the dark water of the stream that edged the Cooper property, replaying his conversation with Emma—whatever her name was—an hour ago. He groaned. The memory was clearer than it had any right to be. He'd been rude and maudlin, and to top it all off, he'd admitted he had the hangover from hell because he'd drunk too much champagne.

That made him a jerk, a loser and a wuss all rolled into one. He could have at least told her he'd gotten drunk on beer. Or Scotch. What normal red-blooded American male drowned his sorrows in champagne?

F. Blake Weston, Esq., Wall Street shark on his way to the top of the food chain, brought low by a woman and a six-hundred-dollar bottle of wine. He groaned and shut his eyes against the sparkles of sunlight that glinted off the water and sent tiny arrows of pain shooting through his brain.

He'd have to apologize to the cinnamon-haired woman at the B and B. That is, if she didn't turn on her heel and walk out of the room the next time she saw him. He'd showered and shaved and taken a handful of aspirin, but it hadn't done much to improve his appearance, if his wavering reflection in the pool below the bridge was anything to go by.

"Good morning, Mr. Weston. I didn't expect to see you again so soon."

"Oh, hell," he muttered under his breath, turning slightly toward the silky voice that was every bit as intriguing now as it had been an hour ago. He grunted a reply and went back to staring at the water, trying to get his thoughts in order. The sooner the better didn't necessarily mean right then and there.

"You aren't contemplating suicide, are you?" she asked cheerily, leaning both elbows on the stone wall and following his gaze into the water. "There are lots of rocks, I admit, but at this time of year the water's only about two feet deep, even under the bridge."

"That would be just my luck if I were thinking about doing myself in. But even if I did jump and hit my head on a rock, I doubt it would hurt any more than it does right now."

"Champagne hangovers are the worst," she said, nodding sagely, a hint of laughter lacing her words.

Blake felt a shiver skitter up his spine. God, her voice was sexy. And tantalizingly familiar. Where had he heard it before? He chanced another glance in her direction. She was wearing a thick, softly woven sweater in shades of green over faded jeans that hugged her long legs and cupped her rounded bottom as though the fabric had been spun to their exact dimensions. She was looking at him, her generous mouth curved into a smile, her intelligent sherry-brown eyes narrowed against the sun. She was even more intriguing outdoors than in. He couldn't be that far gone, he mused, if he could still recognize a good-looking woman when he saw one.

She wasn't beautiful, this Emma person. Not if you judged her by Heather's supermodel standard. But *pretty* was too pale and tame a word to describe her. So was *cute* or anything else that came to mind. *Intriguing.* That one word fit her best. There was a scattering of freckles across her high cheekbones, and her nose just missed being snub. Her hair was between red and brown, the color of some exotic spice. Wavy and long, it was pulled off her face with gold clips and shot through with fiery highlights that hadn't been as noticeable in the dining room as they were in the sunlight. She was tall and slender but nicely curved in all the right places, as he'd already noticed. The kind of woman any man would be proud to have by his side—or in his bed.

Where the hell had that thought come from?

He clamped his teeth together and put a rein on his overactive imagination. It had been little more than twenty-four hours since he'd found the woman he loved coming naked into their living room to meet another man, and here he was thinking about a perfect stranger in his bed.

Well, maybe not quite the perfect stranger. She seemed to be laughing at him again.

"At least you only drank a magnum of champagne. I remember my father telling me about a series of dinners he attended on his first diplomatic mission to one of those tiny, fabulously wealthy enclaves that only career foreign service personnel and jet-setting billionaires ever heard about before the Travel Channel came along. The dinners were hosted by twin brothers, hereditary princes who were politically powerful and huge rivals in business and love—'' She broke off. "I'm sorry. I tend to get carried away sometimes telling stories. You're probably not in the mood…."

"No, go on," he said, ignoring the voice inside his head that told him this was a perfect opportunity to break off the conversation and go slinking back to his room— the one with the big four-poster bed he should be sharing with Heather. "Your story sounds interesting, and I'm sure there's a moral, or a temperance lecture, at the end of it somewhere."

She laughed. "I don't think there's a moral, and there's certainly not a lecture. It's just a good story. Are you sure you want to hear it?"

She waited with the eagerness of a born storyteller with a captive audience. He leaned back against the stone parapet and crossed his arms over his chest. "Fire away."

"Okay. You asked for it." Bracing her hands behind her, she levered herself onto the parapet. He watched, approving. The wall was a good four feet high. She was stronger than she looked. "The first night when it came time for the mandatory toasts, a magnum of champagne appeared at each place setting. One of the first things a rookie diplomat learns is not to insult his host. The princes were notorious sticklers for protocol, and my father and the others did their best to keep up with their host and his brother through round after round of flowery toasts. Sadly, the champagne was a very indifferent vintage, but needs must."

"The sacrifices one makes for his country."

"Exactly." She smiled at him across the small distance that separated them. "The next night it was the second brother's turn. And when it came time for the toasts, he produced jeroboams of the same indifferent vintage.''

"A jeroboam. For each guest? I'm impressed.''

"My father was horrified. His head was still pounding from the night before, but he did his best to make inroads on the stuff and couldn't get out of bed until noon the next day. The third dinner was a nightmare. They were on the elder prince's yacht, and you'll never guess what he presented his guests.''

"Two jeroboams each of cheap champagne?" He hadn't the foggiest notion what bottle of champagne could be bigger than a jeroboam.

"No. A Salmanazar each.''

He might have an MBA from Harvard but he had no idea what she was talking about. "What the hell is that?''

"Surely you know a Salmanazar is more than twice as large as a jeroboam?" She laughed again, and he found the note of self-deprecation endearing. "Oh, dear. My one year of finishing-school trivia is leaching out again, isn't it. Or maybe, that's what happens when you spend half your growing-up years in embassy compounds.''

"Twice the size? Drinking one of those would kill a man.''

"It nearly put my father in the hospital. He had nightmares of Balthazars and Nebuchadnezzars showing up at the table.''

"You've lost me," Blake said truthfully. "Aren't they the names of biblical kings or wise men or something?''

"They're also gigantic bottles of wine. The Nebuchadnezzar holds fifteen liters of wine. Twenty regular bottles. I've never seen one, but I'm sure they're impressive.''

"And give the waiter a hernia pouring them.''

"Exactly. Drinking more than two glasses of champagne gives me a headache," she confessed.

"Tell me about it." He turned and rested his elbows on the stone wall, staring into the water. "I doubt there's a Nebuchadnezzar of champagne in the entire state of Indiana," he said in all honesty.

"How did you find your way to Cooper's Corner from Indiana?" she asked, obligingly changing the subject.

"I live in Manhattan now." If he kept the answers short and sweet, maybe he wouldn't make a bigger fool of himself than he already had.

"Manhattan for me, too, the last few years," she said. "Before that, all over the world. Were...were you there when the towers fell?"

He nodded shortly. It was still hard for him to talk about that terrible day. He'd lost too many friends. More even than in war. Except, of course, it was a war, just a different kind from the ones he'd served in in Saudi Arabia and Somalia.

"Me, too." She fell silent.

"How does your story end?" he asked, steering the conversation back into shallow water.

When she spoke, she sounded relieved. She, too, had memories she didn't want to dredge up in the light of the late fall morning. "After that night, the embassy liaison officer took the prince's major domo aside and explained that it was unnecessary to be quite so...generous. Most Americans, he explained, weren't capable of...assimilating...so much culture at one sitting. Both princes laughed and congratulated themselves on one-upping the foreigners, and each other, and were perfectly satisfied to go back to serving a single bottle at each place setting. They'd made the Americans look slightly foolish and got rid of a lot of poor champagne that was cluttering up their cellars at the same time. It took my father a week to recover from the hangover."

"All in the service of Uncle Sam."

"Well, at least the State Department. And yes, you're right. My dad's boss said he was ready to give his all for his country, but he damned well wasn't going to ruin his stomach with cheap champagne. Not without drawing hardship pay."

Her laugh was carefree and bubbly, as heady as a good champagne should be. "I bet they didn't teach you to laugh like that at your finishing school."

"They didn't teach me much of anything. Can you imagine—my parents paid thousands of dollars to send me to a school that taught such nonsense but didn't even offer calculus or physics on the curriculum?"

"I wouldn't be surprised at all."

Her eyes narrowed, and her tone was challenging. "Are you suggesting my parents didn't have my best interests at heart when they sent me to St. Catherine's?"

He lifted one hand as though to ward off an attack. He found he was enjoying their verbal give-and-take despite his pounding head. "No. I'm sure they thought the school would benefit you greatly, just as I'm sure you made a stink about going."

The sternness around her generous mouth relaxed, and she smiled again. "You're right. I did make a stink. A big one. But St. Catherine's wasn't about to change their curriculum for a student whose math grades were mediocre at best, which made my objections somewhat suspicious in the administration's eyes. They politely asked my parents to enroll me, posthaste, in a school where I could fulfill my ambition to major in math and enter MIT."

"MIT?"

She cleared her throat. "I was trying to make a point. My paternal grandmother was mortified. St. Catherine's was her alma mater. I was the fifth generation of her family to go there and the only one not to graduate and enter into an advantageous marriage.''

''You're not married?'' He'd already noticed the absence of a ring.

''No.'' This time she cut him off. ''I went to live with my mother's parents. I graduated from high school in Connecticut. Then I went to India to be with my parents for a year before I came back to New York to go to college.''

''NYU? Columbia?'' He didn't usually spend this much time in small talk with a woman. Hell, he rarely had time for small talk, period, but he didn't want her to go.

''Columbia. I'm a psych major.''

He groaned. ''That explains it.''

''Explains what?'' she asked, slipping off the parapet. ''My storytelling prowess? I can assure you I didn't learn that in college. It comes naturally from my grandfather.''

He shook his head, watching as she dusted off the seat of her jeans with both hands. His breath caught for a quick, hard second in his throat and he had to pull his eyes away before the hardness moved lower in his body. ''No. Your knack of asking just the right questions to keep a guy talking whether he wants to or not.''

''I'm sorry. That's wasn't at all what I was trying to do.'' She turned and took a step away from him in the direction of the village.

He reached out and grabbed her hand, circling her wrist with his fingers. ''That's not what I meant to say.'' He'd boxed himself into a corner. If there was any way he was going to salvage the situation, it would have to involve telling her the truth. ''I…it's just… It's this damned headache and the fact that the last day or so—'' He broke off.

"You had your heart broken," she said softly.

"Maybe not broken." He gave a short laugh that came out more of a growl. "But it's beat up pretty bad. I'll get over it. I just don't want to talk about it, okay?"

She looked at her hand, encircled by his larger, stronger fingers. He supposed he should let her go, back off and give her space, but he didn't want to, so he held on to her. "I do tend to talk a lot. And to ask nosy questions. You're not in the mood to talk about your broken heart. I can understand that. Although, if everyone felt that way, I'd be out of a job—" She caught herself up short.

"Look, I told you I don't have a broken heart."

She made a noncommittal sound. "I think a hangover cure's in order, though."

"A cure? I've already taken as much aspirin as the law allows."

She laughed again, and the sound carried over the bridge and toward the village. "No, not aspirin. A real cure. Guaranteed hundred percent effective. Made of all kinds of strange and wonderful things."

"No thanks, I'm not up to some quack cure."

"It's not a quack cure. It works. And you'll be glad to hear it's the invention of a real, authentic medical doctor." She looked at him, and the sparkle was back in her rich brown eyes and a smile curved her generous mouth. His heart thudded in his chest. Lord, she had a kissable mouth. He wondered what she would say if he blurted out the fact that he'd be willing to bet every cent he had that kissing her would cure his hangover for sure—and maybe his broken heart. "I think it's time you met my grandparents. You'll like them." She hesitated and squared her shoulders, her glance sliding past his to a point somewhere next to his left ear. "Visiting them is the reason I'm here in Cooper's Corner this week."

CHAPTER THREE

TELLING BLAKE WESTON she was in Cooper's Corner to visit her grandparents wasn't exactly a lie. She was there partly for that reason. It was the other part Emma didn't want him to know. That she was supposed to be there to plan a party to announce her engagement to one of the town's favorite sons. Or at least the favorite son of Lori and Burt Tubb, the owners of Tubb's Café.

She didn't want to talk about her heartache and indecision to a stranger. But she'd almost done just that. She was acting as desperate and needy as the people who called her show. The moment Blake Weston had touched her, any semblance of reasonable thought had left her brain, and she was functioning on pure emotion. She wanted to tell him she knew how he felt, how he hurt...and how angry she was for him—and for herself.

That's what shocked her most. The realization that the terrible knot of coldness inside her wasn't pain. It was anger, pure and simple. That's why, even though she'd denied it to herself long before this moment, she'd begun to doubt whether she truly loved Daryl. If she did, shouldn't she be sad and weepy and feeling as if her world had come to an end? Instead, she felt her hands curl into fists. She'd like to poke him in the nose. She wished she'd stuck around that awful night she'd seen him at the restaurant and done just that. Or maybe pulled the shimmery silver hair of the woman whose breasts had brushed his arm, whose eyes had stared so intimately into his—

"Hey, at least give me a chance to put on the gloves." Blake raised his free hand in a defensive stance as though they were getting ready for a round of boxing. He sounded as if he was only half joking. "I know I'm not at my best at the moment, but—"

Emma blinked, bringing his rugged face into focus. "No. No. I'm sorry. I'm not angry with you. I…I was thinking of someone else." Her hand was still wrapped in his much bigger one. She tugged it loose, feeling heat rise in her cheeks. She should have done that right away. She started walking. "C'mon, let's get you something for that hangover. My grandparents' home is just up this street."

It only took him half a dozen long strides to gain a step on her. He turned slightly toward her. "I'm sorry. I shouldn't have grabbed you that way. I missed that session in sensitivity class, I guess." He angled his head enough to catch her eye. He was trying to look chastened and humbled and not doing a very good job of it, unless he was trying to look like a chastened and humbled highwayman or pirate.

She couldn't help herself. She smiled. "You never took sensitivity training."

"I beg your pardon. Everyone at Braxton, Cartwright and Wheeler, from the mail room boy to the partners themselves, has been enlightened to the signs and symptoms of lingering patriarchal attitudes, as well as the dangers of potential lawsuits for sexual harassment," he added dryly.

"It happens," Emma replied. She'd had enough women call her show to complain, as well as some men. She told them all the same thing. Start a paper trail. Take it to the proper authorities. Follow through. She even had one or two callbacks to tell her the advice had worked.

"I know it does," Blake replied. "I offended you again. It was a pretty lame joke. I'm really batting zero this morning."

"That said," Emma continued briskly, "I'm not one of those women who hollers rape or sexual harassment every time a man touches her. And I'll give you the benefit of the doubt about being off your game until after you've recovered from your hangover."

"Thanks."

"Truce, then?"

"Truce. I'll confine myself to comments about the weather and the scenery until your grandfather's potion can turn me into a prince among men." He held out his hand. Emma braced herself for some kind of shock of awareness. The electric zing she'd felt the first time she'd touched Daryl. The current she thought she'd detected a few moments before with this man. But Blake's hand was hard and warm, his grip firm, and withdrawn in a moment—nothing more. She'd obviously overreacted to his touch back there at the bridge. She really did have to confront Daryl and put this all behind her. The stress was getting to her.

"Don't you mean turn you *back* into a prince among men?" she teased, hoping she hit the right note. Her voice sounded slightly off pitch even to her own ears.

He angled his head a little further toward her. "You caught that, huh?"

"I did. I told you it could cure hangovers, not work miracles." She had herself in hand as they walked along the edge of the village green with its big old oaks and maples and the stern-visaged statue of the ever vigilant Minuteman. "Oh, look. They're advertising cider doughnuts at the diner," she said, pointing to a small sign on a telephone. "I love cider doughnuts almost as much as Clint Cooper's walnut griddle cakes."

"Then let me buy you one or two." He looked at her with a grin that was as wickedly sexy as—she was back to pirate or highwayman, although she guessed Wall Street shark was more accurate. Even she, who cared little about the stock market and whose small trust fund was invested in rock solid blue chips, had heard of Braxton, Cartwright and Wheeler. Blake Weston might not be a partner in the world famous international investment firm, but he definitely didn't work in the mail room, either. She'd bet a week's salary on it.

She opened her mouth, ready to take him up on the offer when a horrifying thought hit her. She couldn't go into the diner with this man—with any man—and face Lori and Burt until she had come to terms with Daryl. "No, thanks," she said hastily. "I couldn't eat another bite." She changed the direction of the conversation. "There's my grandparents' house. Just at the end of the block."

"Good. I don't think my stomach's up to cider doughnuts at the moment." They'd reached the outskirts of the picturesque village, and her grandparents' yellow Cape Cod was just ahead, its small front yard nestled behind a picket fence freshly painted to match the equally dazzling white shutters at every window.

Her grandmother, still trim at eighty-three, was in the small front yard mulching her prize rose bushes. A stack of foam cones sat by the sidewalk, waiting to be placed over the plants to protect them from the heavy snow and icy winds of a long Berkshire winter.

"Hello, Nana," Emma called, quickening her step. She

stopped just outside the gate of the picket fence and waved as her grandmother turned toward her.

"Emma, sweetie. You weren't supposed to be here until late this afternoon." Martha Dorn propped her rake against the dark trunk of the huge redbud tree that dominated the yard and held out her arms. "It's so good to see you. It's been too long."

Emma returned her grandmother's hug. "I was here just three weeks ago." It had been a beautiful fall weekend, the maples and oaks in all their glory, the bed and breakfast filled to the rafters with guests. It was the weekend she'd accepted Daryl's proposal of marriage—just days before she'd seen him with the woman in the restaurant.

"I miss you," Martha said, tightening her embrace. "It seems longer. Have you heard from your parents?"

"Last Wednesday. They're fine and they send their love."

Martha stepped back, her bright gaze zeroing in on Blake Weston. "I'm forgetting my manners. Introduce me to your friend, Emma."

Emma stopped herself from saying Blake wasn't a friend—that would only complicate the situation even more. "Blake Weston, this is my grandmother, Martha Dorn. Blake is a guest at Twin Oaks and he's badly in need of Granddad's restorative."

Her grandmother removed her gardening glove and held out her hand. "A little under the weather, are we, Mr. Weston?" she inquired.

Emma held her breath, hoping Blake wouldn't squeeze Martha's fingers too tightly and cause her pain. She should have warned him about her grandmother's arthritis, but there hadn't been time.

"I'm afraid so, ma'am," Blake said, equally polite as

he folded Martha's small, arthritis-ravaged hand gently within his own.

The slightly wary look in Martha's gray eyes vanished as she withdrew her hand. "Then you came to the right place. My husband's restorative works wonders. I can tell you so from my own experience—many years ago, of course. I don't drink alcohol anymore these days. Too many medications to take. The bane of growing old, Mr. Weston," she said, gesturing toward the house, her movements graceful despite her condition. "The body can no longer keep up with the desires of the mind or the heart. At least until Viagra came along." She tilted her head to gauge Blake's response to her slightly risqué comment, seemed satisfied with the momentarily stunned expression on his face and continued, "Does it surprise you I'd be familiar with the drug, Mr. Weston?"

"No, ma'am," he replied, and wisely left it at that.

"A response worthy of my son-in-law," she said with the same chiming laughter that had attracted Emma's grandfather more than half a century earlier. "He's in the diplomatic corps, you know. Please, come inside. I'll tell my husband we have visitors. Or more precisely that he has a patient."

"Granddad's officially retired," Emma informed Blake as they moved up the brick walkway to the recessed front door with its antique, leaded-glass fanlight. "But Cooper's Corner is too small to have a doctor of its own, so he spends a lot of time looking in on friends and neighbors. And he's a member of the town rescue squad, too."

"Then he must value his leisure time," Blake said, hanging back a step. "I'll survive this hangover without the restorative."

"Don't be silly. Felix couldn't be prouder if he'd invented penicillin. He loves to see that concoction work, right, Emma?''

"Yes, Nana.'' Emma hurried to open the heavy oak door for her grandmother. Blake reached out a long arm and pulled it shut behind them as they entered the small, narrow foyer with its shining pine floor and pale green walls.

"Felix. Guess who's here? It's Emma Martha. And she's brought a friend in need of your elixir.'' Martha turned her smile on Blake once more as she motioned them to follow her through the doorway under the stairs into her husband's study. The sound of a college football pregame show could be heard coming from the enormous entertainment center that dominated the far wall of the small, low-ceilinged room.

"What?'' Felix Dorn unfolded his frame from the depths of an old wing chair, the TV remote in his hand. He hit the mute button and straightened slowly to his full height. Eighty-four, white-haired and bushy-browed, her grandfather was still an inch or two over six feet. Her father was only five feet eight, and Emma had shot past him her junior year in high school. She got her height from the Dorns.

"Grandfather, this is Blake Weston.'' Emma made the introductions. The two men shook hands. "Mr. Weston had a run-in with a magnum of Dom Perignon,'' Emma explained, raising her voice slightly to compensate for her grandfather's failing hearing and his refusal to wear a hearing aid. "I brought him for a dose of your elixir.''

"I'm sorry for the intrusion,'' Blake said. His color wasn't good, and there were deep lines carved nose to chin on each side of his mouth. "I see you were getting ready to watch the game.''

"Kickoff isn't for another twenty minutes, and in fifty

years I haven't seen an entire football game from beginning to end. Why should today be any different? Follow me, young man. My office, such as it is, is right through that door.''

Blake looked as though he might refuse, but he was standing next to a table with a bowl of her grandmother's rose potpourri on it, and with each breath he took, he turned a shade paler, and a shade greener around the gills.

''Go with Granddad. He'll fix you up in no time flat, I promise,'' Emma said in her best advice-giver tone.

Blake's eyes narrowed. He tilted his head, staring a little past her, as though trying to recall something he'd forgotten.

''Yes, go with Felix, Mr. Weston,'' Martha urged. ''You'll feel much better soon, I promise.''

''Come on, man. Time waits for no one.''

''My husband has never been known for his bedside manner,'' Martha said dryly.

''I haven't got all day. This is just like Emma Martha,'' Felix muttered under his breath, but loud enough for them all to hear. ''Always bringing home strays and birds with broken wings. It's no wonder she's in the business she's in. Talking to the Lord knows who on the radio about sex and what-all and more sex, just as if she'd known them all their lives.''

Blake stopped dead in his tracks. ''Talking on the radio?'' His green-gold eyes bored into her.

''Emma's on the radio, Mr. Weston,'' Martha explained. ''In New York City. Didn't you know that?'' Her grandmother gave Emma a puzzled glance. Emma shrugged. This was going to take some explaining.

''I listen to your show in Manhattan,'' Blake said, a dull red flush overlaying the pallor of his skin. '' 'Night

Talk with Emma Hart.' That's why your voice was so familiar.''

"I should have taken a pseudonym when I started out," Emma murmured. It was an omission she was coming to regret more frequently as *'Night Talk'*s popularity grew. She hoped she wasn't blushing, too.

Martha took a protective step toward Emma. "He didn't know who you were? I thought you said he was your friend?"

"We met this morning, Nana. At Maureen's. I—"

"Taking in strays," Felix muttered louder than before. "Well, it makes no difference if you're suffering. Took an oath fifty years ago. Not about to break it now. C'mon, young man. Before I forget what I came in here for."

"I—" Blake said helplessly.

"Go on. You really will feel better in no time," Emma said, the shocked expression on Blake's face sending a bubble of laughter into her throat. He must be mentally reviewing each and every word he'd said to her in the last three hours. "I promise I'll never mention this on my show. You have my word on it."

BLAKE LOOKED at the foaming brown liquid in the glass and swallowed hard. He'd be damned if he'd lose the contents of his abused stomach in front of Emma's grandfather. And from the look of unholy glee on the old man's face, that was exactly what he was expecting him to do.

"Go on son, drink up. Won't do your hangover any good just staring at it that way. It's made to work internally, you know."

"That's the problem," Blake muttered. "I'm not sure it will stay put long enough to do me any good."

"You can suffer for a few minutes or you can suffer

the rest of the day. Makes no difference to me.'' Felix Dorn folded his arms across his chest.

Blake had the decided impression he was being tested by Emma's grandfather. He took a tentative swallow of the contents of the glass. The concoction tasted surprisingly good. He'd expected bitter or sour, but it was sweet, almost syrupy, with a pungent aroma and aftertaste he couldn't place.

''Ether.'' The doctor pulled a chair away from a scarred and dented metal desk and sat down. ''That's what you're tasting. No one uses it for much anymore, but a little goes a long way to settling your stomach. Learned the secret from a Navy medic I served with in Korea.''

''Emma didn't mention you were in the military.''

''Chosin Reservoir,'' the old man said flatly. ''Seems to me you haven't known my granddaughter long enough to get into family history that deep.''

Blake stiffened his spine. Chosin Reservoir was the scene of some of the US Marine Corps's hardest fighting. Four years in the Marines had paid for Blake's education. The pride of the Corps was at stake. He lifted the glass in salute. ''Semper Fi,'' he said, and downed the contents in one swallow.

Felix narrowed his eyes. ''Desert Storm?'' he asked, taking a shrewd guess at Blake's age.

He nodded. ''And Somalia.'' And the World Trade Center, too, the worst of them all.

''Some bad times there. Still, nothing to compare with a real war,'' Felix said with the absolute conviction of a man who knew whereof he spoke. ''But it'll do until another one comes along.''

Blake smiled. He was pretty sure the old doctor's concoction was going to stay down. ''Hooyah.''

A knock sounded on the closed door. ''Grandpa?'' It

was Emma's distinctive voice. How could he not have recognized it? He'd listened to it for twenty-seven solid hours after the attack on the World Trade Center. She'd been calm and collected, keeping the WTKX field reporters on track and coherent. She'd helped keep him sane, too. "Nana wants to know if you're going to keep Mr. Weston shut up in there all morning?"

"We'll be out in a minute, Emma Martha. Don't want your friend vomiting all over your grandmother's Persian carpet, now do we?"

Blake felt color rise to the level of his chin, but he held himself in check. He wasn't about to let the old devil dog get to him. "I'm fine," he called to Emma. "You could make a fortune bottling this stuff."

Felix made a growling sound in the back of his throat. "I could tell you I had all the money I want or need," he said, "but that'd be lying. Not many of God's children have the moral fiber to say no to the temptation of the world's riches. My guess is you make your living with other people's money."

"I manage an investment fund."

Felix nodded. "You have that Wall Street look about you."

Blake didn't think the old man meant the observation as a compliment, but he didn't respond. Age had its privileges, and besides, he was feeling better by the moment. He owed Emma's grandfather his silence for that reason, if no other.

"I'm too old to start a new business. I won't sell the secret to that elixir. That's to go to Emma. She can do with it as she pleases. Though I have a feeling that fiancé of hers wouldn't be averse to trying his hand at making a million or two."

Fiancé? Emma Hart was engaged to be married? She

wasn't wearing a ring. He'd already checked. Engaged? His stomach dropped. He wondered for a moment if he was having a relapse of his hangover.

The old man didn't seem to notice Blake was standing in the middle of his office like a stone pillar. He opened the door. "Here we are, Mother." The tone he used to address his wife held warmth and humor, unlike the gravelly timbre he affected in dealing with Blake. He bent and placed a kiss on her cheek.

"I hope he didn't browbeat you too badly, Mr. Weston."

"Call me Blake, please," he said automatically, his eyes going once more to Emma's ringless fingers.

"You look as if you'll survive," Emma said.

Engaged. Taken. Off-limits. He'd better start getting that through his head.

"He's Corps, Martha," Felix informed his wife. "Emma should have told me that straight off."

"I didn't know."

"'Course you didn't. Barely known the man an hour."

Blake took that as another not so subtle warning that Emma was taken. Was she engaged to a local, or was she meeting her lover from the city for a weekend tryst like the one he'd planned with Heather? He'd have to watch his step. If she was seriously involved with another man, he was going to have to keep his distance. He'd only known her a couple of hours, and already she was making an almost indelible impression on his heart. There was more wrong with him than a hangover. He must be losing his mind. He'd just ended a two-year relationship with a woman he'd thought he would make his wife, and already he was letting his imagination project a virtual stranger into her place.

Well, maybe he wasn't that far gone. So far he'd only

imagined her in his bed. He hadn't actually pictured Emma Martha Hart with his ring on her finger or his baby in her arms. But he was close.

There was no such thing as love at first sight. And the sooner he got that irrefutable fact through his thick skull, the better off he'd be.

EMMA WAS beginning to wonder if her grandfather's potion was as effective in curing Blake's hangover as he'd professed it to be before they left her grandparents' home. He'd barely said a word since they'd left the little Cape Cod house, and now they were nearly halfway to Twin Oaks. His silence was beginning to bother her. She couldn't say exactly why, but didn't want to delve that deeply into her feelings at this point.

"How did you come to find Cooper's Corner?" she asked when the silence had stretched out longer than she thought was comfortable. "It's off the beaten track."

"I was driving through last spring, looking for a place to buy in the area. It caught my fancy." Blake had been staring at his shoes as they walked. He raised his head and surveyed the picture-perfect New England village spread out before them. "It's the kind of place you could put down roots in."

"That's what my grandparents thought when they first saw it. But, of course, they were ready to retire. Slow down. This is a long, long way from Manhattan, even if more and more people from the city are buying property around here."

"You sound as if you know something about it."

"My…my friend is a real estate broker here." She couldn't bring herself to say "my fiancé." She turned her thoughts inward and felt the acid of resentment and anger that had so shocked her that morning stir again.

He stopped walking and turned to look at her. They were almost at the old bridge, where they'd met earlier. Emma stuck her hands in the pockets of her jeans and kept on going. Blake didn't reach out to halt her as he had before. Instead, he fell into step beside her and waited until she stopped and rested her hands on the stone parapet. She chanced a glance at him from beneath her lashes. The deep furrows that had bracketed his mouth had smoothed out. His chin was strong and square and his gaze direct and totally male. Her pulse kicked up a beat or two, and she turned her head away.

"I got the impression from your grandfather that you were here to meet someone a little closer than a friend. I think he said a fiancé."

Emma sighed. Leave it to her grandfather to make sure Blake knew she was off-limits. He was so protective of her. "Not officially…yet. Do you mind? I'd rather not talk about it." How could she explain to this man, this stranger, that she had decided to call an end to her involvement with Daryl merely because she had seen him with another woman in a restaurant? It sounded ridiculous even to her own ears. But she couldn't help herself.

"No one wants to talk about a love affair that's gone bad, including me. But that didn't stop you from asking me what happened to mine this morning."

Her gaze flew to meet his. "You didn't tell me what happened," she reminded him. "Not in detail, anyway. I think I should be able to expect the same courtesy from you."

"I found her with another man in my living room."

"That doesn't sound so terrible." A more intimate setting than a neighborhood restaurant, she'd grant him that. But had her hand been resting on his arm? Had her eyes been locked to his as though they were the only two people in the room—

"She was stark naked." Blake's clipped words cut into her thoughts.

"Oh, heavens. I'm…I don't know what to say." She would have, though, if he'd called her show. She would have had an answer ready a heartbeat after he'd finished speaking. But this was different. He was standing beside her, and the pain and hurt pride were just as visible on his face as they were in his tone. She could feel the tension in him, and she ached, too. The realization, the proximity erased the distance she needed to be objective, dried up the source of her thoughts and rendered her speechless.

"There's not much more to say, is there. It's hard to explain a scene like that."

"Did she try—" His brow furrowed, and she realized how silly the remark sounded. "I mean…did you give her a chance? It might have been a moment of weakness…." She let the words trail off. What moment of weakness could justify betraying the person you professed to love in such a way? "You didn't just walk away?"

"We talked. After I threw the guy out on his ear."

"But you didn't believe what she told you?"

Blake laced his hands in front of him on the parapet. They were big hands, tanned, with strong wrists and lean forearms sprinkled with dark hair. His nails were clean but clipped short, as though he did a lot of physical labor. Not at all the kind of hands you'd expect to see on a Wall Street corporate shark. "She explained, all right. In her world these things happen all the time. It wasn't supposed to mean anything, and if I hadn't come home unexpectedly, I would never have known about it. She didn't say it wouldn't happen again. She can't understand why I was so upset. She thinks it's my provincial upbringing." He

gave a rough snort of laughter. "My upbringing was anything but conventional. My parents are the last of the die-
hard hippies. They live in a commune in Florida. They
eat bean sprouts and tofu and wear all-natural fibers. But
they've always been faithful to each other. And that's
what I expect from the woman I love."

"You still love her, don't you?"

Blake was silent for a long time. The sounds of cars
going by on the main road could be heard in the distance.
A tractor engine roared to life in the barn beyond the
meadow that bordered the stream. At the edge of town,
the church bell rang out, announcing the noon hour.
Emma waited, her eyes narrowed against the sparkle of
sunlight on the water. "I don't know," he said at last.

"That's how I feel, too," Emma whispered, as much
to herself as to the man beside her.

"What did he do to you, Emma?" Blake asked quietly.
She watched as a car drove up the winding lane to Twin
Oaks. There was lettering on the side, dark green, discreet.
Although it was too far away for her to read from where
she was standing, she recognized it immediately. It was
Daryl's car. He was coming for her. She felt a shiver of
apprehension slip across her skin. She wasn't ready for
this. She turned her head away and stared over the brown
and gold hills, capped with the green of cedar and pine,
that rose above the town.

"Nothing as terrible as what happened to you. I found
him having dinner with a woman, and he hadn't told me
he was going to be in the city that night. Nothing more
sinister than that. But there was something about the way
he was looking at her...something about the way she
touched the sleeve of his coat, the way her hair brushed
his shoulder. She was all silver and shimmer—" She

heard what she was saying and shut her mouth with a snap.

"Good grief, how maudlin I must sound." She took a deep breath and cleared her throat. "The long and short of it is, I don't trust him now. I may be overreacting, but I can't help it. I don't want to announce our engagement this weekend. I need time to sort out my feelings. And that's what I intend to tell him the minute I walk through the door of Twin Oaks." She nodded toward the man walking up to the house.

Blake turned his head to follow her gaze. "That's him?" he asked, a sharpness in his deep voice she hadn't heard before.

She nodded. "That's him."

"Berkshire Realty." His eyesight was much better than hers if he could read the lettering on Daryl's car from this distance.

"Yes. He owns the business. He has a branch office here in Cooper's Corner. It's his home town. His parents own the diner with the wonderful cider doughnuts. His main office is in Williamstown, though. He doesn't live here anymore—"

"What's his name?" Blake asked, interrupting her without apology.

"Daryl," she said, surprised by the abruptness of his tone. "Daryl Tubb. Do you know him?"

CHAPTER FOUR

THERE WAS NO ONE around except for Maureen and Daryl when Emma came through the front door of Twin Oaks a few minutes later. Blake had left her at the bridge, explaining he wanted to walk into the hills and clear the last vestiges of champagne fumes from his brain.

He'd denied ever meeting Daryl, and he sounded sincere, but something nagged at Emma. There had been a tightness around his mouth and in his tone that made her wonder. Hadn't he said he'd found Cooper's Corner while looking for property in the area? Berkshire Realty was the premier real estate firm in the county. Daryl had clients in New York and Boston. Wealthy men and their wives and girlfriends. She'd carried the familiar doubts with her to the bed and breakfast, growing angry with herself—and Daryl.

"Hi, there," Daryl said, coming toward her. He gave her a hug and a kiss on the cheek. He took a step back but still held on to her hand, regarding her warily. She hadn't seen him since the night of the incident in the restaurant. They'd talked on the phone, but she'd avoided being alone with him. He'd been astute enough to recognize how deeply hurt she was, and kept his distance. "I didn't expect you this early. God, I've missed you."

His smile was genuine and infectious, as always. Emma couldn't help but smile back, though her heart was troubled, and the tiny seed of conjecture that had germinated after Blake's reaction to Daryl's arrival continued to grow.

"I couldn't sleep so I got up early and beat the weekend traffic out of the city. How did you know I was here?"

"Mom gave me a call. Said she could have sworn she saw you walk past the Village Green with some guy an hour or so ago." He was still smiling, but the smile didn't reach to his honey brown eyes. "What was that all about?"

"A mission of mercy," Emma said, and let it go at that.

Daryl took the hint. He was trying very hard to make things right between them, Emma knew. "You should have called me on your cell phone. I would have met you here for breakfast."

"Then I wouldn't have been able to rescue Mr. Weston from his hangover. And, actually, I left my cell phone back in the city. I'm on vacation, remember?"

Maureen had been making notations in a large book at the front desk. She looked at Emma and Daryl. "Would you like Clint to fix you a box lunch? I'm sure he wouldn't mind."

"I promised Mom we'd eat at the diner with her and Dad," Daryl informed the two women. "That's okay with you, isn't it?"

It wasn't okay, but Emma didn't say so. She had no desire to air their problems in front of their friend. "That's fine."

"Your room's ready," Maureen said, "if you want to freshen up a bit. It's number four. The one you like best." She picked up an old-fashioned brass key and handed it to Emma, her face carefully neutral. If Maureen had sensed the tension between Emma and Daryl, she didn't let on.

"We'll see you for tea, then."

"I wouldn't miss it." Emma hoped her smile didn't look as shaky as she felt.

She could feel the strain in Daryl as they walked toward his car. He pulled her into his arms and leaned against the door, holding her loosely. "I've missed you." She didn't pull away but raised her hands to his chest to keep a small distance between them.

"I'm not ready to go back to the way we were, Daryl. I've told you that more than once these last couple of weeks." She gave a little push against him, and reluctantly he let her go.

"How long do I have to do penance for taking a woman to dinner without telling you about it? It was a business meeting, for God's sake."

When he put it that way, it made her feel small and petty, but it didn't dispel the nagging sense of distrust that ate at her. "You lied to me, Daryl. That's what hurts."

"You caught me off guard. I was afraid you'd think there was more to it, that's all." He raked a hand through his razor-cut brown hair. "I don't always think straight when I'm around you." It was as close to admitting he'd lied as he'd come so far. When he reached for her again, she stepped out of his way. "I'm sorry, Emma. It won't happen again. How much longer are you going to keep me at arm's length?"

Emma assessed Daryl silently for a moment. He was wearing khakis and a wool sport coat over a gold-brown sweater that matched his eyes. He looked tan and fit, though his face was a little too round to be called classically handsome and his hair was thinning a bit on top. To his credit he wasn't vain enough to wear a toupee, but then he didn't need to. Daryl Tubb had charisma enough for two men. Everyone liked him. He liked everyone. It was one of the qualities that had drawn Emma to him in the first place.

She considered his question. It was a reasonable one, if she believed the dinner had been completely innocent. But he hadn't convinced her. Not yet. And she was honest enough to admit she could no longer trust her feelings where Daryl was concerned. "Till I get my head straight," she replied at last.

He remained silent on the short drive into town. They parked in front of his parents' diner, and he helped Emma out of the car and shut the door behind her. "I haven't told Mom and Dad about this little rough patch we're going through," he said, shrugging. "I don't quite know how to explain it."

Emma sighed. Her heart felt like a weight in her chest. "I haven't said anything to my grandparents, either. But, Daryl, please. Don't bring up engagement plans."

"I won't," he said, looking grim. "But I can't guarantee my mom won't launch into the subject."

Emma was afraid of that, too. Why couldn't she just forgive and forget? Daryl held out his hand, his brown eyes pleading, and she didn't have the heart to deny him. She let him fold her hand in his. His fingers were warm to the touch, but that was all. There was no spark, no connection. At least the anger was gone, if only for the moment, and she was grateful for that. It would make facing Daryl's mom and dad a little easier.

"Emma," Lori Tubb sang out from behind the counter, where she was directing the operation of the grill. "It was you I saw on the other side of the green."

Emma leaned across the counter for a hug. Daryl's mother was a small woman, only a couple of inches over five feet, with a round figure from years of eating her own good cooking. "Burt," she called out over the background noise of a dozen customers and staff, "come say hello. I told you I wasn't seeing things. Emma's here with Daryl."

Burt Tubb stuck his head around the corner of the small bar nestled at the back of the building. He was round, too, and bald, with a good-natured face and a ready smile. Emma had always imagined that was how Daryl would look in thirty years. "Hello, Emma. We've missed you these past weeks."

"It's good to see you both again." With a wave, he disappeared back into his favored domain.

The decor of Tubb's Café was seriously retro, black and white tile floors, gray Formica tabletops, red vinyl covers on the chairs and stools that lined the long counter. And a real jukebox filled with records from the fifties in an alcove along the far wall.

Today the diner's tables were half empty. It was the beginning of the slow season for Cooper's Corner. The leaf peepers—the tourists who came to see the spectacular change of color in the hills surrounding the town—were mostly gone, and it would be several weeks before the ski season got into high gear. Lori took off her apron and came around the counter. She gave her youngest son a hug. "Sit. Both of you. What'll you have? Yankee pot roast is the special today. I've saved two servings."

"Sounds great, Mom. But easy on the gravy. I've put on a pound or two the last few weeks."

Emma wasn't hungry but she didn't let on. There was a friendly rivalry springing up between the diner and Maureen and Clint's bed and breakfast, even though Twin Oaks only served breakfast to guests and afternoon tea. It would be a real faux pas to say she'd eaten too many of

Clint's griddle cakes to do justice to Lori's cooking. Emma stifled a small sigh. She would probably gain five pounds over the next week.

Daryl's mother served them and then dropped into one of the empty seats at the table. "I've been meaning to call your grandmother and check with her on plans for this weekend," she said, watching Emma eat with an eagle eye.

"We haven't made any," Emma said, swallowing a mouthful of succulent beef. She took another bite, stalling for time to find the right words, hoping against hope that Daryl would step in and rescue her. But he remained silent, concentrating on cutting a potato into bite-size pieces.

"Good. Let's plan on dinner Sunday night. Daryl's oldest brother, Mark—you've met him, haven't you?" Emma nodded. "I thought so. Well, both he and his sister Rosalie are coming up for a few days. I thought it would be nice if we were all together for the announcement."

Emma kicked Daryl under the table. He dropped his fork. "That's great, Mom. But you know what monsters Mark's kids are. And Rosalie will bring those damned poodles of hers—"

Rosalie was Daryl's oldest sister. She was a nursing administrator in Philadelphia and had never married. She had three tiny, yapping dogs and they were the loves of her life. Emma felt another sigh welling inside her. If she married Daryl, she would have something she'd always wanted, a big extended family. Daryl had four older brothers and sisters and eight small nieces and nephews. None of them lived in Cooper's Corner any longer, but they visited often, and most, if not all, were around for summer vacations and major holiday celebrations.

Emma loved her parents and her grandparents deeply,

but she had always wanted brothers and sisters, a big family. Maybe that was part of the reason she'd fallen so hard and so fast for Daryl. He had all those things, and if she married him, she would have them, too.

"We aren't announcing our engagement this week," Emma heard herself say. The words had tumbled out of her mouth before she could stop them. Obviously they'd been trapped behind the lump in her throat for too long and they were determined to fight their way to freedom.

"Why not?" Daryl's mother looked at her, then at Daryl, her eyes narrowed, the corners of her generous mouth pulled down in a slight frown. "What's wrong?"

"Nothing's wrong, Mom." Daryl didn't sound convincing to Emma, and not to his mother, either, it seemed. He dropped his gaze and went back to cutting up his potato. Lori folded her arms on the table and continued to stare at Daryl.

"Something's wrong. Not two weeks ago you were telling me you'd already picked out a ring and set a date."

They hadn't set a date, not a specific one, anyway. They'd only talked of a summer wedding at the local church. And that was before Emma had stumbled on him with the silvery-haired woman in their favorite restaurant. And he'd never given her a ring. Had he lied about that to his mother the way he'd lied to her? What did that say about his character? On the other hand, what if he had chosen a ring? Would a man who was being unfaithful spend money on an engagement ring? And what kind of woman would accept it if he did? Those were the questions that kept popping into her mind. And until she found acceptable answers for them, she wasn't marrying Daryl or agreeing to set a date.

"It's because of Emma's job," Daryl was saying. "She's got a lot on her mind right now." He gave her one of his great smiles, but his brown eyes were pleading, and his fingers shook slightly when he covered her hand with his.

Lori sat up a little straighter. She wiped at a dribble of water on the tabletop with the corner of a towel she had thrown over her shoulder. "What about your job, Emma? I thought you would be trying to find work here. There are several radio stations in the area, you know."

Emma tried not to wince. The radio stations Lori was referring to were easy listening or golden oldie stations with programmed play lists, canned news reports and on-air talent that never did more than read the weather reports and the obituaries. Daryl gave her hand a squeeze.

"Emma's been offered a syndication deal. It's a great chance for her, Mom. Her show will be aired all over the country. She'll have a chance to reach a million people a night." Daryl was exaggerating the numbers, but Emma didn't correct him.

"So that means you'll be staying in New York," Lori said, cutting to the heart of the matter.

"Yes." Emma softened the one-word answer with a smile. "It's a great opportunity. One I've been working toward." That wasn't quite the truth. She'd thought about syndication, of course, everyone with a talk show did. Who wouldn't want to make as much money as Howard Stern or Rush Limbaugh or Dr. Laura? What wasn't true was that being successful at her job was the main goal of her life. It was important, but it was a distant second to what she really wanted in her heart of hearts—a home and family of her own. A man she could love and honor…and trust.

"How can you run your business from another state?" Lori asked Daryl.

"I'll work it out somehow, Mom. But right now it's

Emma I'm thinking of. She's got a lot of decisions to make. A lot of negotiations these next few weeks and promotions and meetings to attend. She doesn't have time for parties and wedding showers and that kind of stuff.''

"Well," Lori said dubiously. "I can see where all that's going to keep you busy. But I still don't see why we can't have a nice family dinner. With Martha and Felix, of course, and you can show us the ring."

Emma felt the room closing in around her. She was being trapped by the affection she felt for Daryl's mother and her reluctance to make a scene in public. The diner was beginning to clear out, the midday crowd drifting away to enjoy the cool, sunny afternoon or browse through the end-of-season sales in the shops, but there were still a number of people easily able to overhear their conversation. Daryl remained silent. He wasn't going to make this easy for her, and she couldn't blame him.

"I'm sorry, Lori," she said. "But—"

"Emma needs some time, Mom." Daryl broke in at last. "You know, we haven't known each other all that long. It's been a pretty whirlwind kind of affair. She needs to be sure."

His voice cracked a little on the last word. Lori gave Emma a sharp look, one that clearly said, *What's going on here?* But she nodded slowly. "I don't understand this business of needing space and whatnot. But jitters I can understand. In this family we get married for the long haul. Not one divorce in three generations. I don't want my baby to be the first." She smiled and gave Daryl's arm a playful slap, but beneath her teasing words there was a serious undertone, and Emma noticed that Daryl didn't quite meet his mother's gaze.

"Well, I'm sure enough for both of us, Mom," he said with a smile as he leaned over to brush a fleeting kiss on

Emma's cheek. "I've been sure from the moment I laid eyes on her."

Emma might have been reassured by the sincerity of his tone and the warmth of his hand on hers if she hadn't flashed back to the scene in the restaurant. He'd been looking at the silvery-haired woman in just that way, and she had gazed at him with the same intensity.

"I need to get back to Twin Oaks," Emma said, sliding her hand from beneath Daryl's. "I haven't even unpacked yet."

"I thought—" Daryl began, then broke off. "That's fine. I have some work to finish up at the office this afternoon. I'll pick you up for dinner at eight."

She gave Lori a quick hug and waved goodbye to Burt. They made the short trip to Twin Oaks in silence.

"Where do you want to go for dinner?" Daryl asked as he pulled into the shaded parking area along the side of the farmhouse. Emma stared through the branches of the century-old oak that sheltered the house. The leaves were a dozen shades of gold and brown, clinging stubbornly to the branches long after the maples and hickory had shed theirs. "I can get reservations at the country club if you like."

"Not tonight, Daryl. I'm tired." She was going to suggest they have tea together at the inn so she could turn in early, but Daryl's patience was at an end, and he interrupted before she could finish her sentence.

He shifted in his seat, the rich leather upholstery sighing with the movement. He drummed his hand on the steering wheel. "You're blowing this incident way out of proportion."

"I don't know if I am."

"You've been paying too much attention to the women who call your show."

"What women are those?"

"The ones who always pick losers."

"The ones with broken hearts because they gave their love to a man who wasn't trustworthy?"

"No. I mean the ones who can't see the plain truth in front of their faces. They're making you gun-shy. I'm no loser, Emma. I love you. I'll always love you." He reached out and brushed her cheek with the back of his hand. "God, I want to kiss you and make love to you and make you forget you ever saw that woman in the restaurant."

"It's not that easy." She wished it was. It would have been if he'd been honest with her from the beginning.

"Saying you love me shouldn't be hard." He waited. She couldn't say she loved him. She wanted to but she couldn't. Because despite all his reassurances, he still hadn't admitted he'd lied to her when he'd denied having dinner with that woman, and until he did, she could never be sure anything else he told her was the truth.

BLAKE STOOD on the deck that overlooked the fields and meadows stretching up the hillside behind Twin Oaks. The night was quiet, as quiet as the nights of his Indiana boyhood, as silent as the deserts of Saudi Arabia or the ravaged Somalian countryside. The stars were high and bright, cold and far away. The scent of fallen leaves and dried grass mixed with the tang of spruce and pine from up the hill, and a chill hung in the air, the harbinger of frost before dawn.

He'd been standing there long enough to notice the chill. Turning up the collar of his worn leather jacket, he faced away from the starlit vista of shapes and shadows, his attention captured by the scene in the inn's gathering room, just beyond the French doors.

Emma Hart was sitting cross-legged on the floor, playing dominoes with Maureen Cooper's small twin daughters, Randi and Robin. Blake had met them the evening before when they'd put in an appearance at teatime. He'd avoided tea this afternoon in case Daryl Tubb came by. He didn't want to be in the same room as the bastard.

The twins were three or three and a half, Blake guessed, sturdy little girls with chestnut hair and blue-green eyes that sparkled with health and mischief. They were well-mannered and well-behaved, but not above wheedling one or two of their uncle Clint's chocolate chip cookies off a guest's plate.

The domino game was proceeding with what seemed to be little regard for the rules. There was much laughter and jumping up and down on the twins' part, and lots of smiles and hugs on Emma's part. From Blake's perspective, she looked to be a natural with kids. He bet she wanted a big family of her own, though how he knew that, he couldn't say. It was something he wanted in life, and had been yet another sticking point with Heather, who thought two kids were more than enough, and then only someday in the distant future.

Finding her naked with Daryl Tubb had been a blessing in disguise.

For him.

But for Emma Hart, it was going to be a heartbreaker.

If she found out, that is.

Should he tell her?

He couldn't quite see himself in that role. How did you go about breaking a woman's heart? Over breakfast the next morning, perhaps? Just come out with it? *Oh, by the way, that guy you're with—the one you're going to marry... Well, the damnedest coincidence. Remember the guy I told you I found my girlfriend naked with? It's him.*

Your Daryl. Do you need a little more maple syrup on that griddle cake?

God, how had he gotten himself into such a mess? He supposed if you thought about it, the odds of him meeting up with Emma weren't as astronomical as they seemed. Cooper's Corner was a small town, after all. He could accept the chain of events that had brought them into each other's orbits. She'd met Daryl through her grandparents. He'd met Daryl because he wanted to buy property in the area.

Heather had betrayed Blake with Daryl. Daryl had betrayed Emma with Heather.

And then fate had brought Blake and Emma to Twin Oaks at the same time.

Was he supposed to save Emma from marrying Daryl and getting her heart broken? Because if there was one thing he was sure of in this whole fiasco, it was that Heather wasn't the first woman Tubb had betrayed Emma with. He was as certain of that as he was of the sun coming up in the east the next morning. And from what he'd seen of the bastard, she damned sure wouldn't be the last.

Maureen had come to end the domino game and get the twins ready for bed, it seemed. He wondered for a moment what events had led her to leave the city and take up innkeeping in Cooper's Corners. Had she just grown tired of the rat race, as he was beginning to? Or had there been other reasons behind the move? Whatever the circumstances, she seemed to have made the right choice.

With a smile, he watched the little girls throw their arms around Emma's neck, nearly knocking her over onto the carpet as they begged and pleaded to be allowed to stay up a little longer. But Maureen was firm, and soon the girls, lower lips trembling just a little, were busily putting the dominoes back in the tin. As they worked,

Emma teased and cajoled, and by the time the game was put away, the pouts had disappeared and smiles wreathed the girls' chubby faces. They each gave Emma a hug and kiss and followed their mother out of the room into the small library, where Blake had noticed the lower shelves were filled with children's book. They'd obviously cajoled their mother into reading them a bedtime story. Sure enough, a minute or two later they emerged, each clutching a story book in her pudgy hands.

Emma stood up, dusting off the seat of her jeans, and Blake felt himself stir and harden. He felt the same strong pull of attraction he had at their first meeting. An afternoon spent avoiding her company had done little to lessen the intensity. He doubted anything would. Something about her called to him. She was everything in a woman he'd always wanted, strong yet feminine, smart, witty and sure of her own mind. As different from Heather as night from day. Heather's dalliance with Daryl Tubb had enabled him to break off a relationship that would only have ended in disaster, and for that he was grateful.

But what of Emma? Should he be the one to bring her dreams of a future with Daryl crashing about her ears? She sure as hell wouldn't want anything to do with Blake after that. He was caught on the horns of a dilemma. Stay silent and watch her get hurt by a man unworthy of her, or tell her of Daryl's unfaithfulness and be forever connected in her mind with heartbreak and betrayal? It was a no-win situation as far as he was concerned.

Maybe he should just get in his car and head to the city.

But if he did that, it would mean giving up his plan to buy the old McGillicuddy farm. He didn't think he could stand running into Daryl Tubb whenever he ventured into town—not if the bastard ended up marrying Emma Hart.

CHAPTER FIVE

"It's GOOD to have you with us again, Emma."

"Thank you, Father." Emma shook hands with the minister of Cooper's Corner's Episcopal church. "I always enjoy the service."

"That's what we like to hear. Come again, soon." Father Tom Christen smiled and turned to greet the person in line behind Emma, his robe and stole blowing in the breeze coming down off the hills.

"Father Tom's been a real blessing to the church," Martha Dorn confided as they paused for her to pull the hood of her all-weather coat over her hair. It was a cool morning, with a bite in the wind but a promise of warmth in the afternoon. Emma took her grandmother's arm to help her down the steps of the white clapboard church, whose steeple soared into the blue New England sky. "Not that I don't miss Father Ude, I do. But he was ninety-six, God bless him, and it was his time. And the work was getting to be too much for him. Some people had started to fall away. Now it's more like the days when your grandfather and I first moved here. Young couples with children, families with teenagers. Enough bodies in the pew every Sunday to resurrect the youth group and start two new Sunday school classes."

"He certainly has a great rapport with the congregation."

"And he's not hard on the eyes, either."

"Nana," Emma said, pretending to be shocked. "What a thing to say about your minister." Privately she agreed with her grandmother. Father Tom wasn't hard to look at early on a Sunday morning, with his sunshine blond hair and sky blue eyes that twinkled with good humor and compassion.

"I really do enjoy coming to church when I'm here with you."

"When you and Daryl are married you'll be able to attend more often, I hope." Martha looked at Emma as they moved onto the sidewalk and turned toward her grandparents' home, just a block away. "You are planning to live in Williamstown after the wedding, aren't you?"

Emma had been dreading this moment but she knew she couldn't put it off. It was probably better that she tell her grandmother first, and let Martha break the news to her grandfather. He tended to treat Emma as if she were still sixteen, and if he thought Daryl had behaved badly toward her, he wasn't above picking up the telephone and giving him a piece of his mind. Emma wanted to avoid a scene like that if at all possible.

"There's something I want to tell you, Nana. Two things actually. About my job. And something else."

"I'm all ears, dear." Martha gave her a long, assessing glance. "I have the feeling this isn't all good news. Am I right?"

Emma nodded. "I'll tell you about my work later. But first I want you to know Daryl and I aren't announcing our engagement this week. As a matter of fact, not any time soon."

"What happened?" Martha's hand rested on the sleeve of Emma's sweater.

"I...I saw Daryl having dinner with another woman in a restaurant in the city one night a few weeks ago."

"I'm assuming she was a business client," Martha said sharply.

"She was. At least Daryl said she was."

"And you didn't believe him?"

"He lied about being in town that night when I first questioned him about it, then he said it was because I had caught him so off balance. And he didn't want it known that he was meeting his client's fiancé behind his back, trying to convince her that going through with the deal was in her best interests, as well."

"I suppose that's possible." Martha said, but she couldn't quite remove all the doubt from her voice.

Emma stopped walking. They were just outside the white picket fence that bounded her grandparents' property. Sunlight filtered through the branches of the trees lining the sidewalk and fell in dappled patterns on her grandmother's white hair. "I know it's possible it happened just that way. I want to believe it's the truth—"

"But there's something else besides."

"Yes." Emma opened the gate and waited until her grandmother passed through. She shut the gate and lowered the black, wrought-iron latch carefully into place while she sought to put her doubts into words that would convey the depths of her uneasiness. "Beyond the fact that he denied it ever happened, there was something about the way they were sitting there. As though they were the only two people left in the world. Her hand was on his sleeve. She was gazing into his eyes—"

"How was he looking at her?" Martha asked. And of course that was exactly what was bothering Emma.

"The same way. I can't get that scene out of my mind. I can't help doubting everything Daryl told me about that night because he was looking at her in exactly the same way." Emma shrugged, unable to explain her feelings in any clearer terms. "Am I being an idiot, Nana? Should I give him the benefit of the doubt, just forget it ever happened and move on?"

"It's not like you to be fanciful, Emma. His explanation sounds reasonable, although I must say I'm very disappointed in the way he came to it. Maybe you've just been hearing too many sad stories from women on your radio show. Heaven knows, when your grandfather and I are in the city and listen to the program, it seems to me that's what the majority of the calls you get are about. Love affairs gone bad for this reason or that. A lot of them for things that might not be any more serious than this."

"You do think I've overreacted." Emma felt a little shiver of dismay. In her heart of hearts she'd been expecting her grandmother to reinforce her argument. But maybe she shouldn't have made that assumption. After all, Martha and Felix had fallen in love at first sight and never looked back. She probably expected the same certainty from Emma.

"I didn't say that," her grandmother said tartly as she opened the front door. It took both hands to twist the brass knob, but Emma didn't try to do it for her. Her grandmother refused to make any more concessions to her arthritis than absolutely necessary. "Those women with the unhappy love affairs are one thing, but the ones with broken marriages who call you are truly sad cases. I don't want that to happen to you. I'd rather you were single with no regrets than married with a lifetime of them to deal with."

"Others would say it was such a small thing. Not important enough to walk away from a relationship."

"Does your heart tell you that?"

Emma shook her head. "My head tells me that. But my heart tells me differently. My heart tells me if he lied to me about this, he could lie to me about other things. And from now on, every time something happens, I'll wonder and doubt his word. Trust is essential in a marriage, I believe that very strongly."

"I said you had a level head on your shoulders. You get that from the Dorns. But you're also my granddaughter, and the Braintrees make decisions with their hearts as often as their heads. If you don't trust Daryl Tubb anymore, then *I* trust your intuition. He may very well be leading you down the garden path. If he is, he'll have me and your grandfather to answer to. If he isn't, well then, this will all come out right in the end. You take as long as you need to decide to marry him. And if Lori Tubb starts to pressure you to make up your mind, you just send her over here to me. I'll soon set her straight."

"What's the matter with me, Nana? I love Daryl—" She stopped talking at the sympathetic, knowing look on her grandmother's face. "Don't I?"

Martha's touch on her arm was gentle, and so was her tone. Gentle but firm and full of conviction. "Perhaps that's the true question you should be asking yourself."

"KEEGAN, stop raking more leaves into Randi's pile. It's your turn to help me," Robin fussed. "Emma's not raking fast enough." The twins were dressed in denim coveralls and long-sleeved T-shirts, one green, one pink, with matching ribbons in their hair. Emma thought they were the cutest little girls she'd ever seen, and felt the familiar stir of longing to have a child of her own. Sometimes she wondered if that soul-deep desire hadn't had something to do with how quickly she'd fallen in love, or thought she'd fallen in love, with Daryl.

"Hey, I'm raking as fast as I can," Emma said with a groan.

"Girls just aren't as good at this. They don't have the upper-arm strength us guys have. You can look it up." Clint Cooper's twelve-year-old son, Keegan, spoke with all the superiority of his sex. He sent a huge rakefull of leaves skimming over the grass into the pile to illustrate his point. A tall, sturdy boy with his dad's dark chestnut hair and green eyes, he was settling into life in Cooper's Corner with little difficulty, and Emma knew from her grandmother that it was a relief to both Clint and Maureen that he was doing so well. The first time or two Emma had met him, in the spring before the B and B was opened, she'd had the suspicion he'd like to do some matchmaking between her and Clint. But then she'd met Daryl, and Keegan had abandoned the effort.

"Them's fightin' words, pardner," Emma said. "I take that as a personal challenge to my sex."

"This looks like the perfect activity for a beautiful autumn afternoon," Blake Weston called from the deck. "Sunshine, blue sky, the Patriots playing the Ravens on the radio and healthy exercise."

"The exercise part is starting to get to me," Emma said, a little breathless from trying to keep up with Keegan's energetic raking—and, she had to admit, from the sight of Blake Weston standing tall and tanned against the achingly blue New England sky.

"Stop talking and rake," Robin interrupted. "I want to be able to jump into a great big pile of leaves."

"Mine's still too small." Randi regarded her pile with dismay. "I'll hurt myself if I jump into this one. Hurry, Emma, we have to rake faster. Keegan's helping Robin too much."

"I'm raking as fast as I can." Emma laughed, giving her taskmaster's pigtail a tug.

"What if I help you ladies rake all the leaves into one big pile?" Blake offered.

Emma leaned on her rake and looked at him. He was wearing a black pullover and snug, faded jeans that looked as if he'd had them for years. The midday sun picked out gold highlights in his dark brown hair.

"A really big pile," Randi and Robin chorused in unison, jumping up and down, pigtails flying.

"I'm not doing this just for the kids, Weston. I want a pile big enough for *me* to jump into. So grab a rake and put your money where your mouth is," she said, rushing her words a little. He looked good enough to eat, standing there, one hip resting on the deck railing. And she could think of all kinds of places she'd like him to put his mouth. She turned the direction of her thoughts hurriedly away from the visions she'd conjured in her mind. What had gotten into her? She never had that kind of lascivious thoughts about Daryl and the things they could do in the darkness and privacy of the night.

He vaulted the deck railing in one smooth, easy motion. Emma watched with her heart in her throat, and Keegan gave an appreciative whistle. "Not bad," he said, pumping his fist in the air. "Not bad."

Certainly not the moves she'd expect from a Wall Street financier, but then she remembered he had grown up on a farm and been a Marine.

His wristwatch and running shoes were expensive, but his jeans had probably been new when he left the Marines, and he drove a pickup—not very practical for the city, but not as pricey as an SUV. He had money, but he spent it wisely. She liked that in a man, too. He didn't look out of place raking leaves and playing with children in the back yard of a New England farmhouse. In fact, he looked just right. She could imagine Keegan and the twins as his—as hers. Once more her unguarded thoughts had led her into unacceptable realms, and she vowed not let it happen again. She attacked the carpet of oak leaves with renewed vigor.

Robin handed Blake her rake and started tossing handfuls of leaves on the pile. "You're bigger. You can do it better than me." Her sister watched in silence for a couple of minutes and then set her rake against a tree trunk and began to do the same thing. Everyone worked in earnest, and in five minutes they had a truly impressive waist-high pyramid of brown and gold leaves.

The twins dived in head first with whoops and hollers that echoed into the hills, and came up looking like denim-clad wood sprites with red maple and yellow oak clinging to their auburn hair.

"You too, Emma."

Emma propped her rake against an Adirondack chair and let herself fall backward into the pile. She came up laughing and brushing leaves from her hair and the front of her dark purple sweater.

"You look like you're having as much fun as the twins," Blake said, leaning on his rake.

"Second childhood." Emma felt color steal into her cheeks. She bet the women he was used to being around in Manhattan never jumped into a pile of oak leaves. Certainly not if they were like the polished and sleek woman she had seen with Daryl that night at the restaurant. Or, from what little Blake had said about her, the beauty who had broken his heart.

"Let's cover Emma all up," Randi said in a stage whisper that carried halfway to the village.

"Yeah." Her sister in crime giggled. "Cover her aw up. So you can't see anything at aw."

"Hey, you little monsters know you're not supposed to do things like that to paying guests," Keegan warned, but his green eyes sparkled with gleeful anticipation.

Blake had much the same expression on his face, but the look in his eyes was darker, more determined and far more exciting. Emma felt her breath catch in her throat.

"Oh, no, you don't. I have allergies. I'll be sneezing for days."

"You're just saying that," Keegan accused her. "You don't have allergies, do you?" Disappointment was writ large on the faces of all three young Coopers.

"All right." Emma laughed, scrambling to her knees as she looked around for the nearest escape route. "I don't have allergies but I'm not giving up without a fight." She pulled Randi close and tickled her belly. Laughing, the little girl wiggled away, scattering leaves in all directions.

"Get her, Keegan. Help us, Mr. Weston," she squealed. "She—"

"She's a wicked witch in disguise. Oh, help! Save us," Robin begged, laughing delightedly as she got caught up in the spirit of the game.

Blake handed his rake to Keegan, but his eyes remained locked on Emma's face. "I think the little girls are right. You are a witch in disguise."

His gaze was scorching, and she burned at its touch. Deliberately she made herself look away from the man to the boy. "What? You're turning on me, too?" Keegan began to furiously add more leaves to the pile. A rakefull landed in Emma's lap, and she brushed the leaves away.

"I have to protect my little cousins," he said piously, and dumped another armload of leaves onto her feet.

"You just got through telling me you wanted a pile of leaves big enough for you to jump into," Blake reminded her.

"Jump into, not be buried in." Emma covered her head with her arms and attempted to stand. The twins had seen their opportunity and were scooping handfuls of leaves in Emma's direction.

"Too late. Haven't you ever heard that old saw about being careful what you wish for?" Blake moved so quickly she couldn't get out of his way. He tackled her, wrapped both arms around her and pulled her down into the dry leaves that smelled of warm, damp earth and memories of summer sun.

"Keegan! Randi!" Robin shrieked "Now we've got them both. Hurry! Hurry! Cover them up!"

Leaves rained down over both of them. Blake rolled on top of Emma, shielding her from the onslaught. "Those little turncoats." He laughed, his face inches from hers, his shoulders taking the brunt of the assault unleashed by their giggling attackers.

Sunlight filtered through the leaves. Dust tickled her nose. But those things were only peripheral distractions. For Emma the world momentarily narrowed to exclude everything but the two of them. She was aware with every fiber of her being of the hard length of his body so close to hers, of his arms holding her safe.

He smelled of earth and the spice of a rich cologne. His eyes were dark and unreadable in the gloom of their almost weightless prison. Her fingers itched to bury themselves in the silky hair at the nape of his neck, and she wanted to run her hands over the corded muscles of his arms and the rock solidity of his back. She wanted to feel his legs tangle with hers, his lips on hers.

To be alone with him. That's what she'd wanted since

they'd first met. It didn't matter where or how. She'd never even known you could construct a lovers' cocoon from fallen leaves, but for the moment that's what they had.

She had Blake Weston to herself, and any thoughts other than that refused to take root in her brain.

She stared at him. She didn't close her eyes as his head came nearer, his lips mere inches from hers. "Now what?" he asked, and his voice was as warm and earthy as the scents and textures that surrounded them.

"Kiss me." She didn't wait for him to do as she bid, but lifted her head, brushed her lips across his. He angled his mouth just slightly, enough for her to know that he wanted inside, and she wanted that, too. Opening her mouth to his, she tasted strength and desire. A heated rush swirled through her veins, pooling low inside and sending tiny arcs of sensation to every nerve ending she possessed. She wanted time to stand still so that their kiss could last forever.

Blake lifted his head and broke the kiss. He reared out of the leaves, scattering them to the four winds, pulling her up with him. Keegan had been standing above them with another armful of leaves. He went head over heels backward, and the twins leaped on him like playful wolf puppies, laughing and pummeling him with their fists, giving Emma and Blake a moment of near solitude in a chaos of autumn splendor.

"Oh, hell," he muttered. "That's the last damned thing we should have done."

Emma didn't know what to say next. She wanted to tell him he was wrong, that incredibly enough, it was exactly the right thing to do, but she never got the chance. Clint was standing on the deck, arms braced on the railing. "Emma, Daryl Tubb is on the phone for you. He said he'll be here in twenty minutes. He wants to take you to Williamstown for dinner.''

Blake's hands were still clasped lightly around her forearms. He stiffened, and his grip tightened almost painfully for a split second. Then he let her go.

She wished he hadn't.

But then, she would have stood there staring at him all day if she had her choice.

She didn't want to have dinner with Daryl. She wanted to be alone in her room and think about what had just happened to her. Because something had happened. She just couldn't tell what. ''I...tell him I can't be ready in twenty minutes, Clint. There are so many leaves—''

Clint waved her objections aside. ''You're a guest, not the gardener. I'll help Keegan finish the raking.''

Blake stepped away, brushed leaves out of his hair and off the front of his sweater. ''Go,'' he said, not looking at her as he bent to pick up the rake he'd discarded earlier. ''He's waiting for you.''

CHAPTER SIX

THE HOUSE WAS QUIET when Emma let herself in, shutting the heavy oak door behind her as softly as she could. She leaned against the wooden panel for a moment, drinking in the silence and the scents of wood smoke, furniture polish and potpourri from the bowl on a table beside the door. The dining room was deeply shadowed, the silver and glass of the breakfast settings shining fitfully in the reflected light from the gathering room beyond. A figure stirred in one of the wing chairs flanking the massive stone fireplace, which still held the glowing embers of the evening's fire. It was Maureen, her auburn hair gleaming in the lamplight. She put down the yellow legal pad she'd held in her lap and stretched her arms over her head.

"I must have fallen asleep."

"I'm sorry if I disturbed you, coming in so late."

"Don't apologize, Emma. It isn't late. I came in here to work because Clint's watching an old western and the noise was distracting me. I guess the fire and the quiet were too much for me."

She didn't look as if she'd been dozing. Her eyes were clear and alert, watchful. Emma had noticed that quality about the older woman before. It sometimes made her wonder what Maureen's life had been like before she came to Cooper's Corner. Clint had been an architect in New York. That was common knowledge in the village. But Maureen's past was a blank page. Lori and Burt Tubb weren't even sure if she was divorced or widowed. Philo and Phyllis Cooper, the owners of Cooper's Corner General Store and Daryl's parents' biggest rivals in the town's gossip race, either didn't know or weren't telling. They were, after all, distant cousins of Maureen's and Clint's. As a doctor's wife, Emma's grandmother had long ago learned to keep information to herself, but that didn't mean she wasn't above speculating on her friends' and neighbors' lives when she had Emma for an audience. "There's a story in Maureen's past," she had said more than once. "Mark my words. And it's not a happy one, I think."

"Am I the last guest in tonight?" Emma asked.

"Yes. There's only you and Mr. Weston, and the couple from New Jersey who are visiting their grandson at Williams College. They'll be leaving tomorrow. It's a slow time until the holidays and the skiing season get in gear. Or so I've been told by the other merchants in town." Maureen moved past Emma and turned the dead bolt on the door. It slid into place with a heavy, satisfying click. "There, all safe and sound for the night. Would you like a cup of tea or hot chocolate before you turn in?" she asked.

"Please, don't bother."

"It's no bother. It's hospitality. Personalized service with a smile. It's what we intend to build our reputation on here at Twin Oaks. Besides, it's already made."

"If you insist."

"I'll bring it right out, and if you don't mind I'll join you."

"I'd like that."

"While you're waiting, there are some pictures on the coffee table you might like to see. They're of Bonnie

Cooper and Jaron Darke's wedding reception. You've met Bonnie, haven't you?''

"Yes, I have. She's your plumber, isn't she?"

"And our shirttail cousin."

"Philo and Phyllis are her parents."

"You're learning your Cooper's Corner family trees very well."

Emma grinned. "My grandparents keep me well informed of what goes on in town."

She picked up the photo album, grateful for the reprieve from having to climb the stairs to her empty room. The room she was still refusing to share with Daryl. Emma had been mulling over the idea of leaving Twin Oaks to stay with her grandparents for the rest of the week. But now that Maureen had mentioned a slowdown in business, she was reluctant to be the cause of lost revenue.

Daryl had been as charming as usual at dinner. He'd kept his hands to himself, but she could tell his patience was wearing thin. He was tired of explaining himself, tired of apologizing. He didn't understand why she could not forgive and forget, and since she couldn't explain it herself, the evening had been filled with awkward silences and stilted conversation about nothing in particular.

Until Daryl had told her he wouldn't be able to spend time with her on Monday. He had two prospects to show the old McGillicuddy farm.

"The deal I've been working on for the past few months is going to fall through," he'd said. "It's been shaky for weeks. I told you that's why I was having dinner with Heather that night in the city—"

A chill shivered its way down her spine, lifting the short hairs at the nape of her neck. He had called her Heather. Not Ms. Whatever Her Name Was. Not my client's fiancée. *Heather.* As though they'd known each other all their lives.

When he'd seen the look on her face, he dropped the subject and began to talk of something else.

A few minutes later he'd driven her to Twin Oaks, angry and frustrated once more, and they'd parted in silence.

Maureen came into the room with a steaming silver pot on a tray and cinnamon-sugar toast cut in wedges on a flowered china plate. "You look as if you could use a little nourishment."

The cups and saucers were flowered china, too, but the patterns were different, one pastel daises and ivy tendrils, the other a riot of pink roses and forget-me-nots. Emma watched as Maureen poured hot chocolate for both of them. She wasn't hungry but took a slice of toast anyway, grateful to have something to think about other than her troubled relationship with Daryl. She took a bite and then another, hungrier than she'd thought. She'd eaten very little of her expensive dinner, she realized.

When she finished her toast, Emma opened the album and glanced through the photos of a smiling, brown-haired woman and the tall, dark-haired man at her side. Emma recognized Bonnie at once, and was surprised to see her wearing a designer gown and three-inch spike heels. Whenever Emma had seen her in Cooper's Corner, she had been wearing jeans and a tool belt.

Maureen saw the look of surprise on her face and interpreted it correctly.

"Bonnie cleans up well, doesn't she," she said with a smile. "The wedding was here in Cooper's Corner. Very simple. Just as she wanted. But Jaron's mother planned the reception in New York—or rather, his mother and Bonnie's aunt did. It was very top drawer. Very posh.

Clint had to wear a tux. He hasn't had it out of the closet since we moved up here."

"He looks very good in it." Emma tapped one of the photos showing Clint, smiling broadly, with his arms around both newlyweds. "I don't see you in any of the pictures."

'Oh, I was there. We all went up and back by bus."

"I hope they'll be very happy."

"I hope so, too. They're planning to split their time between New York and here. You'll probably meet Jaron sometime soon."

Emma put the album on the table. She found she liked being able to put names to faces around town. She'd never lived in a small place like Cooper's Corner, but she was beginning to think she could adjust to it very easily.

She spied the legal pad Maureen had put down. It was filled with carelessly scrawled notes and what looked like a menu. "Perhaps I'll get the opportunity to meet Jaron over the holidays. Thanksgiving is just around the corner. I imagine you're booked solid for that weekend," Emma said, taking her cue from the underscored heading at the top of the page.

"We do have bookings." Maureen's smile was tired, but laced with satisfaction. "And our father will be here for a visit. It's his first trip home in a year. He's been teaching in France since our mother died." The rhythms and cadences of her speech were pure New York. Emma had noticed her accent intensified when she relaxed and settled into a conversation, as she was doing now. She looked less edgy than she had the first time Emma had stayed at the inn. Once or twice Emma thought she'd seen a haunted look in Maureen's eyes, an uneasiness that had little to do with the day-to-day problems of getting Twin Oaks up and running.

Of course there had been that business of the guest who had disappeared from his room, but he'd later been found safe. And her grandmother had mentioned vague rumors of a private detective nosing around town, asking questions about Maureen and Clint that the locals considered none of his business. If Twin Oaks had been hers, Emma decided, she would also sit up each evening to make sure her guests were tucked in safe and sound and the house was secured, just as Maureen did.

"We're planning a big party. Turkey, chestnut stuffing, oyster stew, pumpkin pie. All the trimmings. We're making a real celebration of it. We'll ask Ed Taylor, the man who raises those marvelous free-range chickens. He hardly has any family left and he always looks as if he could use a good meal. Grace Penrose, too. You know her, I believe. She'll be neck deep in planning for the Christmas Festival, so I thought it would be nice to save her the trouble of cooking a big meal. And Beth Young will be dropping by later, I hope, to play piano for those of us who simply cannot sit through another football game on TV. Will you be spending Thanksgiving with your grandparents?"

"I hope to," Emma said carefully.

Maureen watched her closely for a moment over the rim of her cup. "We'd love to have you all join us here. I know how much of an effort cooking a big dinner would be for your grandmother. And—"

"And you know I can't boil water," Emma said, laughing.

Maureen opened her mouth as if to protest, then she laughed, too. "I was going to phrase it more delicately," she admitted. "Please come—unless you've already made plans to join the Tubb family."

Emma took a deep breath and set her cup on the saucer

with a click. She might as well get used to making this speech. "Daryl and I have hit a rough patch. I don't know where we'll be in our relationship by Thanksgiving."

"I see." Maureen looked into her cup for a moment before returning her gaze to Emma's face. "I couldn't help but notice he's...not around much. I won't ask you any more questions, but if you do ever want to talk about it, I'm here."

"Thanks, Maureen. I'm having trouble explaining to myself what's wrong. It's damned near impossible to make sense of it to anyone else. Including Daryl. His mother is more than a little peeved at me for postponing our engagement announcement."

Maureen lifted a brow. "Ah, so there *was* going to be an announcement this week. Forgive me, but Lori Tubb has been dropping hints all over town."

Emma winced. "I was afraid of that."

"I know this one is so old it has a white beard longer than Rip Van Winkle's, but better safe than sorry. Take it from a woman who knows, to her sorrow, what can happen when you leap headlong into love with the wrong man."

"The twins' father?" Emma asked carefully.

"Yes. But it's long over and done with, and I won't bore you with the sad details." Maureen, too, set her cup on the saucer with a little more force than necessary. "You look tired. I'll leave you to go to bed now. Pleasant dreams, Emma."

"Thank you. That would be a nice change of pace." So there was an unhappy relationship in Maureen's past, Emma thought. She hadn't been certain if Maureen was widowed or divorced, or had ever been married at all. It wasn't any of her business, but she did wonder what exactly had happened in her new friend's past. Maureen's voice and expression had hardened when she spoke of the twins' father. There was sorrow in her eyes, and regret, deep and heartfelt. Emma remembered her grandmother's words. *Not a happy story.*

Maureen spoke with the sincerity of a woman who knew what she was talking about. Her words were a warning that Emma was more than a little inclined to heed. She didn't want to end up with the wrong man, be it Daryl Tubb or anyone else.

SHE COULD SEE his silhouette outlined against the many-paned dormer window at the top of the stairs. He was sitting with one leg propped on the window seat, his hand resting on his knee. And he was watching her, as silent as the sleeping house.

At the top of the steps, she hesitated, knowing she wouldn't be able to move past him to her room, pretending they had nothing to say to each other beyond a polite good-night. She gave it a shot anyway, and got as far as putting the key in the lock.

"Emma." His voice was quiet, low-pitched and as arresting as a hand on her arm. Turning slowly, she faced him. "We need to talk."

She sighed. "I know."

He straightened and patted the cushioned seat beside him. "Come, sit down. The view is spectacular."

She did as he asked, settling gingerly onto the window seat as far from him as she could manage. But the dormer was narrow, and his thigh was mere inches from hers, so close she could feel the heat of his body and sense the strength in the bone and muscle of his leg.

The view *was* spectacular, so she concentrated on that and not on Blake's nearness. The village was spread out below them, sleeping in the moonlight. Starlight flickered on the water of the creek as it wound its way through the meadow. The steeple of the church was touched with gilt, and the almost bare branches of the trees bowed and curtsied in the light wind.

"There's a weather change coming," Emma said. "Tomorrow will be the last of the warm days, I believe."

He ignored her attempt to keep the conversation in shallow water. "The first thing I want to say is I'm sorry for what happened this afternoon."

"You didn't have to wait up to tell me that," she said.

"Yes, I did. I'm not good at apologizing, but I'm getting better at it with you. It seems like just about every time we meet, I end up saying I'm sorry for one thing or another." There was a trace of amusement in his deep voice. "I shouldn't have kissed you."

Emma felt a flare of temper. "I think I had something to do with that kiss." She was amazed at the note of challenge that had crept into her voice as if of its own accord. Her eyes were becoming accustomed to the darkness of their alcove, and she saw him open his mouth as if to deny her words, then shut it abruptly. "As a matter of fact, I distinctly remember asking you to kiss me. I'm the one who should apologize. I took advantage of your broken heart."

Blake made a strangled noise that sounded suspiciously like someone choking back laughter. "My broken heart?"

"Yes," she said. "It was wrong of me. Just because I've got myself in a bind over a man doesn't mean I should take advantage of the next one who comes along."

"And just because I'm mad as hell at one woman— not brokenhearted over her, mind you—doesn't mean I should take advantage of the next woman who crosses my path."

He had leaned closer. Only a little, an inch or two, but

it was too much for Emma. She'd been trying to forget that explosive kiss among the leaves for the last six hours. Now his nearness brought it back in vivid detail, and her insides tingled with longing and desire just as they had when it happened. Perhaps even more strongly than before. She panicked and started to rise. "Then no apologies are necessary from either of us. No harm done, right?" His hand closed over her wrist, and he tugged her gently down beside him again.

"Emma, we have to talk. This isn't just about Heather's infidelity—"

"Heather?"

"Heather Markham. The woman I was living with."

Emma's breath tightened in her chest. *Heather.* That Blake's faithless lover had the same name as the woman Daryl had been with that night was only a coincidence, wasn't it? Women with the name of Heather were thick as fallen leaves on the ground these days.

She tried to relax. Another coincidence. That was all. But his mention of Daryl's name coupled with his ex-lover's had started a chain reaction in her mind.

"There's something between us, Emma. Something that doesn't seem to want to go away."

Something like love at first sight?

But that was what she'd experienced with Daryl, wasn't it?

She was so confused she couldn't think straight. She felt as if she'd drunk an entire bottle of wine instead of a cup of hot chocolate. Being near Blake Weston addled her brain and inflamed her body.

Her skin burned where he touched her. Her body vibrated to every sound he made. She wanted to throw herself against his chest, steady her ragged breathing with the strong, solid beat of his heart. She wanted to pour out her problems and, heaven help her, let him solve them for her. She wanted Daryl Tubb to drop off the face of the earth, never to darken her pathway again.

"Emma," he said, running his palm over her hair, cupping her cheek. She wanted to turn her face into his hand and snuggle close, like a kitten. "Admit it. There is something, isn't there?"

"Yes. But I don't know what it is. And since I'm in the middle of one messed-up relationship, I sure as hell don't want to start another one."

He didn't pull back as she almost hoped he would. He was still close enough that if she lifted herself just a little, their lips would touch. And heaven and earth would trade places again, if only for a moment. "Fair enough. I'll wait. I don't have unanswered questions about what happened between me and Heather. It's over. It had been over a long time before she walked naked into my living room to meet another man."

"I...I don't know what I feel now." She wasn't ready to make the almost unbelievable connection between Heather and Daryl, to wonder at the amused Fate that had brought her and Blake to Twin Oaks the same week. She wasn't ready to start tugging on all the ends of her unraveling relationship and follow the strings to their implausible, but seemingly more and more likely, end. *Heather and Daryl. Daryl and Heather.* The names repeated themselves over and over in her mind.

"Go to bed, Emma," Blake said quietly. "We can't resolve anything tonight. And if I sit here watching you in the moonlight any longer, I'll just end up adding more complications to the situation."

"Like kissing me again?" She was losing her sanity, saying those words aloud.

Blake chuckled. "I thought you kissed me."

Her head was whirling, half with delight at the anticipation of feeling his lips on hers again, half with dread
for the dark hours of the night when she was bound to
wake up and start worrying all over again. It was so much
easier to give advice on the radio. There she was in control. She could tell her callers what she thought was best
for them and be fairly confident she was right.

But this was different.

This was her life, and damned if she knew what was
right.

He stood up, pulling her with him. There would be no
kiss, she could tell, and bit back a sigh of mingled disappointment and relief. He wasn't going to solve her dilemma for her. She was going to have to do that for herself. He turned the key she'd left in the old-fashioned lock
and opened her door on silent hinges. He gave her a little
push inside and closed the door.

"Good night, Emma," she heard him say, very softly,
as he headed down the hall. "Tomorrow we'll talk."

CHAPTER SEVEN

EMMA WAS UP EARLY the next day, and like the coward she felt herself to be, sneaked out of the inn through a side door, ignored the beauty of the cool morning that was exactly suited to a brisk walk into town and drove her car straight to her grandparents' house.

Her grandmother was opening the garage door. She was dressed in wool slacks and the turquoise all-weather coat she'd worn to church the day before. "Want a ride?" Emma asked, rolling down the window.

"You don't even know where I'm going," Martha responded with a smile.

"I don't care. I'll drive you to the ends of the earth." Away from the two men she was caught between.

Martha put her hand over her heart and rolled her eyes. "What a dutiful granddaughter you are. I'm just going to the hairdresser and the market, so you're off the hook. But you might ask if your grandfather wants a ride. He's going out to make a few house calls this morning."

"I imagine the AMA frowns on retired doctors making house calls."

"He calls it visiting old friends, but he always takes his bag. I think he's going to check on Ed Taylor and one or two others." She waved her hand in the air. "I've forgotten who. Must be the beginning of Alzheimer's."

"Or maybe you're thinking of errands you've got to run two hours from now, and whether or not you should take the pork chops you're planning to have for dinner out of the freezer before you leave, right?'' Emma said, laughing.

"That might be the case, too."

"How would you like a houseguest for the rest of the week? I promise to help with the dishes." She wasn't going to spend any more nights alone at the inn, no matter how much she liked the place or the people who owned it.

Her grandmother refrained from any overt comment on her leaving Twin Oaks, although her smile was tinged with relief. "I have to admit I've missed you staying with us your last few visits. So has your grandfather."

"I've missed you, too."

"Your room is ready whenever you want to move in." Martha's eyes shone at the prospect of having Emma to herself for five whole days.

"I have to tell Maureen I'm leaving. I'll bring my things with me this evening. Is that okay?"

"Wonderful." Emma watched as her grandmother maneuvered the little import out of the garage and onto the street. She rolled down the window and called to Emma. "Will you join us for dinner? That is, if you don't already have plans?"

"I'm free as a bird today."

"We'll eat at eight, then."

"It's a date." When her grandmother said they would eat at eight, dinner would be on the table at precisely that time. Martha and Felix were punctual to a fault. Emma pulled her car into the driveway and went into the house through the back door. Her grandfather was sitting at the table in the bay window that formed a small alcove at the far end of the kitchen. Her grandmother's rock garden, all ready for winter's long sleep, was framed by large trees and a view of the hills above town.

"Morning, Granddad," Emma said, giving him a kiss on top of the head. "Want some company on your rounds today?"

"I don't do rounds, but I am heading out to check on Ed Taylor and maybe have coffee at the diner with another couple of old geezers. Think you can handle that?"

She slid onto the chair beside him and read the headlines in the paper over his shoulder. There was a school bond issue coming up for a vote in a few days, and pictures of the new rest rooms at the village park. The paper came out only once a week and had long ago given up reporting anything but births, deaths and school sports, along with town council news. "Yeah, I think I'm up to that. Need a lift?"

"Nope. Going to ride my bike. Might be the last nice day we get. You can use your grandmother's bike, if you want to tag along. She doesn't get much use of it these days."

"I can't talk you into a nice drive?" Emma put on her most cajoling smile, the one she'd used to get her way with him as a kid.

"Nope. Can't harangue my patients on good cardiovascular habits and then not practice what I preach."

"The things I put myself through to spend time with my grandfather," Emma grumbled.

Felix gave a nod of satisfaction. "Be good for you. And just 'cause half the ride's up hill, don't think you're going to get away with not telling me what in Sam hill's going on with you and the Tubb boy."

EMMA SCATTERED GRAIN to the fat pullets in the fenced-in run and watched her grandfather and Ed Taylor talk from the corner of her eye. Ed was tall and stooped and terribly thin. Emma didn't think he looked well, at all. From the way her grandfather was shaking his finger under Ed's nose, she suspected he was voicing the same opinion.

Finally Felix threw up his arms and shoved some bottles of pill samples into Ed's reluctant hands. He snapped the lid of his old-fashioned black bag shut, settled it firmly in the basket of his ancient and highly prized Schwinn Corvette and pedaled over to where Emma was standing.

"Let's go," he said, his brow creased in a frown. "That damned stubborn fool won't listen to a word I say. He's not taking care of himself and not getting enough to eat, but he's too damned bullheaded to get any help from the county or his daughter. Something's wrong there, too. She's always been good as gold at helping the old coot out, but I haven't seen hide nor hair of her in months."

Her grandfather's gruff exterior hid a heart of gold, but he would deny it to the end and act even more cantankerous and bad-tempered if she insisted it was true. He'd developed his tough outer shell, Emma was convinced, to protect himself from feeling too much of his patients' pain over the years, and it was second nature to him now. Her grandmother had seen through the ploy from the beginning and, Emma suspected, so had most of his patients over a half century of practice.

They rode in silence toward the village. The sun had climbed higher into the sky, but the morning was still pleasantly cool. Long wisps of clouds arched across the sky from low on the horizon—the weather change Maureen had spoken of. A cold front was coming to blow away the last of the warm Indian summer weather and usher in the beginning of a long, cold New England winter.

There was almost no traffic on the side road they were traveling. A few grasshoppers chirped in the dry grass that edged the roadway, and a couple of woolly worm caterpillars were making their way across the pavement, one brown, one the color of melted vanilla ice cream. Emma could never remember if it was dark for a hard winter or light. Regardless of which meant what, she did her best not to squish them as she rode by.

Black and white cows grazed in a nearby pasture, raising their heads to watch the humans pass before going back to their leisurely meal. It was so quiet Emma could hear a dog bark in its kennel at the vet's farm over a mile away. They stopped on the crest of the hill leading into town, and her grandfather leaned his bicycle against the remnants of a stone fence, then settled himself on the lichen-covered boulders beside it and pulled his ball cap low over his eyes. "Damned proud old fool." Felix muttered.

"Do you mean Ed Taylor?"

He took a deep breath. "He's going to neglect himself right into his grave." Emma looked over her shoulder at the run-down farm they'd just left. The only things that had been well cared for, she thought, were the chickens she'd been feeding.

"I'm too damned old for this, Emma Martha. I can't take on the world's problems anymore."

Emma remained astride her bike, her feet braced in the gravel. "You shouldn't have to, Granddad. You've looked after other people for most of your life. It's time you concentrated on you and Nana for a change."

He sighed. "Ed Taylor's as stubborn as I am, so I might as well stop trying to change him now. Don't worry about me and your grandmother, though. I've been grousing about my patients since Eisenhower was in office, and your grandmother's been listening to me do it for almost as long. Enough of complaining about what can't be changed. We'll start discussing you now,'' the crafty old man replied. ''Spill it, Emma. What's going on between you and the Tubb boy? And while you're at it, what's this about changes in your job, too?''

Emma folded her arms and leaned on the handlebars of her grandmother's shiny red three-speed. She remembered the Christmas her grandfather had presented it to his wife, wrapped in a glittering silver bow. It was just after they'd moved to the tiny Berkshire village. They were going to spend their retirement years tooling around the countryside. And they still did, for short rides in warm weather. Emma had always loved spending Christmas with her grandparents, no matter where they were, but most especially since they'd made their home in Cooper's Corner.

''I'll start with the good news. My show's being picked up for syndication at the first of the year. One hundred stations, good markets, close to a million listeners and the potential, someday, to grow the show to five times that many. It's not the big time yet, but it's a good start.''

''I'm proud of you. I don't always agree with what you tell your callers. Entirely too much sleeping around and such goes on these days. But for the most part I have to say it's good advice.''

''First, do no harm,'' Emma said, quoting from the Hippocratic oath.

''Exactly. And I don't doubt you'll be as big as Limbaugh someday. I hope I live to see it.''

''I hope you live forever, Granddad.''

''Don't know about that. Not as appealing a notion as it was thirty years ago.'' He plucked a stem of grass and inspected it closely before putting it between his teeth.

"So that's the good news. Now for the bad. And that involves Daryl, does it?"

"Yes. I imagine Nana gave you the particulars."

"She told me you caught the young fool with another woman, or some such." A gust of wind, stronger than the light, steady breeze that had followed them into town, began sighing through the meadow and roadside grasses, kicking up dust as it passed, attempting to take Felix's Red Sox cap with it. He settled it more firmly on his head and fixed Emma with a steely glare.

"Yes, and for some reason I don't believe it was only a business dinner. I have no proof…except what's in my heart."

"A most unreliable organ at times."

A crow winged past, cawing raucously, and the call echoed back and forth among the hills. Emma watched the big black bird for a moment, then returned her gaze to her grandfather's face. "I can't help how I feel."

"He's given you an explanation for his being with her?"

"Yes."

"And?"

She took a deep breath. "I don't believe him." The more she said it, the more convinced she was. But it was still hard for her to voice her argument to others. In her heart of hearts she knew Daryl had been unfaithful. She just didn't know what to do about it.

"So the wheels have come off the wagon, eh? I wondered how long it would take you to come to your senses."

"What do you mean?"

"Nothing, just that Lori and Burt Tubb spoiled that boy rotten. I can't say as how I've got a lot of respect for him."

"Why didn't you say so before, Granddad? I was planning to marry him." She caught herself with a start, and her heart thumped a little faster in her chest. She hadn't hesitated a moment in using the past tense to describe their relationship.

Felix gave a little nod, letting her know he'd caught the certainty in her voice, too. "Wanted to give him the benefit of the doubt. I was relying on your good judgment to rein you in before it was too late. And to tell the truth, I wasn't looking forward to being the heavy unless I didn't have a choice. Putting my opinion aside, what proof do you have that he's lying to you?"

"That's the million-dollar question. All the proof I have is gut instinct, woman's intuition, call it what you will...." She let the sentence fade away. She'd studiously avoided trying to make any connection with Blake Weston and the woman who'd betrayed him.

"And what?" her canny old grandfather demanded.

"It's just coincidence. I doubt there's even a connection, but still—"

"I hate riddles," Felix said flatly. "Spell it out, girl."

"You remember the man I brought to the house Saturday morning? The one with the hangover?"

"The Marine."

"Yes. His hangover was caused by a broken heart. He found the woman he'd been involved with naked in his living room. With their Realtor."

"And you jumped to the conclusion that the man was Daryl?"

"Not really," Emma said doubtfully. "Not right away. But the woman's name was Heather. Daryl said the client he'd been with was named Heather, when he finally admitted he'd been with a woman at all," she added. "And he was meeting her because the deal he'd been working on to sell the McGillicuddy place to her and her significant other was going sour—''

"And this Blake Weston found his way to Cooper's Corner because he wanted to buy property in the area," Felix finished for her. "Well, I'll be damned. If it turns out to be true, it's bigger odds than hitting the lottery. No wonder Tubb thought he could get away with it."

"So you think he was unfaithful, too?"

"Let's just say I hear things around town. Nothing I'd ever repeat. But he was noted for being a ladies' man before he met you."

"I wish you'd told me this last summer."

"Hey. You're my granddaughter. My pride and joy. I wanted to think young Tubb was smart enough to know he'd captured a real prize. But seems he's still thinking with his—never mind."

"His penis, Granddad?"

"Hell's bells, girl. If I'd wanted to say the word, I would have."

Emma laughed. She couldn't help herself. "Granddad, you're a doctor. I'm a thirty-year-old woman. I've heard the word before."

Felix ignored her little joke and scowled even harder. "If you want my opinion straight up and unvarnished—''

"Do you ever give it any other way?" Emma said, swallowing her smile.

"Course not. Plain and simple—dump him. As for you ending up at Twin Oaks on the same day as the man who's the other injured party... Well, I guess there have been stranger things happen."

"Not to me."

Felix rose stiffly, using a hand on the old stone fence to lever himself upward. "Did you ever think it might be meant to be?'' He waited a moment, but she didn't answer. She couldn't, because she was remembering Blake Weston's mouth on hers, and the memory left her breathless and slightly addled. *Meant to be*. That kiss had felt as if it were meant to be. ''Better get moving or I'll stiffen up so bad I won't be able to ride.'' Felix righted the bike and settled heavily onto the seat.

''What do I do next?'' Emma said, hearing the note of desperation in her voice.

''I just told you. Dump him.''

''It sounds so final that way.''

''It is final.''

''But I thought—''

''You thought you loved him.''

''Yes.'' She sighed.

''You don't look heartbroken to me. You look mad.''

Emma couldn't help herself. She laughed, a sound filled with longing and sadness, not joy. ''You know, I came to that same conclusion.''

''Good. Then move out of the inn and come stay with us.''

She laughed again. ''I'm doing just that.''

''Good. Can't say as I've ever approved of you shacking up with him like that.''

''But—''

''You thought it was love at first sight? And it would last for fifty years or more like your grandmother and me?''

''Yes. At least I let myself believe it was.''

''It was just lust. Hormones. Chemistry. Whatever you call it these days. When the real thing comes along, you'll know.''

A picture of Blake Weston as he'd looked yesterday on the deck at Twin Oaks filled her thoughts before she could stop it. She pushed the image into the corner of her mind and slammed the door before another memory of the kiss could follow on its heels. She wasn't even free of her commitment to Daryl yet, and already she was fixating on another man. What was wrong with her?

Her silence alerted her grandfather, but for the wrong reason. "You want to give him one more chance?" Felix sounded incredulous. He frowned so hard his eyebrows disappeared under his ball cap.

"I need to find out the truth. For my own peace of mind." How could she go on giving advice to hundreds, even thousands of other women if she was wrong about this? She'd never trust herself again. If she lost confidence in her instincts, she'd begin to second-guess every word that came out of her mouth. And soon, she had no doubt, the words would dry up altogether. She would have ended not only her engagement but possibly her career.

Felix pushed off on his bike, his words coming to her as he gained speed on the downhill slope. "If you want the truth, don't hold your breath that Daryl will all of a sudden turn out to be a hero. It doesn't happen that way. Your best plan might be to talk to that devil dog, Weston. I'll bet he's got it all figured out."

BLAKE DIDN'T FEEL as if he'd figured anything out, even after a night of tossing and turning. He'd finally fallen asleep as dawn was beginning to lighten the eastern sky. By the time he awoke, groggy and slow, it was ten o'clock and the dining room was empty. He refused Clint's offer of griddle cakes and ham, settled for coffee, toast and juice and then headed outside to clear his head.

Emma's car wasn't in her parking place. He hadn't expected it to be. He'd damned near scared her off last night. But then, he could hardly believe it himself. Less than a week ago he'd considered himself committed to Heather. It may not have been a match made in heaven, but he had figured it would work. Now all he could think about was the copper-haired, sharp-tongued beauty who was every bit as captivating in the flesh as she was on the radio.

But Emma, stubborn and loyal as he had already come to believe she was, clearly still considered herself committed to Daryl Tubb, at least for the time being. At least until she figured out for herself what a jerk he was.

That Blake could make that happen by uttering one simple, declarative sentence had been what kept him awake all night.

His churning thoughts had carried him across the footbridge and into town. He found himself two doors down from the diner. Parked in front of the clapboard building was a dark green car with a Berkshire Realty sign affixed to the door. Daryl Tubb was entering the restaurant, briefcase in one hand, cell phone in the other. It wasn't such an amazing circumstance, since Clint had told him Daryl's parents owned the place.

Blake hadn't spoken to Daryl since the night he'd thrown him out of his apartment. He didn't much want to see him now, except for one reason. Emma.

F. Blake Weston had decided to play the knight in shining armor and give the two-timing SOB one more chance to win back his lady love.

Or, more precisely, he hoped, give the bastard enough rope to hang himself.

Blake stepped into the diner and back into his parents' childhood. Red vinyl, black and white tile floor and gleaming chrome trim. Little signs of wear and tear and a few dents and nicks told him that Tubb's Café wasn't the product of some designer's interpretation of a by-gone day, but the real thing. A busy café whose owners hadn't worried about fashion's decrees through the years, but concentrated on providing good food for loyal customers. Too bad he wasn't here for the cider doughnuts Emma loved, piled up on a glass-topped cake stand, or even the meat loaf special.

He gave the big jukebox along the wall an appreciative glance, then zeroed in on the man seating himself at a table near the back of the long, narrow room. It was too early for the lunch crowd, so they were alone except for the plump woman stirring a soup pot on the stove and a burly, bald-headed man polishing glassware behind the bar along the back wall of the dining room.

The sun was behind Blake, shining through the big plate glass window, and Daryl gave him only a cursory glance before going back to the paperwork he'd just finished spreading out before him on the table. It wasn't until Blake stopped directly in front of him that Daryl looked up, blinking. Recognition was followed swiftly by alarm.

"Where the hell did you come from?" Daryl pushed his chair from the table and looked around, as though seeking a means of escape. Blake took grim satisfaction in the reaction. He leaned both hands on the table, bringing his nose within six inches of the other man's.

"I'm staying at Twin Oaks." Outright fear replaced the flicker of alarm Blake had glimpsed in Daryl's eyes. "We need to talk. We can do it here in front of your parents, or we can go someplace more private. It's up to you."

"The office." He motioned to a narrow hallway that ran between the back of the bar and the small kitchen. "Dad, I need to use the office for a few minutes to speak with my client. Is that okay?"

"Sure, son. Take your time." The bald man went on polishing glasses with a snowy white bar towel, but the look he gave Blake was long and considering.

"Thanks, Dad."

Blake followed the younger man into the office, which evidently doubled as a storeroom. Metal shelving stocked with restaurant-size cans, and bottles lined the walls. A cluttered desk was wedged between the shelving, facing a wall filled with handwritten notes, receipts and invoices held in place with colored pushpins. Daryl didn't make the mistake of sitting in the only chair, giving Blake the advantage of height as well as bulk; instead, he leaned against the desk and folded his arms over his chest. "I don't imagine you want to talk about the McGillicuddy place," Daryl said.

"My option's good until the fifteenth. I'll let you know what I've decided then." Blake watched as another wave of disquiet flickered across Daryl's face. Tubb probably had another prospect on the line and didn't like the idea of Blake holding up the new deal. But he hadn't yet made up his mind about the place. He wasn't about to let it go in a fit of pique over breaking up with Heather. "But you're right. It's not the land deal I want to talk about."

"Look, man. I'm sorry about Heather, all right? It was just one of those things—"

Blake cut him off with a wave of his hand and took a menacing step forward. He had the advantage of several inches, twenty pounds and five years, and he'd learned his intimidation techniques from some of the best teachers in the world—the drill instructors at Parris Island. "Do you think if I'd really cared about what you did with her, I wouldn't have broken your damned jaw that night?"

Daryl swallowed hard. "Then if it's not the Mc-Gillicuddy place, and it's not because you caught me with my fly undone in your living room, what are you doing here?"

"Forty-eight hours ago I met the woman you're proposing to marry."

"Emma?" Blake was gratified to see Daryl turn pasty white under his carefully maintained tan.

"Yes, Emma Hart. And I don't like the idea of her getting hurt by the likes of you."

"Did you tell her about me and Heather?" Daryl dropped his hands to his sides and licked his lips.

He looked scared, and Blake was glad. He kept his expression carefully impassive. There was no way he would let Daryl Tubb know he wished to God he could do just that. This knight in shining armor business was for the birds. "I thought I'd give *you* a chance to do the right thing."

"Look. She doesn't have to know anything about it. It was just one of those things. We met a few times. Had a few drinks. Heather cried on my shoulder about you dragging her out here to the boonies to live." He shook his head as though to clear it. "Man, I half think she seduced me to get me to renege on the deal."

The lying weasel wasn't telling him the whole truth, he could see it in his eyes, in the tense set of his shoulders and jaw. But what difference did it make now? That night he'd been too busy dealing with an indignant, then furious, then hysterically tearful Heather to get all the sordid details of the tryst he'd walked in on. To be damned honest, he hadn't wanted to hear them, but Blake figured Daryl was probably telling the truth about one thing. Heather knew how to use her body to get what she wanted. It was an unsavory trait that Blake had chosen to ignore, to his regret.

Maybe Tubb wasn't wholly to blame for what had happened. But he was still a spineless, two-timing, lying jerk.

And Emma Hart didn't deserve to get saddled with the likes of him.

"I love Emma—"

Blake reached over and grabbed a handful of Daryl's expensive cashmere sweater. "Don't give me that line. If you loved her, you wouldn't have cheated on her."

"I tried to tell her." There was a tremor in Daryl's voice. He heard it and swallowed so hard his Adam's apple jumped up and down in his throat. "I just couldn't find the right words. It'll never happen again. If you don't tell her, she'll never have to know."

He had had enough of Daryl Tubb, but his damnable sense of honor and fair play forced him to offer Emma's lover one more chance. If Tubb didn't come clean by morning, then all bets were off. He would go after Emma himself without a qualm. "You're a fool, Tubb. She's already close to figuring it out on her own. If I were you, I'd get on the phone right now and make it right with her. I'd bet the farm it's your last chance." Blake let go with enough force to send Daryl stumbling backward against the desk. He turned on his heel, walked out of the office and didn't look back.

CHAPTER EIGHT

THE CLOUDS Emma had observed that morning had moved in to block the sun by the middle of the afternoon. She'd left her grandmother puttering around in the kitchen and her grandfather napping in his chair in front of the TV and returned to Twin Oaks, promising to be back for dinner at eight. Sharp.

Daryl had called shortly after they'd finished lunch. He wanted to meet her for dinner but she told him she had plans. He'd been insistent, though, and she'd agreed to join him for drinks at a roadhouse a few miles outside Williamstown at nine-thirty. He said they needed to talk. And if he did convince her he was telling the truth, then what would she do? Forgive him? Try again?

Her thoughts were as unsettled as the weather.

Maureen was in her garden picking the last few mums to place on the table in the dining room. Emma followed her, recalling the riot of blooms and good things to eat that the garden had been bursting with just weeks before. As filled with promise as her future. A future that, in some aspects, now seemed as bleak as the landscape.

"I don't think I'll offer you a penny for your thoughts," Maureen said, straightening from her labor with a hand to the small of her back. "You're wearing such a frown on your face, I'm sure they're not happy ones."

"You'd be right," Emma agreed. "Isn't there something I can help you with that will give me a chance to work off my bad mood?'' She hadn't been good company for her grandparents, though she'd tried, and the worried looks on their faces when she said goodbye told her they hadn't been fooled. Evidently Maureen could read her just as easily.

"There's really very little left to do except for cutting back the mums," Maureen said with a wave that took in the last few straggling pumpkin vines and valiant chrysanthemums. The rest of the garden was raked and composted, rosebushes covered, tomato cages stacked neatly near the garden shed. "I just wanted to save these last few blossoms from the wind and rain. But I could use help putting them into vases."

"I can manage that. As long as you don't expect anything too professional looking." Emma made a face. "I should amend that to say as long as you don't expect anything that looks at all professional."

"That's exactly what I strive to avoid. We want Twin Oaks to feel like home, not like a hotel."

Maureen led the way to the back of the house. They met Blake Weston coming around the corner from the parking area. He was wearing a worn leather bomber jacket and a frown that matched Emma's. A ball cap was stuck in the back pocket of his jeans. It was red, and Emma would bet money that it was emblazoned with the Marine Corps emblem. Her grandfather had one just like it.

"Good afternoon, Mr. Weston," Maureen said.

"I wish you'd call me Blake," he replied, the frown transforming itself into a smile.

"Thank you. And I hope that you'll stop referring to me as Ms. Cooper."

"Thank you, Maureen." His gaze turned to Emma, and

the frown returned. "Hello, Emma. I thought I saw your car back in the lot."

"Emma's looking for something to keep her occupied until teatime," Maureen informed him. "I was just about to suggest a hike up to the waterfall. If you're looking for a little exercise, why don't you go with her?"

That was the last thing Emma wanted at the moment. She had too much on her mind to be distracted by Blake Weston's unsettling company.

"That's up to Emma," Blake said, shifting his gaze to the hills above the house.

She looked at her sturdy walking shoes. Blake was wearing hiking boots, too. No help there. "It looks like rain, and I don't have a raincoat." It was the only excuse she could think of.

"I can help you there," Maureen announced. She handed Emma the basket of purple and bronze mums and stepped into the back porch for a minute. When she emerged she had a sage green raincoat and a long orange-red scarf, the color of bittersweet, in her hands. "We're nearly the same size. This ought to fit." The raincoat had a soft flannel lining, and Emma's last objection evaporated. She couldn't refuse to go with him because she wasn't dressed warmly enough.

"The trails are well marked until you get above the waterfall," Maureen reminded them. "You should be able to get there and back before tea." She squinted at the lowering clouds. "And before it rains." She smiled and gave a satisfied nod, the universal reaction of an innkeeper who has successfully disposed of two bored guests.

Blake was already moving across the yard, but after a few strides he turned and waited for her to catch up. "I won't be having tea with you," Emma said hastily. "I'm having dinner with my grandparents. And then I'm meet-

ing Daryl for drinks.'' She had told Maureen earlier she
would be moving down the hill to her grandparents' house
and had attempted to pay for the rest of the week, but
Maureen had brushed aside the offer, saying she knew
how happy that would make Felix and Martha, and that
Emma would always be a welcome guest at Twin Oaks
in the future.

"We'll expect you when we see you, then,'' Maureen
said, making a shooing motion with her hand. "Go, get
some exercise.'' She turned and went into the house.
Emma was alone with Blake.

THEY STARTED OUT in silence, walking through the
meadow behind the house, one of the last remnants of the
farm that Clint and Maureen had been left by their great-
uncle. Their passing stirred up a few grasshoppers, swaying heavily on grass stems, as seemingly oblivious to the
change in the weather and the onset of winter as their
fictional counterparts in the old nursery story. Overhead,
the same noisy crows Emma had observed that morning
winged their way into the trees and the shelter of their
nests.

The afternoon was melting into an early twilight, and
the wind carried with it the scent of rain. The fire in the
massive stone fireplace in the gathering room of Twin
Oaks would feel especially welcome tonight.

Blake set an easy but steady pace and kept his own
counsel. Emma turned up the collar of Maureen's coat,
then pushed her hands deep into the pockets. The trees
closed around them and the pathway rose sharply as they
moved into the hills behind the house. Blake pointed out
a squirrel busily gathering the hickory nuts that had fallen
onto the pathway. The animal watched them with bright
black eyes, unafraid, until they were only a couple yards

away. Then he bounded up the trunk, climbing swiftly and noisily into the lower branches of the big shag bark to scold them with chattering long after they were out of sight.

The waterfall that was the preferred destination of the B and B's casual hikers was a small one at the top of the first rise behind the house. With the leaves off the trees, Emma could see the roof and chimneys of the big old farmhouse from a boulder at the base of the falls once they arrived. Somehow it didn't seem as if they'd gone far enough for her to overcome her reluctance to say what was on her mind. She sat on the rock and tried not to think about the summer kisses she'd exchanged with Daryl in this very spot, because she had the feeling they would be washed away like footprints in the sand by newer, more sensual memories of a single kiss exchanged with the man she was with.

"Not much water running this time of year," Blake said. His deep voice blended well with the browns and grays of the hardwoods and the somber green of the pines.

"It's beautiful in the summer, though, cool and green, with a sound like…I don't know—"

"Water tumbling over rocks, maybe?" he asked, giving her a sideways look.

Emma felt a bubble of laughter pushing its way past the lump of anxiety in her throat. "I was going to say like fairy bells chiming in a secret glade or something equally improbable and poetic."

"You came here with Daryl, right?"

She sidestepped the question. "Everyone who stays at Twin Oaks comes here. Maureen told me they're thinking of bringing a bench up. Something suitably rustic, so you don't get moss all over your hostess's coat the way I've just done." She stood up and glanced over her shoulder, brushing at the stain on Maureen's coat.

"Want to go back?"

She gave him look for look. "No. But I don't think I want to stay here, either."

He nodded. "Okay." He looked around. "This way."

A faint trail led up the ridge, following one of the small streams that fed into the creek above the falls. "I don't think we'll get lost if we follow the water."

"I thought Marines never got lost."

"That's true," he replied without missing a beat. "But we do occasionally misplace the objective."

"How did you go from the Corps to Wall Street?" Emma asked, watching her steps carefully as they worked their way into the woods. The light was failing a little, and she didn't want to twist an ankle.

"My hitch in the Marines paid for my education. Didn't know what I wanted to do when I got to college. I just knew I wanted to make something of myself. I was good with numbers so I took an economics course. My professor liked to dabble in the market on the side. He set some of us up in a dummy investment club. I made a mint on paper that semester and decided I wanted to do it with real money. I ended up with a double major in business and economics. Did my postgrad work at Harvard and never looked back."

"You make it sound easy." She knew there was much more to his life story than he had revealed, and found herself wishing he would tell her more.

"About as easy as getting your own radio show in one of the biggest markets in the country."

"In other words, you worked your butt off."

"Exactly."

He turned and offered his hand and a smile that was so

electrifying it almost blew her socks off. Emma hesitated. She wasn't altogether certain sparks wouldn't arc through the air between them if she touched his hand. Taking a deep breath, she let him fold his long, strong fingers around hers. Warmth. Solidness. No sparks, but a slow deep tingle that started somewhere low in her middle and rose steadily toward her heart.

She moved along in a fog after that, not really paying attention to where they were going. She found herself standing on the edge of a narrow, tree-filled ravine. Blake was surveying the rise of ground on the other side. ''I think if we can get around this ravine we'll come out of the woods just about where I want to be.''

''Where's that?'' she managed to ask without sounding too winded. They were higher into the hills than she had ever gone. There wasn't a sound to be heard that didn't belong there except their own footsteps. The wind sighed through the trees, another squirrel scolded them from a high branch, a grouse drummed somewhere off in the distance. It was hard to believe Cooper's Corner and the farmhouse were little more than two miles away as the crow flew. They might have been in another world, even another time.

They left the faint path and scrambled into the ravine at its shallowest point. The climb up the other side was strenuous, and more than once Emma found herself needing a helping hand. Even Blake was breathing hard by the time they reached the top. ''I think we'll look for another way back to Twin Oaks. There's probably an old logging road around here somewhere that will lead us down toward the village.''

''Good idea.'' Emma was panting. ''I wish I'd thought to ask Maureen for a bottle of water when she brought me the raincoat.''

"We can get a drink right down there." Blake had moved ahead of her a little way. He was standing on a rocky outcropping and held out a hand to pull her up beside him.

An old homestead was spread out in a tiny valley below them. The house was very large, four-square and unpretentious, the paint faded away to gray. Five double-hung windows marched across the upper floor, and below the overhang of a ramshackle porch, four more windows flanked a wide front door with a fanlight. Behind the house a steep-roofed barn stood forlorn and neglected, listing a little away from the relentless winds that blew off the hillside. A chicken coop and garden shed squatted in the lee of the barn, and what was unmistakably an outhouse occupied the corner of a ruined garden behind the house.

Stone fences ran their course through meadow grasses and disappeared into the trees on the far hillside. A small creek meandered through the front yard and crossed the road under a narrow humpbacked bridge. It had been a substantial property in its day, but time and the elements had taken their toll.

A Berkshire Realty sign was prominently displayed near the driveway. Emma's heart began to pound like a drum inside her skull, and she hung back, reluctant to cross the gravel lane that fronted the property. This was McGillicuddy place. She knew it in the very marrow of her bones.

Blake led the way into the overgrown yard. "I was driving through the area one day last spring and came across this place. I thought it was going to be my escape from the rat race. Or more precisely, a return to my roots."

"I thought you said you're from Indiana."

"You remembered that?"

She felt her cheeks grow hot and was glad the rise in color could be attributed to exercise and the cool wind that had freshened to a stiff breeze while they were in the woods. "I have a very good memory."

"I've made an offer to buy this place," Blake said as he walked up the rickety steps to the front porch.

Emma followed him and tried to peer in through the wavy glass of one of the windows. "It's too dark to see inside. I wish we had a key."

"We don't need one." He put his shoulder to the door, gave it a mighty shove, and it swung back on rusty hinges. "I guess the agent figured putting a shiny new lock on this old place would just invite trouble. Anyway, there's nothing left inside worth stealing."

They stepped over the threshold. The house smelled of mildew and dust and age. A central hallway ran down the middle of the house, and small, high-ceilinged rooms opened from either side. A narrow stairway disappeared into the shadows above.

"The kitchen's through here." Blake led the way into a room that ran the length of the house. Dingy linoleum covered the floors and countertop, and the walls were stained with damp, but the cupboards were glass fronted and went all the way to the ceiling.

The orange and gold wallpaper was peeling off in long strips, a blessing, to Emma's way of thinking. But there was a fireplace of warm redbrick at the far end, flanked by windows that looked out over the small valley. Here the shabby linoleum had been torn away in spots, and the wide-planked wooden floor that lay beneath showed through. If the sagging ceiling were pulled down, hand-hewn beams would also come into view, Emma surmised. She could imagine sitting in front of the blazing fireplace, a kettle of soup simmering on the stove behind her. She would watch the deer come out to feed as darkness crept across the snow-covered meadows to wrap the old house in winter solitude, sealing the family inside in a cocoon of warmth and comfort. Suddenly, it was clear to Emma what had drawn Blake to this place.

She blinked away the fantasy and focused once more on the atrocious flowered wallpaper. Blake grinned at the look on her face. "I'm sorry," she said, grinning back. "It's...it's so sixties."

"My parents would be right at home in here."

He crossed to the chipped enamel sink and began to work the handle of an old-fashioned pump fixed to the counter. A rush of clear, cold water poured into the sink. "Go on. Take a drink. It's safe. I had it tested."

Emma cupped her hands under the flow and drank deeply. "It's good."

Blake copied her motion.

"I remember what you said about your parents. That they had stayed true to the Sixties."

"Yep. They're the original flower children. The last of the hippies. They met in the summer of love. They don't care a fig about money or investments. They live close to the land, and close to the bone, and are happy doing it. But it's a hell of a way to raise three kids. Hand-me-down clothes, goat cheese sandwiches and bean sprouts in your lunch sack when everyone else is eating burgers and fries. A dad who had a ponytail and an earring when everyone else's old man wore a suit and tie to work, or at least jeans and boots, not bell-bottoms and sandals. It was hardest on my sister, Summer. My mom despises makeup. She still wears granny dresses and tie-dye, and she hasn't shaved her legs...well, ever, I guess." He stopped talking abruptly. "Sorry. I'm making it sound like some kind of nightmare."

"No, you're not. Flared legs and tie-dye are very chic again. But ten years ago it must have been hard on your sister."

"My poor folks still don't know where they went so wrong. They want nothing to do with what they still think of as the Establishment—the military-industrial complex. They raised us to be self-sufficient and at one with nature, as they call it." He gave a rueful chuckle. "They did their damnedest to try to keep us out of the mainstream, but instead they got three workaholic overachievers."

"Three? Another sister?"

"A brother. Ash. He's an engineer. Summer's a pediatrician. Or soon will be. I'm the oldest."

"I'm an only child but I want a big family of my own someday. Three kids at least." She didn't know why she was telling him all this, but somehow it was making it easier to ask what she needed to know.

"And what about Daryl?" His voice had taken on a hard edge. He shoved his hands in his pockets and looked out the small window above the sink.

"He comes from a big family—the youngest of five children. He says two are more than enough. And he wasn't in any hurry to have those."

"Wasn't?"

"A slip of the tongue." Daryl had said he wanted to talk tonight. To get things settled between them, to make things right. She had to focus on that. Not on the width of Blake's shoulders or the deep timbre of his voice as he talked of his family.

She turned and walked out of the kitchen into what must have once been the living room or, more likely, the parlor of the old house. There was another fireplace, with

glazed tile edging, and a mirror over the mantel that was
wavy and dull where the silvering had worn away.

Emma swiveled from the mirror. She looked lost and
apprehensive in its wavering reflection, so she moved to
look out the smudged and dusty front window at the Berkshire Realty sign. A car came into view from around a
curve and drove slowly by the house. The man inside
stared at Emma for a moment through the dusty glass,
then accelerated with a spurt of gravel and disappeared
along the winding road. The car had the look of an airport
rental, nondescript and plain. Perhaps the barely glimpsed
man behind the wheel was a city dweller looking for a
place to put down roots just as Blake had done. He would
go back to his motel and place a call to Berkshire Realty
inquiring about the dilapidated old farmhouse at the end
of the gravel lane.

"He'll be back," Blake said, coming up behind her.
"It's a dead-end road." She could feel the heat of his
body in the cold room, and she longed to lean into it, lean
into him and be warmed by his strength.

She didn't care about the man in the car or where he
was going. "It was Daryl you found with your Heather,
wasn't it?" she asked in a voice she hardly recognized as
her own.

Blake remained silent. Emma could feel her pulse beating in her throat, in her head. She counted the beats, fifteen, twenty. "Yes," he said at last.

That had been only a few days ago. Two weeks after
Emma had seen them together in the restaurant. "And
she's beautiful and sleek, with hair the color of moonlight." Here was her proof Daryl had been lying all along.
Emma braced herself for the pain she thought would
come, but there was none.

"She's one of the most beautiful women I've ever seen."

She was cold and wrapped her arms around herself, breathing in the stale air of the old house. Suddenly she wished she were outside. "What do you suppose the odds are of us meeting this way?"

"Pretty steep, I imagine. I've always stayed in Williamstown when I've come up here before. The last time I drove through town, the B and B wasn't even open, but I liked the look of the place and decided to bring Heather here to propose and close the deal on the farm."

"Daryl told me the deal was going sour. He said he was showing it to a couple of prospects in the next few days. Are you going to let your option lapse and walk away?"

"I don't know. I've certainly had second thoughts. Cooper's Corner's a small place. Hard not to run into Tubb now and then."

Daryl and Heather's philandering had ruined more dreams than hers, Emma realized. Blake's plans for his future were as cold and dead as the ashes in the fireplace.

"Poor Daryl. He must feel like the most unlikely guy on earth. One-in-a-million chance I'd see him with Heather. One-in-a-million chance you and I should meet."

Blake spun her around so quickly she stumbled against him. He steadied her with his hands on her arms. "He's a damned fool. A lying idiot. Don't waste your sympathy on him. He betrayed you with Heather."

"More than once, do you suppose?" she asked. As she watched, his eyes darkened with anger and hurt pride before he shuttered the emotions that lay behind them.

"Would it make a difference?"

"It might have if he'd told me the truth in the beginning. People make mistakes…they do foolish hurtful things they regret.''

''You said you were meeting him tonight. Do you think he finally plans to tell you the truth?''

She wanted to ask him why it was so important to him to know what she was going to do next. Was it because he was beginning to care for her? Was that why he'd brought her here? So that she would come to the conclusions she had? She was too unsure of her careening emotions, her reaction to him, to ask outright. ''I hope so. We can't resolve anything between us until he does.''

''Are you saying you're willing to forgive and forget?''

''No. I'm not ready to do that, either.''

''Then what are you going to do?''

She wished he would take her in his arms and kiss her the way he had the day before. Then she would tell him she and Daryl were through. That she had already made arrangements to move out of the room Daryl had booked for them and into her grandparents' home. But he didn't move a muscle, didn't make a sound. His eyes, which usually held the warmth of a green and gold summer's day, were as bleak as the November sky overhead.

The room grew even colder as she felt his withdrawal. She was chilled to the bone and shivered, hunching her shoulders inside Maureen's coat. ''I don't know. But whatever it is, I can't make the decision here. Please, will you take me back to Twin Oaks?''

CHAPTER NINE

HE SURE AS HELL had made a mess of things. He should never have given in to the impulse to bring Emma to the farm. So much for doing the honorable thing. He made a lousy knight in shining armor. He hadn't come right out and told Emma that Daryl was sleeping around on her, but that was only a technicality. He'd dropped enough hints to make even the most trusting of women suspicious.

He wanted Emma to know the truth about the creep she'd been planning to marry, but he hadn't had the patience or the guts to get out of the way and let her come to the right conclusions on her own. Now she was mad at him, and she had every right to be.

She hadn't spoken a word since they'd left the house, just stared down the gravel road that skirted the hillside and headed into town. He knew what she was thinking. She didn't want to hike through the woods with him. She was going to take the long way back, on her own.

"It'll be raining before you get halfway there if you go that way," he said, pulling his hat out of his back pocket and settling it on his head to give him something to do with his hands.

She nodded. "I know," she replied grudgingly. "Maybe someone will come along like that car a few minutes ago, and I can hitch a ride."

Even in Cooper's Corner it wasn't a wise idea to accept rides with a stranger, and she knew it. "That was probably the only car that's been down this road all day, and he was going in the wrong direction.''

Emma gave him a slanted look. "It's not going to be a piece of cake hiking back through the woods, either. It's already getting dark. The clouds have thickened a lot since we set out.''

"I shouldn't have brought you so far.''

"You didn't bring me. I agreed to come along. There's a difference,'' she said with the stubborn tilt to her chin he was coming to recognize. "There's no use standing here arguing about it. We'd better start walking, or you'll be late for tea.''

"I don't give a damn about tea.''

"But I give a damn about keeping my grandparents waiting for their dinner.''

She set off across the road and into the trees, straight-backed and silent once more. Blake dropped back a step or two and let her lead the way. She entered the woods without once looking back, but stopped on the top of the ravine and peered into its shadowy depths. "It looks even steeper from this angle,'' she said, biting her lip.

Blake moved past her and held out his hand. She hesitated, a frown wrinkling her forehead. "C'mon,'' he said. "You can be mad at me again on the other side.''

"I'm not mad,'' she insisted, then shut her mouth and concentrated on getting down the steep, rocky slope.

They crossed the narrow bottom of the ravine in a dozen steps, skirting a fallen pine tree and using its slender trunk as a base for a quick scramble up the less steep side. Blake halted at the top and put his hands on his knees to catch his breath. "Whew,'' he said. "I don't think I'll make this hike again.''

Emma was breathing hard, too. "Next time we drive.''

It was just a figure of speech, he told himself. She didn't really mean there would be a next time.

From the direction of the road, of the farmhouse, he heard a car approach, then idle. A car door slammed. The guy they'd seen before coming back to get a closer look? Or Tubb, bringing a prospective buyer to check out *his* house? The sounds were faint, distorted by distance and the trees on the far side of the ravine.

Emma heard them, also. "Do you want to go back and see who it is?" she asked, still a little breathless.

"No."

"I don't suppose it's anyone I'd be comfortable asking for a ride into town."

She meant Tubb, and they both knew it. "Probably not."

She made a little face. "I don't want to climb down into that ravine again today, anyway."

He scaled the big rock that blocked their path, then reached down and pulled her up beside him. The birds had quit singing. The day was over as far as they were concerned. Even the squirrels had ceased their querulous chatter. Emma's cheeks and nose were pink with cold and exertion, but her hair was still gloriously copper-tinged even in the fading light. It framed her head like a crown and begged a man to run his fingers through the silky strands. She'd pushed it behind her ears, and the wink of tiny amethyst studs drew his attention to her earlobes. Small, curved, just the right size and shape to nibble on before stringing kisses down her throat and lower, to her breasts. In Maureen's sage green coat with the dark orange scarf framing her face, she looked as if she belonged to the earth, to the forest, to this place.

To the farmhouse behind them. He had a sudden image of her before the kitchen fireplace, turning to greet him as he came in from the cold, her hair and eyes as softly luminous as they were now, her belly round with child.

His child? Or Daryl's?

He tightened his grip unthinkingly, and she gave a grunt of pain, stumbling a little on the uneven surface of the rock. He pulled her close. "I'm sorry, Emma."

"It's all right." She flexed her hand a little. "I wasn't going to fall, you know."

He couldn't come right out and tell her about his vision. He had no right to say such intimate things to her. He'd told Daryl he'd give him one more chance to tell her the truth, and evidently he'd taken it. Until she'd heard him out tonight, she was as off-limits as if she were wearing his ring. "I thought I felt you slip," Blake lied.

She looked at him for a long moment, and a little furrow appeared between her softly arched eyebrows. He could feel her sizing him up, trying to read his thoughts. "That's not it at all. Something's bothering you. It has been all afternoon. And I'm not leaving this rock until you tell me what it is. Did seeing the farmhouse upset you that much? Were there memories of Heather there that put you in such a bad mood?"

"I told you, I'm over Heather. And even if I wasn't, she only saw the place once. She never got five feet past the front door. A bat came down the stairway and scared the bejeezus out of her." His tone was too harsh, his words little more than a growl. Her frown deepened.

"Then it has to do with Daryl."

"You're good, Emma." She didn't give up easily, and her instincts were dead on. That's what made her so successful at what she did. He could almost be enjoying this if he wasn't aware, deep inside himself, that his whole future hinged on her meeting with Daryl Tubb in just a few hours. He was tired of dancing around the truth. He was tired of guerrilla tactics. Sometimes a straight-on frontal assault worked best. ''I brought you here with the express purpose of getting you to ask me if Tubb was the guy I caught screwing around with Heather. I couldn't take the chance you'd make the connection yourself.''

''You don't pull your punches, do you.''

''Not when it's important.''

''I knew it was Daryl you caught with Heather that night,'' she said quietly. ''I've known in my heart for a while now.'' The whole woods seemed to have gone silent around them except for the wind sighing high in the tree branches and the idling car engine that lingered at the edge of his senses and reminded him they weren't the only two people left on earth.

''I figured as much, but I couldn't leave it to chance. I couldn't keep my nose out of your business. And that makes me as big a jerk as Tubb.''

She watched him closely, not blinking, the wind lifting tendrils of her glorious hair to curl them around her cheek. ''Why?''

He couldn't just blurt it out. What sane, intelligent woman would believe he'd fallen in love with her in forty-eight hours? Especially when he'd met her hungover from mourning a broken love affair? It was insanity to even admit it.

''I didn't want you to make a mistake that would haunt you the rest of your life,'' he said, sounding pompous and hating it.

''How noble.'' He deserved the sarcasm he caught in her tone. Her eyes were locked on his face, the tiny frown still in place on her forehead.

''Yeah, real noble. In a pig's eye. I feel like some kind of low life, sneaking around in the back yard waiting for Tubb to leave the house so I can steal the silver.''

"Considering I'm the silver in that metaphor, I think I should remind you that I'm no man's property."

He pulled off his red ball cap and raked his hand through his hair. "Oh, hell, Emma. You know what I mean. I feel like a jackass. Don't make me worry about being PC, too." There was too much at stake. He wanted desperately to know if she felt the same way. But he couldn't push her any further. This wasn't war. She wasn't a hill to be taken at any cost. Hell, this wasn't even Wall Street, where he'd wine and dine a client and agree with him on everything from politics to penne to close a deal. This was his future standing before him, and she was still promised to another man.

She lifted her hands and rested them on his chest. Her touch was light, but the heat of it burned through his shirt like fire. "I want the truth, Blake. I'm tired of evasions and lies from the men in my life."

"I didn't just bring you up here so you'd realize Tubb was the two-timing bastard he is. I wanted there to be no doubt in your mind he was a worthless SOB. I wanted to make sure you'd send him packing tonight."

"How did you intend to convince me of that?"

He didn't know if it was an invitation or a challenge. He didn't care much which it was, but he was damned certain he wasn't going to answer it with words. "Like this." He pulled her close and covered her mouth with his.

She didn't open to him, not right away. She stiffened a little and he gentled his touch. He didn't want this to be the hurried, furtive coupling it had been in the pile of leaves. He wanted this to be a kiss that she would never forget, a branding, a claiming. Pulling back slightly so their lips barely met, he lifted his hands to her face, twining his fingers through her hair to hold her still. Before returning his quest to her mouth, he brushed his lips across her cheek, her eyelids, the curve of her earlobe, which had so intrigued him earlier. At last he touched his lips to hers once more, lightly, testing.

She opened slightly to his touch, tasted his bottom lip with the tip of her tongue. Blake felt control begin to slip out of his grasp and clamped down on it with an iron hand. He slanted his mouth across hers, sliding his tongue between her teeth, drinking deeply of the silky moistness within. She tasted of cinnamon and spice and the sweet heat of desire. Her hands clenched handfuls of his shirt as she strained toward him, letting her tongue duel with his. She wanted him. He knew that as well as he knew his own name and exulted in the certainty. She didn't have to tell him with words that she was through with Tubb. He could sense it in her response to him. Emma Hart was not the kind of woman to play one man against another.

But God help him, he wanted to hear her say the words. To tell him aloud that she was free of her obligation to Tubb. Free to love again, completely and until the end of time.

His heart beat like a drum in his chest. His blood pounded in his ears. But it was no longer from the intoxication of physical desire. Something wasn't right. The atmosphere around them had changed subtly, ominously. He could feel it in his gut, in the primitive brain at the base of his skull. Responses embedded in his bones and psyche by the unrelenting taskmasters at Parris Island many years before, and honed to a fine edge by Desert Storm and the street fighting of Somalia, kicked into high gear.

He lifted his mouth from hers and scanned the darkening woods beyond the ravine.

Emma stood rooted to the spot, her eyes closed, her

mouth still open slightly as though waiting for another kiss. "Don't stop," she whispered, and lifted herself on the tips of her toes to bring his mouth to hers. "Not yet."

"Emma, we're not alone." The hardness in his voice got through to her.

Her eyes flew open, the dreamy desire that had darkened them to burned sugar giving way to unease. "What do you mean? Is someone watching us?"

"I don't know. It just doesn't feel right," he said as she spun to follow his gaze, peering into the gathering darkness of a short November twilight.

"I don't see anything."

Neither did he. Not that he could pinpoint. But the prickling at the base of his skull wouldn't go away. And once again he noticed the silence of the creatures who called these woods home. There should be a grouse drumming for his mate off in the distance. A squirrel or two scolding the human intruders away from their treetop nests. Crows noisily settling in for the night. But he heard none of those things. Nothing but the wind in the trees. He couldn't even hear the car idling out on the road anymore.

He'd been more than a little preoccupied with kissing Emma, but he couldn't remember hearing it drive away.

The short hair at the back of his neck stood on end.

"Time to go, Emma," he said gruffly. A flicker of movement through the trees on the far side of the ravine added a harsh urgency to his words.

Emma gave him a narrow look over her shoulder. "I still don't see anyone," she said in the tone of voice he already knew presaged an argument.

He wasn't about to stand on top of a six-foot-high granite rock and discuss the finer points of Marine survival training with her. He wanted to get low and keep moving.

The farther into the trees they went, the less of a target they presented. He reached out and grabbed her hand, spinning her around as the unmistakable sound of a shotgun shell being loaded into the chamber broke the unearthly silence. Dragging Emma along with him, he launched himself off the rock. It was a split second too late.

He never heard the shot that caught him low on his left side.

There was a jumbled confusion of sound and sensation. He would recall until the moment he died the swirl of green and red-orange as the skirt of Maureen's coat billowed around Emma's slender form, the look of disbelief on her face as the force of the slug tearing through the fabric and into his flesh threw them backward off the rock.

They landed hard, knocking the air out of both of them. His mind eddied with darkness and white hot pain, a nauseating combination that kept him on his knees for too many precious seconds. They had to get moving, away from the shooter in the trees.

Emma was curled into a ball beside him. She moaned a little, and he rolled her onto her back. Her face was white, and a tiny smear of blood marred her cheek where it had been scraped raw by a twig or branch. When he pressed his fingers to the pulse in her throat, it was fast, but steady. Her eyes opened, and she stared into the trees with a blank expression. "How did I get on the ground?"

"Emma, are you okay?"

She turned her head and winced with pain, then lifted her hand to the back of her head. "Ouch. What happened? Was that thunder? Did we get struck by lightning?" It had started to rain sometime during their kiss. He hadn't even noticed.

"Someone took a shot at us." It was an effort to speak.

All his senses were screaming for them to get out of there, but he was in no shape to pick Emma up and carry her, and she wasn't making any effort to get to her feet by herself. He pressed his left hand to his side, and it came away covered with blood. He had no idea how badly he'd been hit, but it was a safe bet he wouldn't last long out here in the woods, bleeding like a stuck pig.

"Took a shot at us?" Emma struggled to one elbow. She turned even whiter and moaned in pain. "My head hurts."

Blake reached around with his right hand and felt along the back of her neck. A bump was already forming. "Look at me, Emma." She did, and her gaze was clear and focused, but unbelieving. No concussion. That was good. She was dazed by the hard landing.

"Someone shot at us?" she repeated, as though she hadn't heard him right the first time.

"Damned straight."

"But who? Why?" She tried to lever herself into a sitting position, but he held her down.

"Keep your head low. The shooter may still be out there."

Her attention shifted to his side, and her mouth dropped open in horror. He didn't follow her gaze. He didn't have to. He could feel the blood trickling out between his fingers. Even in the failing light it had to be a frightening sight.

"You've been hurt," she whispered.

"I've been shot, Emma. And the guy's still out there. We've got to get moving. Put some distance between us." The speech left him panting for breath.

"Who in the world would have a gun out here? Now? It's not hunting season yet, is it?

She didn't seem able to take it all in. He could feel the

darkness that had been lurking at the edges of his vision begin to move inward, stealing his sight and his strength. "Keep low and follow me," he said through clenched teeth.

She tried to shake off his restraining hand and stand. He clamped down tight on her arm. "Surely whoever it is knows they've made a mistake. That they—" she faltered a moment "—shot you." Once more she looked in horror at the blood spilling through his fingers. "We have to get help. The hunter, or whoever it is, has to help us." Her voice was rising in frustration and fear. "He must know he made a terrible mistake by now. Listen. I can hear him coming this way through the ravine." She opened her mouth and yelled at the top of her lungs. "Over here. Help us. My friend's been shot."

The silence was so intense he could hear the raindrops splashing on the big rock, feel it pelting on the top of his head. His hat was gone. He spotted it lying ten feet away, but he wasn't about to go after it.

"He isn't answering. He must not have heard us down in the ravine. I'll try again."

Blake jerked on her arm, hard. It startled Emma enough that she shut her mouth for a moment. "Don't say another word," he hissed, trying to get enough oxygen into his lungs to keep breathing and talk at the same time. He was losing too much blood and he had to do something about it. Fast. But not here. It wasn't safe. He didn't need the ominous silence that had greeted Emma's call for help to tell him that. They had maybe three minutes until the shooter worked his way through the ravine. Thank God he wasn't just staying put and waiting for them to put their heads up so he could take another shot.

She stared toward the ravine with a look of mingled alarm and fury on her face. "He didn't answer."

"If he wanted to help us he'd have called out by now. This isn't some kid shooting squirrels after school with a twenty-two. My guess is he's a poacher, out for a deer before the season starts. He's not going to rescue us and get caught." He was wasting breath and time trying to explain. "We've got to move. Put some distance between us and him." Before she could get another word out, he gritted his teeth and stumbled to his feet, pulling her with him. "Keep low and keep moving, no matter what. Do you hear?"

"You can't travel with a bullet in you."

"Emma, I haven't got the strength to keep arguing with you. Do you hear? Keep moving. Don't stop for anything until you get to the inn." He stumbled on a branch, or maybe over his own two feet.

The continued lack of response from the gunman must have convinced her. She was beside him in a heartbeat. Sliding her arm under his shoulders, she took his weight with only a tiny grunt of surprise. "I'll keep moving as long as you do."

It would have to do. They could both hear the sounds of the gunman climbing the ravine, moving fast but making no effort at all to call to them.

It was too dark to try to circle the ravine to find the road. He could barely stay on his feet. They limped through the thickening dusk, downhill, toward the water and the trail to Twin Oaks. Every breath was agony. He couldn't hear anything above the drumming of his blood in his ears.

He stumbled once, twice. The third time he fell heavily to his knees, dragging Emma with him. "I can't go on, Emma. Do what I told you. The stream we followed can't be far ahead. You can find your way to the falls from there."

"Shh," she warned, as breathless as he was. "Do you hear anything?"

He tried to quiet his harsh breathing and listen. He lifted his head and closed his eyes against the swoop and swirl of tree branches against the pearl gray sky, calling on skills he hadn't used in a decade. He waited for a full minute, two. Nothing. "He's given up the chase."

"I know. We're safe, I think," Emma whispered in case they were wrong about the lack of pursuit. "Safe enough to take time to try to stop the bleeding." She pushed him against the tree trunk he'd slumped in front of. "Lean back a little." He did, but the pain was exquisite. "Do you have anything we can use to make a pressure bandage?"

"Handkerchief. Coat pocket." Even one-word responses were getting to be too much effort. They had to keep moving. He grunted and tried to sit up, but she held him down with a hand on his chest.

"Stay still." Leaning forward, she reached into his coat pocket. She eyed the linen square. "Not big enough." Emma was biting her lower lip again. She did that when she was agitated. He could barely see her face, a pale oval in the twilight. She stuck her hands in the pockets of Maureen's coat. "I don't think—my Lord." She was looking at the bullet hole she'd found in the fabric. "He almost shot me, too?" When her eyes rolled back, Blake reached out and pushed her head between her knees.

"You're okay, Emma. He didn't hurt you."

She lifted her head, her eyes flashing fire. "I wasn't worried about myself. If he'd shot us both, I wouldn't have been able to help you." She pulled Maureen's orange scarf from around her neck. "I'll use this. Take off your belt."

"I'm not wearing one."

For a moment he thought she might cry. Then she squared her shoulders. "Okay. Plan B. I...I'll use my socks. They're heavy cotton." She tried for a smile and almost managed one. Sitting in the wet leaf litter, she began untying her shoes. "They're clean—I just put them on this morning."

"You can't walk in those shoes without socks."

"Let's see," she said with a definite touch of sarcasm in her voice. "What would I rather have? Blisters? Or a lifeless Marine on my hands?" She slanted him a look from beneath her lashes. "Now, that's a hard choice." She pulled off the heavy crew socks and folded them into a pad, took his handkerchief and put it on top of them. "This should work. Can you get your coat off?"

He shook his head. "Can't." One-word answers were the easiest.

"Okay. No problem." She pushed aside the ruined leather and sucked in her breath. His shirt was black. The light was almost gone, so the blood wasn't as obvious as it might have been, except on his hands. "Is—is the bullet still inside?" she asked, her eyes narrowed against the gathering darkness.

"No. And it wasn't a bullet. It was a slug," he said. Another inch or so to the right and he'd have been gut shot. There weren't many worse ways to die.

"Are you ready?" she asked with just a tiny quaver in her voice.

"When I take my hand away, press down hard. Then wrap the scarf around my waist and tie the knot as tight as you can."

"I can do that." She took a deep breath and went to work. Blake sucked in his breath and tried to think of anything but the pain.

It didn't work. The agony coalesced in a blinding white light behind his eyes. He couldn't get away from it. The light expanded until it filled his brain and then it exploded into darkness, and he sank thankfully into its depths.

CHAPTER TEN

EMMA DIDN'T KNOW how far they'd come. Or how far they had to go. The last of the daylight had faded into the silvery gray of twilight, and most of that precious light had been washed away by the rain. In ten minutes she wouldn't be able to see her hand in front of her face, let alone where to put her feet.

They weren't going to make it to the waterfall. In fact, they'd stumbled across the feeder stream they'd followed to the ravine moments before. At least she hoped it was the same stream. There was no way to tell. And if it was, that meant they were less than halfway to their goal. And if it wasn't—they were well and truly lost. That didn't bear thinking of.

Blake's weight dragged at her shoulders. She knew he was doing the best he could to keep on his feet, but it was a losing battle. She was going to have to find some kind of shelter for him, then try to find her way back to the house on her own.

It didn't matter that it was raining hard. It didn't matter that it was going to be pitch dark in a handful of minutes. It had to be done. She wanted to sink onto the wet pine needles and bawl like a baby, but she wasn't going to do that, either.

A splotch of color caught her eye. Blue. Not the blue of the autumn sky, or a jay winging its way home for the night, but a definite flicker of a neon-bright, decidedly man-made shade of blue. The same color as the plastic tarp her grandfather used to cover the woodpile behind the garage. She narrowed her eyes against the rain. It was a tarp, and it covered the roof of a small lean-to. The only reason she had seen it was that it had frayed loose from its bindings and was flapping in the fitful breeze.

"Blake." He was starting to sink to his knees. She shouldn't have stopped even for a moment. "Don't quit on me now. Keep moving, Marine. We're not there yet."

"Ex-Marine," he mumbled.

She bit back a little sob of relief. She hadn't been certain he was still fully conscious. "My granddad says there no such thing as an ex-Marine, only inactive ones."

"Dead Marine, then."

"Blake, don't say such a thing. Please, don't give up on me now."

"I'm moving." But just barely. Panic jabbed at her, and she beat it back. He lifted his head. "Where are we?" he asked.

"Not where I thought we were," she admitted, and the panic level increased a notch or two. She ignored it. "There's some kind of lean-to or hunter's shelter over here. I don't remember seeing it when we came up this afternoon. That's why I don't know where we are. Sorry. I have a lousy sense of direction." The long speech winded her. She shut her mouth and concentrated on getting her breath.

He tried to follow her pointing finger. "Can't see it." His words were more slurred than before. The panic was beginning to feel like sheer terror.

"Just a few more steps, Blake. Please."

"I'm moving, Drill Sergeant." He did keep going, but she didn't know how. A half dozen faltering steps brought them to the lean-to.

Emma peered inside. It was made of slender, rough-cut pine logs. Three-sided and about the size of a tollbooth, the lean-to was just big enough for two men to take shelter in from the weather if they were out hunting or snow-mobiling. The roof had been covered with the blue plastic tarp for extra protection, but that must have been years ago because it was faded and flapping in the wind, and thankfully so, or she would never have seen it in the gloom.

There was no floor, but the ground was covered with six inches of fallen leaves and wind-blown pine needles and seemed relatively dry. There was even a small pile of kindling-size wood pieces in the far corner, ready for a fire. Unfortunately there were no matches in Maureen's coat pockets.

"Do you have a lighter?" She'd never seen Blake smoke, so he probably didn't have one, but it was worth asking. "There's wood here, and I could start a signal fire. If it didn't bring us help, we could at least keep warm." It was so cold she could see her breath when she spoke. Soon it would be too dark even for that.

She felt rather than saw him shake his head. "Sorry. Can't help." His words trailed off, and Emma could have cried with frustration and disappointment.

"I swear I'll never leave home again without a compass and matches and a cell phone. Maybe even a global po-sitioning system."

He made a sound that might almost have been a chuckle. "Isn't that what Scarlett said in *Gone With The Wind?*"

Emma managed to laugh at his joke, but she was torn. Should they stop and wait for rescue or try to keep walk-ing? Her anxiety for Blake's safety urged her to keep moving. But since she wasn't certain where they were, that might mean courting disaster from a fall or a tumble into a ravine like the one near the McGillicuddy farm.

In the few moments she'd stood hesitating, Blake's weight had brought her almost to her knees. It was too dark to see much more than her hand in front of her face. She faced the inevitable. She couldn't go on with Blake or alone. They would have to take what little shelter the lean-to offered and wait for the town rescue unit to come find them.

Somehow Emma got him inside the lean-to. His bitten-off groan of pain as he slumped against the rough logs made her heart twist in anguish. She propped him against the wall furthest from the slanting rain and scooted in beside him, checking to see if the makeshift pressure bandage was holding. It was soaked with blood, but there no longer seemed to be fresh bleeding. Emma took a long, deep breath of relief. If she kept him quiet and warm, maybe they would get through this with no lasting damage. She had no idea how badly Blake was injured and she wasn't about to loosen the bandage to find out. But she had nightmare visions of internal injuries and a ruptured spleen. She wondered if she shouldn't head off into the darkness and try to find help.

Once more her common sense told her to stay put. Let the experts come to them. Surely in a couple of hours they would be found. Her grandparents would start inquiring into her whereabouts when she didn't show up for dinner promptly at eight.

There were enough leaves and mounded pine needles behind Blake to keep the rain and wind from coming through the lower portion of the lean-to, but the front was completely open. It would only be a matter of minutes before they were soaked, and hypothermia would become an added danger.

"I'm going to try to untie the tarp and use it to make an awning or something to keep the rain out," she said, reaching out to touch his face because she could no longer see him in any detail.

She felt him nod. "Okay. There's a knife in my pocket. Just a penknife. My dad gave it to me when I was ten—"

"If it's got a point on it, it'll do." She ran her hands down his chest, over the ruined leather of his jacket until she felt the silky knit of Maureen's scarf, then lower to the muscles of his stomach and thigh beneath the soft denim of his jeans. She hesitated. The damp stickiness of blood was everywhere she touched, so much of it. A shiver coursed down her spine that had nothing to do with the chill in the wet air. Her heart twisted again with worry for Blake's safety, but that wasn't the only unnerving sensation she felt. Lower, deeper, she was aware of him as a man, broad chest, narrow hips, and she remembered the feel of him pressed against her as they kissed.

"Left front pocket. I promise there's no surprise waiting for you." Amusement overlaid the pain in his voice, but she could feel him tense and knew that he had felt that same awareness.

"I think I can handle you, Marine," she said lightly, but it took an effort to be so flip. She slipped her hand into the pocket of his jeans, feeling the sharp jut of his hipbone, the coolness of loose change, the heaviness of his sex along the edge of her hand. She was back on the big rock for a split second, remembering the heat and strength of him pressed against her. Her heart beat like a kettle drum in her chest and in her ears, and lower, in the very center of her.

She could feel the muscles of his abdomen contract as he sucked in his breath. Her fingers closed convulsively over the small penknife at the bottom of his pocket and she pulled her hand away so quickly, she jostled the pressure bandage, making him groan. "Sorry," she murmured, skimming the bandage with her fingers to make sure she hadn't dislodged it in her haste. She could feel him shiver beneath her touch. "I'll hurry," she promised, and surged to her feet.

Her hands were shaking with cold and reaction and the unsettling intimacy of the last few moments. After feeling her way around the lean-to, she skimmed her hands over the ruined tarp. It was damp from the rain and she took a moment to wet her hands and wash away the stickiness of Blake's blood. Then she took the penknife he'd given her and began sawing away at the top layer of plastic tarp, behind the half-rotten nylon rope that lashed it to the shelter's roof. She had to be careful she didn't cut the weakened rope and loosen the entire tarp. It would blow away in seconds and leave them completely at the mercy of the elements.

She worked by touch, stopping occasionally to wipe the rain from her eyes, although she didn't know why. She was as blind as a bat. Blake kept the blade of the small penknife well-honed, and it was easier than she thought to free the material from its rivets. She gathered it toward her as carefully as the gusting breeze allowed and lowered it over the opening. It smelled musty and mildewed, but it did stay in one piece. Unfortunately it didn't quite reach the ground.

"Shit," Emma said in heartfelt tones as she knelt inside the lean-to, holding the bottom edge of the tarp so that the wind didn't catch it.

Blake stirred behind her. "What's wrong?"

"I haven't got anything to tie this tarp down with. It's too short to reach the ground, so I can't use a rock." She began to feel along the side poles of the lean-to, hoping against hope that she might find a piece of rope or twine, a vine, anything to tie the ends down.

She was considering taking off her bra and slicing it in half with Blake's penknife when he spoke. "Shoelaces."

"Shoelaces?" she repeated, her brain occupied with the logistics of removing and dismembering her bra without Blake figuring out what she was up to.

"Yes. Use my bootlaces—they're probably longest." Bootlaces. Of course. Why hadn't she thought of it?

Emma laughed, she couldn't help herself.

"What's so funny? They'll work fine." He moved restlessly once more, and Emma was instantly contrite.

"I'm sorry. I'm not thinking very clearly. I never thought of my shoelaces. I…I was going to use my bra."

"Your bra?" She wished she could see his face. She couldn't tell what he was thinking from the sound of his voice.

"Yes. I was going to hack it in two with your knife."

He moved again. She could tell by the rustling leaves. "Maybe we should go with your idea."

"No way. Where's your foot?"

"Here." His hand found hers and guided it to his leg just below the knee. She worked at the laces, her eyes closed in concentration, although it was as dark when she opened them. Again by touch, she found the eyelets at the corners of the half-ruined tarp. With fumbling fingers she tied first one, then the other to the side poles of the lean-to.

By the time she was done she was breathing heavily and shaking with cold. She scooted into the lean-to, away from the bottom edge of the tarp, which was dripping with rain. She bumped into Blake, and he reached out and touched the side of her face.

"You're freezing," he growled. "Change places with me. It's warmer back here."

"Don't be silly. How can it be any warmer two feet from where I am right now?"

"Don't argue with me." She could feel him trying to raise himself to his knees, and her temper snapped.

"For God's sake, stay still. You're the one who's been shot, not me. I'll be fine."

"I don't want…" His teeth were chattering so hard she could barely make out his words.

Emma scooted as close to him as she could and put her hands on his shoulders. He was shivering violently, as much from shock, she feared, as the intensifying cold. Gently, she urged him down beside her and wrapped her arms around him. He tensed against her, then with a bitten-off groan stretched out his long legs and let her take his weight. The leaves that cushioned her backside weren't going to keep out the cold for long, but Maureen's coat was long-skirted, and the warmth of the lining would help. She stuck her hand in the pocket and pulled it over both of them as far as she could. It was little enough protection, but all they had.

She leaned her head against the side of the hut and stared into the darkness, listening to the rain and the rustling of the tarp. Time had ceased to have much meaning from the moment the shot had torn through Blake's side, but Emma began to wonder how much longer they would have to stay in the hut before they were rescued. Hours and hours? All night? She didn't want to think of that possibility. It was going to be very cold by morning. Freezing cold. The thought made her shiver, and Blake stirred restlessly against her.

"You're still cold. I shouldn't have brought you out here."

"I thought we agreed I came of my own free will."
She made very sure her teeth didn't chatter as she spoke.

"I guess I forgot."

"You're forgiven." She tightened her grip on him, being careful to keep her arms above the wound in his side. She tried to remember the one anatomy course she took in college. What organs were on your left side? The spleen, surely, but anything else? She couldn't remember. If the bullet had torn through his spleen, would he still be alive?

Thinking that way would drive her insane. She had to trust in God that nothing vital had been hit. That he was only suffering from shock and loss of blood, and that help would come soon enough to save him from any complications. She reached down. His left hand was pressed against the bandage. She brushed his fingers with hers, and he shifted slightly, flexing his fingers. She skimmed her hand over the bandage, checking for new moistness. Blessedly there was none.

"The bleeding's slowed down," he said. He'd stopped shivering, at least, and so for the moment had she.

"I think so, too. But you need to be in the hospital." Emma lifted her hand. "Damn. I can't see my watch. Add that to the list of things I'm never leaving home without. A watch with a lighted dial."

"I have one." He lifted his left hand and brushed against her breast. "Sorry," he muttered. Emma ignored the tiny burst of sensation that once more stirred inside her. This was not the time or place to begin to contemplate her physical reaction to Blake Weston's slightest touch.

"That's okay." She closed her hand around his wrist, feeling the strength of corded tendons beneath her fingers. "Which button is it?"

"The top one."

She felt for the tiny knob with cold-numbed fingers and found it on the second push. The small blue light from the dial was intense in the near-complete blackness of the hut.

"Not quite seven-thirty."

"Will it take your grandparents long to realize you're missing?"

"About ten minutes after eight they'll be on the phone to Maureen. My whole family is fanatically punctual. I'm the only one who's ever even a few minutes late. And I do mean a *few* minutes." Emma smiled, although he couldn't see her. She felt a little more confident. Cooper's Corner had an excellent rescue unit. She'd met a couple of the team when she was out and about with her grandparents. There was Axel McAlester, the vet. And Alison Fairchild, the town postmistress. Her grandfather wasn't a member, officially, but he often showed up to help out when the unit made a run. They were used to looking for hikers and snowmobilers and cross-country skiers lost in the hills around town.

"With any luck they'll call in the rescue unit by nine or nine-thirty," Blake surmised.

Nine-thirty was when she was supposed to be meeting Daryl. She wondered if he would be as quick to start looking for her as she was sure her grandparents would. He might think she had stood him up. She didn't want to contemplate what might happen to her and Blake if Daryl had been their only hope of rescue.

After that, Blake was quiet for so long, Emma wondered if he had gone to sleep or passed out. She stayed very still, listening to his breathing, wondering if she should take his pulse. She'd tucked her hand into the pocket of Maureen's coat after checking the time. She slid it out again, brushing over the hole the bullet had made in the fabric. She bit her tongue to keep from crying out in distress. It was bigger than she had realized. Her entire index finger fit through it. Again her thoughts circled to the damage the slug must have caused his body, and she pressed her fingertips to his wrist. His pulse was fast, too fast, and light, but steady and even. She breathed a little sigh of relief. It would be thready and irregular if he was in real danger. Thank God, her long-ago first aid class at St. Catherine's had taught her that much.

"I'm okay," he said quietly into the rain-filled darkness.

"I hoped you were asleep," Emma said. "It would make the time go faster until we're found."

"I'd rather stay awake. Right now I don't think there would be much difference between being asleep and being unconscious."

"Do you feel like talking?" she asked. Perhaps it would keep his mind off his pain.

"My mouth's dry."

"I'm thirsty, too." She should have gone up to her room and gotten a bottle of water before they left, but she'd thought they were only going as far as the waterfall, and that was a short enough hike not to need water on such a cool day. "Here, let's see if this works."

Emma held her left hand under the edge of the tarp. It was raining hard enough that water was running off it in steady rivulets. Thankfully the floor of the lean-to sloped downward and the water was running away from them instead of into the shelter. She cupped her hand and let it fill with the cold rainwater, then took a sip, refusing to consider what dirt and debris were washing off the top of the tarp. After all, she told herself, the cleanest portion, the part that had been folded under and protected, was facing out.

The rainwater was cold and sweet with a faintly metallic taste. The residue of Blake's blood that hadn't washed away when she was outside working on the tarp? She refused to think about that, as well, and cupped her hand under the rivulet once more, then offered it to Blake.

"Here," she said. "Drink this."

"Rainwater?"

"Mmm. Don't think about what's in it. Just drink."

"I'm not worried about that. I've had worse."

Of course he had. He'd been in two war zones. But she wouldn't think of that now. No more thoughts of death and disaster. Death was too close tonight, lurking just over her shoulder, waiting to pounce.

He drank thirstily, and the touch of his lips on her palm sent warmth arcing through her. She gave him a second handful, steeling herself against his touch, but the shivery tingle was too strong to be denied, and she finally gave in, holding the momentary warmth close to her heart.

He was quiet again for a while. Emma wanted to ask what time it was, but she knew only minutes had passed since they had checked. She had to be patient, but it was so hard.

"Tell me about your family," she said at last. "What was it like growing up with a brother and sister and hippie parents?"

He made a noise that might have been a chuckle. "It wasn't as bad as I made it sound. My parents are just very simple people with simple ambitions. The part of Indiana where I was raised has a number of Amish families, so we had a lot in common. Except that my dad had half a dozen marijuana plants growing out in the cornfield. He gave it up after a few years when the sheriff came out and told him friendly-like that the Feds were looking to make an example of people in the county. He'd be better off taking care of those exotic weeds next time he made a pass with the cultivator. From then on he had it brought in from friends passing through from San Francisco and New Mexico.''

"Is that where you were born? San Francisco?" That was the place she always associated with hippies. Fragments of old newsreels of girls in long skirts and bare feet, hair down to their waists, and boys in bell-bottoms and sideburns with peace symbols around their necks came to mind.

Blake nodded, and the movement caused his hair to brush against her cheek. If she turned her head only a little, she could touch her mouth to the softness of it.

"I was conceived during the summer of love. My parents lived in a commune out there until after my sister, Summer, was born."

"Summer. What a pretty name."

"Summer Solstice," he said. "She was born on the first day of summer."

"And your brother?"

"Ash."

"I like that name. But does it stand for—"

"Haight-Ashbury Weston."

Emma smiled. "How…original," she said at last.

"My parents were both young and in love with the lifestyle," Blake explained. "If you ever meet Ash, pretend you don't know his full name. He's a biotechnical engineer working on top secret government projects, and his superiors don't appreciate our rather unconventional upbringing."

"I'll remember that." She would love to meet Blake's family. She wondered if she would ever have the chance. "And you? How did you get such an ordinary name?"

Blake chuckled. "I hardly think my name is conventional."

"I think it's very distinguished. F. Blake Weston." She quoted from the careless scrawl on the Twin Oaks guest register.

"How did you know about the F?" he asked.

"You signed in just ahead of me," she reminded him.

"If I tell you what the initial stands for, do you promise never to breathe it to another living soul?"

"Cross my heart," Emma assured him.

"My name is Freedom Blake Weston."

Emma smiled in the darkness. So, he hadn't escaped his parents' eccentric name choices after all. "Freedom?"

"It could be worse. I was named after the midwife who delivered me. Her name was Moonbeam Freedom Blake. My father hadn't completely lost his old patriarchal hangups, thank God. He said there was no way he was going to name his firstborn son Moonbeam. If my mom wanted to encourage gender equality for her children, okay. I could play with Barbie dolls, but he wasn't going to name me after one."

"Did you play with Barbie dolls?" Emma asked. She found it hard to believe someone so inherently male would have played with dolls even as a small child. She shifted her leg to try to get more comfortable. The dampness of the ground was seeping into the shelter. It was going to be a long, cold, frightening night if help didn't arrive soon.

"Sure," he said without hesitation. "My mother thought they were establishment symbols of a male-dominated society, but Summer loved them. My brother, Ash, and I used to take the ones our grandparents sent Summer for Christmas and her birthday and guillotine them with the wood ax. Or we'd play airplane crash with them and pull off their arms and legs and dunk them in red paint and scatter them across the porch. Summer took to hiding them in a tin can under a floorboard in her bedroom to keep them safe.''

"You must have been terrible brothers."

"We were. But we'd have laid down our lives for her. And for each other."

"That's one of the good things about a big family, always being there for each other." She couldn't quite keep the longing out of her voice. A draft of cold air blew under the tarp, scattering raindrops along her leg. Blake obviously felt it, too.

"It's raining harder," he said.

"And it's getting colder."

"Do you want to know what time it is?"

She gave a rueful chuckle. "Am I that obvious?"

He held up his hand, and she fumbled for the right button. Eight-fifteen. She gave a little sigh of relief. "We'll make it," she said, blinking back a sting of tears that caught her unaware. "Just about now my grandparents should be calling Twin Oaks. Help should soon be on the way." She closed her eyes and prayed she was right.

CHAPTER ELEVEN

BLAKE HOPED Emma's grandparents were as reliable as she insisted they were. He didn't know how much longer he could stay conscious. Even if the Cooper's Corner search and rescue squad had the instincts of bloodhounds, he might not make it. He could feel the cold seeping into the marrow of his bones. Not just the chill of the rain and dropping temperature, but the weakness of blood loss and shock.

The warmth of Emma's slender body against his back didn't help. Only the sound of her voice, her laughter, tinged as it was with a quiver of fear, kept him grounded in the here and now. He'd even told her his full name. He felt the ghost of a smile curve his mouth. It had been years since he'd confided that information to anyone.

He'd never told Heather what his first initial stood for. She had never cared enough to ask.

Emma moved slightly, flexing her knee, and another bolt of white-hot pain lanced through him. He groaned. He couldn't help it. The pain simply would not go away. He could no longer focus on distractions to keep it at bay. The discomfort was getting stronger, and he was not.

He wondered if he was going to die.

He didn't think so. But then neither had the guys in Saudi who'd been mortally wounded when their Bradley was hit by friendly fire.

His buddy, Fiegler, had been one of them. Blake had

seen him die. He'd suffered no pain at the end. But Blake still hurt big time, so maybe he wasn't as bad off as he feared.

"Do you miss living on a farm?" Emma asked so quietly he didn't know if he'd imagined the question or not. He knew she was already listening for sounds of rescue, even though it might be hours before the team made it this high into the hills. He wasn't sure where they were on the mountain. Like Emma, he hadn't noticed the lean-to on their climb. It was possible they'd intersected the streambed a short distance above the spot where they'd left it.

Or they could be following another streambed entirely. One that led them into the countryside, away from the village.

"Not for a minute until I saw the McGillicuddy place." Manhattan had such energy. It was the center of the financial universe, and for the first couple of years he'd lived there, he'd reveled in the novelty of it all. He'd enjoyed dining in the finest restaurants, seeing Broadway plays, having seats for the Knicks games and heading off to Yankee Stadium whenever his hectic schedule permitted.

And the women. There weren't women like those back in Fort Wayne.

But too many of them had been like Heather, and he began to think it was his priorities that were out of step, not theirs. When Heather came along, he'd told himself there were trade-offs in every relationship. That's the way it was in the twenty-first century.

He'd had his apartment, a steady rise in his position and responsibilities at Braxton, Cartwright and Wheeler, and Heather. He'd been content. Or at least he pretended to himself that was the case.

And then one day last spring he'd wakened to find that the seasons had changed once again, and he hadn't even noticed. In Manhattan it was easy enough to do. But he was more of his parents' child than he sometimes admitted. He'd taken a good look around, and the concrete and steel and glass surrounding him was suddenly like a prison, not the buzzing, twenty-four-seven hive of energy, talent and creativity it had seemed at the beginning.

So he'd packed up a protesting Heather and headed west into the Berkshires. There he found the McGillicuddy place—the same kind of tumbledown farmhouse he'd spent the first eighteen years of his life trying to get away from—and he felt as if he'd come home.

"What did you say?" Emma's voice seemed to be coming from very far away.

"I...I don't remember." Had he spoken his thoughts aloud? He was farther gone than he'd imagined.

"You said you felt as if you'd come home."

"I must have been dreaming." He was in no shape to tell her what he felt about the McGillicuddy place. Or what he felt for her.

"I was drifting a little myself," she admitted. "It's hard to stay awake when it's so cold. I've always heard you're not supposed to fall asleep if you're very cold. You could freeze to death."

"We're not going to freeze to death."

She gave a tiny rueful chuckle, and the warmth of her breath brushed across his cheek. Her grip tightened on him in a reassuring hug. "I'm not really going to fall asleep. My bottom's too cold. That's all I can think about."

If he didn't hurt so damned bad, it would be all he could think about, too. She had a cute bottom, round and feminine. No jutting hip bones and young-boy angularity for Emma. Her breasts were full, her waist nicely curved. She was every inch a woman. A very opinionated and independent woman, but sexy as hell.

She grew silent again, and he could feel her listening, her senses straining into the distance, trying to distinguish the sound of an ATV engine or the shout of a searcher. He listened too, but there was such a ringing in his ears, he gave up and contemplated the bursts of colored light behind his eyes that pulsated in time with his heartbeat, and focused his waning senses on the warmth and comfort of the woman who held him in her arms.

He must have drifted off again because he jerked to consciousness when he felt Emma stiffen behind him. His mind resisted the effort to concentrate on the here and now, preferring instead to remain in the dreamlike state where he'd been watching Emma fly kites with three round-cheeked, knobby-kneed little boys in the flower-strewn meadow behind the McGillicuddy place. In his fantasy he had looked down and found he was holding an infant in his arms. A little girl, dressed all in pink and smiling at him with Emma's smile. Four children. A possibility Heather wouldn't even discuss.

"Listen," Emma whispered, her voice tight with suppressed excitement. "Did you hear that?"

"All I can hear is the rain on the tarp," he said honestly. He didn't want her to get her hopes up. It might be hours before they were found.

"You didn't hear an engine? Wouldn't they search for us with off-road vehicles?"

"Possibly. But I imagine most of them would search on foot."

"I suppose you're right." She settled against the rough siding. "I'm not going to ask you what time it is. I think

I'll cry if you tell me it's not even nine. And I think I'll cry if it's later, too."

"Are you hungry?" It was getting to be an effort to speak. He kept feeling himself float off. But he was afraid that if he didn't keep her talking about mundane subjects, he would weaken and tell her what was in his heart. If he was dying, he wanted Emma to know he was falling in love with her. That he was already in love with her. He had no idea how it had happened so quickly, but he didn't care. There was nothing like looking death in the face to focus your feelings. He loved Emma Hart.

"I'm starving. When I'm not thinking about my cold bottom I'm thinking about my empty stomach." Her tone was light and teasing, but he wasn't fooled. He could hear the teeth-clenching determination that kept it that way. He liked that about her, too. There was no role-playing with Emma, no attempt to mold herself to the image of what a man wanted, at least until she had what she wanted. Emma was Emma. Not so plain and not so simple, but the woman he wanted most in the world.

He took a breath to answer her question, or perhaps to tell her what was in his heart, when another sharp lance of pain changed it to a groan. Emma laid her cheek beside his. "Hang on, Blake. They'll be here soon." He thought he felt a tear, warm against his skin, but he was too weak to lift his hand to brush it away.

He nodded. He had no strength left to speak. It was too late to tell her what he wanted her to know, regardless of her relationship with Daryl Tubb. It took everything he had to stay conscious.

Emma lifted her head. He felt her tense, and her arms tightened convulsively around his chest. "There. I heard it again. And listen. Isn't that someone shouting?"

"I don't know." He couldn't be certain of anything he

heard any longer. He was too tired of fighting the cold and the pain.

"It is." Emma's voice was full of certainty. "They're looking for us. But they sound so far away."

"We need a signal flare," Blake said.

"Or a whistle," Emma responded. "One more thing I'm going to add to my survival list." She was sliding out from behind him, moving as gently and slowly as she could to keep from jostling him. She cushioned the back of his head with her palm as he leaned back against the rough sapling wall. "I'm going out to try to attract their attention. They could walk right by us in the darkness and not see this place." He could feel her hesitate. "Maybe if I go to the creek?"

He reached out and grabbed her wrist. "No," he said, and it came out more of a croak than an actual word. "Don't leave the lean-to. It's too dark. If you fall you could break a bone or knock yourself out, and it might take hours longer to find you. Stay put. Do you understand?" He didn't have the energy to try to be reasonable.

"Okay. Okay. I'll just stand outside and holler my lungs out."

He shook his head, even though he knew she couldn't see him in the darkness. "Voices get distorted in the woods at night. Echoes come back on you from all directions."

"I'm not keeping quiet a moment longer, Blake Weston." He could hear the exasperation and impatience in her voice, and he smiled.

"I know that. Take one of those pieces of firewood over there and bang it against a tree, the side of the hut, anything. Just use a pattern, so they know it's you."

"You mean Morse Code? SOS?"

"Anything."

"I know SOS."

"You learned it at finishing school?"

"No. I used to bug the Marine guards at the embassy when I was staying with my parents. I told you I could handle a devil dog. I meant it."

He tightened his grip on her wrist. "I'll hold you to that boast."

She leaned over and kissed him on the cheek. Something alerted him to her movement, her nearness, and when he turned his head, her lips brushed his. "I love you, Emma."

He thought he had spoken the words aloud, but she didn't respond, didn't act as though she'd heard him, and he wondered if he was half-dreaming again. But the kiss was real. He could feel the warmth of her lips on his mouth. Heat like the flare of a match seared through him, and he pulled the sensation deep inside him and held it there. He let the darkness close over him and concentrated with all his might on keeping the tiny flame alive.

EMMA'S ARMS ACHED, and her hands were raw. Each blow of the rough-barked piece of firewood against the tree trunk sent shards of pain racing from wrist to shoulder. She was soaking wet and shivering so hard her teeth chattered uncontrollably. She had given up trying to convey any decipherable distress signal. After losing track of whether she was pounding out three long or three short whacks against the tree trunk. She concentrated on keeping the signal going. Three swings and a deep breath. Three more swings and exhale.

She longed to stop what she was doing and listen, but she was afraid that the searchers might lose track of their direction if she didn't keep to her task. And she was scared to death of what might be happening to Blake behind her in the lean-to. He hadn't made a sound in what seemed like hours.

She bit her lip until it bled to keep from calling out to ask how he was. He would probably try to crawl out of the shelter to see why she'd stopped her signaling, and she was certain that much exertion would start his wound bleeding again, if not kill him outright.

He had to be the stubbornest man alive. And, dear Lord, please let him still be alive.

Minutes ran into each other and time stood still. She shut everything out of her thoughts except the rhythmic pounding of wood against wood. Closing her eyes to the steady rain that had soaked through Maureen's coat. *It's ruined,* Emma found herself thinking. *It's ruined. I'll have to buy her another. And a scarf to go with it.* But not another bittersweet-orange scarf. Bittersweet was too near the color of blood.

Lights sparkled behind her eyelids. She shook her head to make them go away. But they didn't. They continued to dance and weave their way closer. She blinked and realized her eyes were open and the lights were real, not phantoms of fatigue and stress. She sucked in a sobbing breath and clutched the piece of wood to her chest.

"Here," she shouted, but it came out a mere croak. She licked her lips, moistening her tongue with rainwater, and tried again. "Here! We're over here. Help!"

"Keep pounding," a voice shouted. "We'll home in on that."

"Blake. Did you hear? They've found us!"

There was only silence behind her in the lean-to. Fear clutched at her heart, but she didn't dare crawl under the tarp to see how he was. She began swinging the stick of firewood against the tree trunk once more. If she didn't, the searchers might move off in the wrong direction, and the consequences could be tragic for Blake.

And for her if she had to go on without him in her life. One. *Love.* Three. Pause. One. Two. *You.* Pause. *I. Love. You.*

Where had that thought come from? Did it mean what she thought it meant? Was she falling in love with him? She couldn't be sure, but she did know that if Blake Weston died, she would never be the same again.

I. Love. You. Pause. *I. Love. You.* Pause.

She closed her eyes against the icy raindrops and narrowed her focus to the simple task at hand. Had she really heard him say those words? If her ears hadn't been playing tricks, did he really mean it? Or was it shock and pain talking, not Blake in his right mind?

And did she love him?

Was that why she was so scared she could barely string two coherent thoughts together? Because she had fallen in love with a virtual stranger? Her. Emma Hart. Who was still tangled up in a love-at-first-sight relationship that had gone oh, so wrong.

I. Love. You. Her arms were numb to the shoulder. She could barely lift the wood to swing it against the tree trunk. *I. Love*— The piece of firewood halted in mid-arc and she lost her hold on it. She whirled, dropping to her knees to find it. She couldn't fail Blake. Help was so close. *I*— Strong arms grasped her by the shoulders and held her upright.

"It's okay, Emma. We're here now." It was Clint's voice. That much she recognized, but her eyes couldn't adjust to the brightness of the high-powered flashlight he held in his hand. She blinked against the sudden glare.

"Clint? Thank God you came. Are there others?"

"Alison Fairchild's with me." Emma stared dazedly at

the short, slight woman who moved into the circle of light. *Cooper's Corner's postmistress. You've met her before, remember?*

"We need help." Her knees sagged, and Clint hauled her upright. "Blake's been shot."

"What the hell?" Clint's voice was incredulous. "Did you say shot?"

"Yes." She was shaking so hard with relief and anxiety that she could barely get a word out. "Someone shot at us. The bullet hit Blake in the side. He's in the lean-to. I've tried to keep him warm and dry." A sob worked its way past the lump in her throat. "He's lost so much blood."

"I'll take a look at him, Clint." Emma noticed the heavy backpack Alison was carrying as she swung it off her shoulders. Alison was too small and slender to be able to carry a wounded man very far, and Emma began to worry how they would get Blake down the mountain. But her first concern was to find if he was still alive.

"Please, hurry." She couldn't erase the terror from her voice and didn't try. "He's seriously injured."

A slim radio appeared in Clint's hand. "McAlester? Castleman? Are you out there?"

The radio crackled to life. "We're here, Clint. Did you find them?"

"Yes. They're about twenty yards west of the stream-bed where we split away from you. There's an old hunter's lean-to. Emma tells me Weston's been shot."

"Shot?"

Emma recognized the voice coming from the receiver. It belonged to Seth Castleman. She'd met Seth, the town's electrician, in the spring when he'd done some rewiring for her grandparents. He was a strong man, well built. If he and Axel McAlester, the veterinarian, were nearby, they would have no trouble moving Blake down the mountain to safety. Emma went a little dizzy from relief.

"Alison's going to take a look at him right now. Home in on my signal. And you'd better alert the unit that we've got a badly injured man to transport, Stat."

"They're already on this frequency."

"Standing by." Another voice, distorted by static and distance. "Doc Dorn is here. He wants to know the condition of his granddaughter."

"She's wet and cold but otherwise appears to be okay."

"Don't worry about me," Emma insisted. "It's Blake who needs your help."

"Someone get on the horn to the state police. Tell them we're treating a gunshot wound."

Clint shrugged out of the big pack he was carrying. He pulled a rectangular package from a side pocket and shook out a metallic-looking sheet that gleamed fitfully in the circle of light. He wrapped it around Emma's shoulders. "It's a survival blanket—like the astronauts use. It'll keep the rain off."

"Clint. I could use your help in here." It was Alison's voice. Calm, but with an edginess that started Emma's heart pounding all over again.

She pulled the rustling folds of the blanket tight around her shoulders and sank against the trunk of a pine tree whose lower branches had long ago given up the struggle to survive in the gloom near the forest floor. Pulling her knees against her body, she wrapped her arms around her legs, trying to hold what little warmth she had left inside the blanket's cocoon. She was dryer only because rain was no longer dripping onto her face and into her eyes.

As she leaned against the rough bark, she could hear Alison and Clint talking in low voices, and then, wonderfully, a reply from Blake. She couldn't hear what he said, but at least it meant he was still conscious, alive.

I love you. She dropped her head onto her upraised knees and began to cry.

CHAPTER TWELVE

I. LOVE. YOU.

The refrain had been repeating itself with every drum-beat of agony that pulsed through his body into his brain.

Had he really said the words aloud?

He didn't know.

He hoped he had.

Darkness swooped and spun around him, thicker than the blackness of the lean-to. Darkness that weighed so heavily on him he could barely breathe.

He clung to the rhythm of Emma's signals to the rescue team, gritted his teeth and hung on to consciousness with grim determination.

Emma called to him, but the words were garbled by the rain and the pain. He opened his mouth to answer, but it took too much effort. His head lolled on his shoulders and he fought nausea and breathlessness to bring it upright again.

There were other voices. And light so bright he couldn't keep his eyes open against it. A woman spoke to him. Not Emma. This person's words were light and calm but laced with authority. He forced himself to focus on what she was saying. Yes, he had been shot. No, he didn't know what kind of gun. A shotgun from the sound of it. Yes, he knew his blood type, and stopped himself just in time from rattling off his name, rank and serial number.

A man joined the woman at his side. Blake couldn't

see him any better than he could her. Strong, sure hands probed at the makeshift bandage. He tried not to pay them any attention but it was impossible to ignore the increasing pain. It gnawed at him like a ravenous snake, wrapping him in ever tighter coils.

''Where's Emma?'' he tried to ask, but once more he wasn't certain he'd spoken the words aloud. Answering the woman's question had drained him of his last reserves of strength. The dizziness and vertigo were growing worse. He clenched his hands at his sides to try to hold on, to keep from crying out. The roaring blackness was gaining on him, promising oblivion. He gave up fighting and let the pain take him.

Once more he was standing at the edge of the ravine where the shots had come from, but this time he was pitching headfirst off the rock. He had lost his grasp on Emma's wrist and couldn't see her. Couldn't find her. He was slipping. Sliding. Falling free. And this time there was no bottom.

THE TRIP to the medical unit was a nightmare. Reaction had set in, and Emma could barely put one foot in front of the other. Alison Fairchild supported her for the hundred or so yards of slippery walking to the faintest of trails, where they were met by a rescue squad member Emma had never seen before. With a minimum of words the man helped her onto the back of an off-road vehicle that jolted and jarred her all the way to the bottom of the trail.

She kept trying to look over her shoulder, wondering how they were going to get Blake off the mountain. She had argued with Seth Castleman over the radio until she was blue in the face, but he wouldn't let her stay.

Finally, it was Alison who secured her cooperation.

They couldn't give their full attention to helping Blake if they had her to worry about, she said matter-of-factly. Once Emma was at the unit, her grandfather could check her out, and if he gave his okay, she wouldn't have to go to the hospital— Alison left the sentence unfinished.

Emma had no problem grasping her meaning. She had no intention of being sequestered in a curtained cubicle, waiting for a doctor and nurses to deal with her scrapes and bruises while Blake's life hung in the balance. She wanted to be near him—to know how he fared.

So she had let herself be buckled into a safety helmet and had climbed on the back of the squat, powerful little vehicle to go meet the mobile unit. Her grandfather was waiting for her, standing in a circle of brightness cast by powerful lamps on the back of the ambulance. He was wearing a heavy parka and a black watch cap, and his breath billowed in the cold, wet air, circling his head like dragon's smoke.

Helping hands lifted her off the ATV and into the brightly lighted interior of the ambulance. Her eyes were tearing from the rain and cold, she ducked her head against the light. "Come on, Emma. Look at me, honey." The words were gruff as always, but gentle, insistent fingers urged her to lift her chin. It was the same touch she remembered as a little girl when some childhood illness or another had made her feverish and fretful.

"I'm fine, Granddad. But Blake—"

He was checking her eyes with the penlight he'd carried in his shirt pocket for as many years as she could remember. He moved his hands over her neck and shoulders, finding the bruise at the back of her head, scowling at the scrape on her cheek. "I don't think that will need a stitch," he said, muttering half to himself, half to her. "But it's going to leave a nasty bruise. No scar, though, or just a tiny one, anyway. Won't need plastic surgery. You can cover it with a little makeup.''

"I'm fine," she said, hearing her voice rise hysterically. What did she care about a little scar? She was in radio, not TV. No one ever saw her face, unless you counted the huge, ugly picture of the WTKX personalities she had to look at every morning on her way to work. She clamped her mouth shut and reined in her careening thoughts. "I'm fine."

Her grandfather nodded, putting his stethoscope into his ears. "Looks like you'll be okay after you get something warm in your stomach and some dry clothes on your bones."

She reached out and clamped his hand between hers. "Blake's been shot."

"I know, honey. I'll check him out the minute they get him down the mountain. The ER at Pittsfield's already on alert. And if he's in worse shape than it sounds from Clint's report, when he's stable we'll Life Flight him into Boston."

"I want to go with him."

"You're going to Twin Oaks to get cleaned up and warmed up, or I'll have Scott here haul you off to the hospital in his squad car whether you want to go or not. And I guarantee you, if that happens, you won't see Blake Weston for the next twenty-four hours—or longer." He jerked his head over his shoulder, and for the first time Emma noticed a tall, broad-shouldered man in the uniform and campaign hat of a state trooper, standing outside the door of the ambulance. "If you behave yourself, he'll take you down to the house and see that you get to Pittsfield ASAP."

"I…" A million arguments jostled in her brain, but she knew voicing any of them with her grandfather would be an even greater waste of breath and time than it had been with Alison. "Thank you. I'll go."

"I need to ask you some questions, Ms. Hart," the state trooper told her. "But first, let's do as your grandfather ordered and get you warm and dry."

"Thank you," Emma repeated automatically. She could hear the roar of another ATV coming down the mountain. She wanted to stay right where she was while they brought Blake to the ambulance, but she turned and walked toward the police car.

Five minutes later she was standing in the entrance of Twin Oaks. Maureen and her grandmother were waiting for her, and in the doorway of the dining room was Cooper's Corner's librarian, Beth Young, who played the piano so beautifully at afternoon teas in the gathering room. She was wearing one of Clint's big white aprons tied snugly around her waist and carrying a tray of sandwiches. Emma caught a glimpse of a coffee urn and stacks of cups on the big mahogany table. Two or three people she didn't recognize were sitting there, eating and drinking. They would be part of the rescue crew, she supposed, called in for refreshments now that the search was ended. Emma wanted to go thank them, but her grandmother's anguished voice distracted her.

"Oh, Emma Martha," she said, holding out her hands. Emma saw the look of horror in her grandmother's eyes and followed the direction of her shocked gaze.

For the first time she saw the damage to Maureen's coat, the gaping tear from the bullet's passage, the bloodstains. So much blood. All of it Blake's. Pinwheels of light and dark whirled behind her eyes. Her knees felt wobbly, and bile rose in her throat. "Nana…" No more words could make it past the tightness in her chest. She started to cry.

Martha opened her arms, and Emma walked blindly into her embrace. "It's all right, baby. It's all right." She patted Emma's back as if she were still a little girl.

"I'm so afraid for him."

"Your grandfather won't let anything happen to him. You know that, don't you?"

Emma nodded and sniffed back her tears. "Granddad's the best doctor in the world."

"Of course he is," Martha Dorn said, recovering herself. She handed Emma a handkerchief. Her grandmother was talking to her as though she were a child, and Emma didn't care a bit. She wiped her eyes and blew her nose, and then she just stood there. She couldn't seem to move her arms or make her brain tell them what to do. "Wipe your tears, then let's get you out of these wet clothes. And get rid of that awful coat."

"I'll need to take the coat," the state trooper said quietly. "It's evidence in the shooting, Mrs. Dorn."

"Oh. Oh, certainly. I…I didn't think of that."

"I'll get a bag. You'll want to secure the chain of evidence." Maureen's voice was tight and hard.

"Thanks, Maureen," he said, then turned to Emma. "Let me help you off with the coat, Ms. Hart. Did you see the shooter at all?" he asked as Emma shrugged out of the garment. The entryway was warm, the fire blazing cheerfully in the gathering room fireplace only yards away, but as far as Emma was concerned, it might as well have been miles. She was cold as ice.

"Scott, can't this wait? Emma's half frozen." Martha reached up and brushed a fresh tear from Emma's cheek with her hand.

Scott. Gears clicked and meshed inside Emma's head. Scott Hunter. Lieutenant Scott Hunter. Yes. She had heard the name before. He'd been married at Twin Oaks not too long ago. Martha's e-mails had been full of the details for weeks. For the life of her, Emma couldn't remember his wife's name, but she had seen her often enough on television in the city. Her brain began to sift through names. Leah? Lisa? Lily? It suddenly seemed very important to remember just who Lieutenant Scott Hunter had married.

"Your wife is Laurel London," she blurted, relieved to have gotten something right.

Scott's rather severe expression softened. "That's right."

"I've seen her on TV."

"And she listens to you on the radio. Why don't you go upstairs with your grandmother and get warmed up and change into dry clothes."

"And she needs something to eat, Scott."

"That, too. I'll go check on Mr. Weston's progress. When I get back we can leave for the hospital. I can ask her what I need to know on the way to Pittsfield."

"You won't leave without me?" Once more Emma's world had narrowed to her anxiety about Blake.

"I won't, ma'am."

Keegan came out of the dining room. He, too, was wearing one of his father's aprons, cinched around his middle and falling to his knees. "I wanted to come and help look for you and Mr. Weston," he said, not quite making eye contact with Emma. He fiddled with the ties of the apron. "Dad said I wasn't old enough to go along on a search and rescue yet. But I wanted to help."

Emma reached out a hand to him, then pulled it back. Her nails were crusted with blood. Keegan saw it, too, and paled a little. He swallowed hard. He looked so earnest and awkward, caught as he was in that stage between boy and man. "Thank you so much for wanting to help.

Someday you'll be a real asset to the team,'' she said, pulling a smile out of the deepest reserves of her heart.

"He's been a great help to me." It was Beth Young speaking. She had come to the entrance of the dining room, and walked forward and put her hands on Keegan's shoulders. She was a striking woman, slender, with pale translucent skin and coal-black hair highlighted with a dramatic streak of white that swept from her widow's peak. "I don't know what I would have done without his expertise in the kitchen."

"All I did was make sandwiches and tell you where to find things," Keegan said, but a dark flush of color on his cheeks betrayed how proud he was of the praise.

"I would like one of those sandwiches before I leave for the hospital," Emma said. "Keegan, would you make one for me, please?"

"Sure. What would you like? We have peanut butter. Or cheese. Or ham. Or roast beef."

Emma's stomach roiled at the mere thought of eating. But her grandmother wouldn't hear of her having only a cup of tea. "Cheese will be just fine."

"Swiss or American?"

Emma felt the confusion and wrenching anxiety she'd been holding back by sheer force of will pulsing behind her eyelids once more. *What difference does it make?* she wanted to scream.

Beth Young noticed it, too, and urged Keegan gently toward the hallway leading to the kitchen. "Why don't you surprise Ms. Hart. And I'll make her a nice hot cup of tea. You can take it up to her room when it's ready."

"I can do that."

"Thanks, Keegan." Emma had control of herself again. Going to pieces in front of Clint's son wouldn't help Blake. She summoned one last smile. "You're a lifesaver.

I need that sandwich just as much as I needed your dad to find me up on the mountain.''

Keegan galloped off to the kitchen, beaming. "Thanks," Beth Young mouthed silently, then followed him with an indulgent smile.

Lieutenant Hunter and Maureen resumed their low-voiced conversation as Emma and her grandmother mounted the stairs. Maureen might as well have been talking in code for all Emma understood, but a small, functioning corner of her brain found it odd that a Berkshire innkeeper should know so much about chains of evidence and ballistics testing. Emma was in no shape to lean over the railing and ask Maureen what was going on. Blake had been shot. By whom wasn't important at the moment. She knew at some point it would become important to her that the man be caught and punished, if not for the shooting itself, then for running away. She knew Maureen's ruined coat would be important evidence. As would her recollections. But none of that mattered at the moment. Only Blake mattered. *Dear God,* she prayed, *let him live.*

And she had so little to tell, really. Heaven knew, she'd racked her brain during those long hours on the mountain. But she'd dredged up so few details. The birds and small forest creatures they'd listened to all afternoon had been silent those last minutes before the shot. She had thought it was because twilight was falling, a natural occurrence. But had it been because a more dangerous human trespasser than she and Blake was nearby?

She continued to sift through small and hazy fragments of memory as she stood under the warming spray of the shower. Nothing had seemed out of place in the cold, gloomy woods. Nothing had intruded on the November twilight except the sound of a car engine idling somewhere near the road. Beyond that, she could tell Scott

Hunter almost nothing. It might have been a truck engine. Or a car. Even the car she'd seen pass by before they'd started back to the B and B. A nondescript car with tinted windows, driven by a man wearing a ball cap pulled low on his forehead. That was all.

Nothing was clear in her mind at the moment.

Nothing but her searing anxiety for Blake.

LIGHTS AND VOICES and pain. He didn't know how much longer he was going to last. The voices were all unfamiliar, except for Clint Cooper. And Emma's grandfather. But Emma was gone. Sometime after he'd lost consciousness they'd spirited her away. Had she gone off to meet with Tubb? He'd dreamed that at some point. That he'd seen them walking hand and hand through the front door of the McGillicuddy place.

"Emma?" The sound he made wasn't quite human. It certainly wasn't recognizable. He lifted his free hand and found an oxygen mask clamped over his nose and mouth. The discovery set his heart pounding. He didn't need oxygen. He could breathe on his own.

"Take it easy, son." Felix Dorn spoke from somewhere just out of view.

He tore at the mask, but someone grabbed his wrist, and to his horror he found he couldn't shake off the grip.

"He's going to start bleeding again if we don't keep him quiet." That came from the small woman with the nose that was more suited to a Roman gladiator than a petite blond with cornflower blue eyes.

"This will settle him down." Emma's grandfather leaned over her shoulder and emptied a syringe into the IV tubing in his left arm. "Don't fight it," he ordered, his face contorted with his habitual scowl beneath the bright lights mounted in the ceiling of the swaying ambulance. Blake blinked and tried to focus on the old man's face. His eyes were surprisingly gentle, in stark contrast to his gruff tone and iron hold. Blake couldn't shake off the grip of an eighty-year-old man. He must be in worse shape than he thought.

Everything was moving in slow circles. He didn't hurt like he had before. The pain had receded to a dull ache in his side. Was that good or bad? Medication? Or approaching death? He made one last desperate attempt to make himself understood. "Emma." He meant to scream her name, but even to his ears it sounded like a whimper. The circles of light began spinning faster. The old devil dog's face began to dissolve in the glare.

"Don't fight it, Marine," Emma's grandfather said from what seemed a long way away. "She'll be there when you wake up. I promise."

THE RIDE to Pittsfield passed in a blur of humming tires and the click of windshield wipers. The rain had turned to big wet flakes of snow while they were at Twin Oaks. It was quiet for the moment, the police radio silent, the questions finished. Emma had done her best to answer each and every one, but she was afraid her jumbled and imperfect recollections of those terrible minutes before and after the shooting were not much help.

She laid her head against the back of the hard leather seat and felt her grandmother's feather-light touch on her arm. A faint smile quirked the corners of her mouth and played across her lips as Martha spoke. "That's it, take a little nap, Emma Martha. We'll be there so much quicker that way." It was the same tactic she'd used on Emma as a child when they were traveling in the car. Sleep and the miles would melt away in a lovely dream. Only this time

Emma was afraid if she went to sleep, her dreams would be nightmares of blood and pursuit.

Emma did as she was told, though, and dutifully closed her eyes.

Martha Dorn could be as stubborn and autocratic as her husband when she got the chance. She had informed Lieutenant Hunter in no uncertain terms that she intended to make the trip to the medical center with Emma. And that he could inform her husband of that fact when he checked on Blake's condition on his radio. When Maureen volunteered to drive them instead, Martha brushed aside the suggestion that she would be more comfortable in the Twin Oaks van. "I jounced halfway across Korea in the dead of winter in the back of a Red Cross truck," she said, her chin high. "I can make it to Pittsfield in the back of a police cruiser."

Emma's fears for Blake kept her from falling asleep, and when they reached the hospital, everything seemed a blur of muted sounds and colors and sharp, unfamiliar smells. Emma felt as if she were floating in a cloud of unreality until she saw her grandfather's beloved, glowering face.

"Granddad?" She was afraid to ask straight out how Blake was doing. What if he had died on the way to the hospital? It didn't bear thinking of.

"He's doing fine," Felix assured her, anticipating her unspoken questions. "Looks like the slug nicked an artery and did a lot of muscle damage. They're giving him blood and he should be out of surgery in an hour or two. He insisted no one notify his family or co-workers, and he was lucid enough to sign his consent papers. He would have been a good man to have at my side in Korea," he added gruffly under his breath.

It was the highest compliment he could pay a man.

Emma dropped her head and let the tears come. Her grandfather guided her to one of the chairs in the surgical suite waiting room and patted her awkwardly on the shoulder. "There, there, Emma Martha. Don't cry. He's a damned tough young man. He'll be up and around, if not exactly kicking up his heels, in time for the Marine Corps birthday ball." No granddaughter of Felix Dorn had to ask what date that was— November tenth. Only a few days away. Emma began to relax a little.

"You're sure he's going to be all right?" she asked, sniffling.

"I said so, didn't I?" he responded in his usual, nothing-out-of-the-ordinary crabby tone. It sounded wonderful. She closed her eyes, aware of her grandmother's hands folded over hers and her grandfather's solid presence with only a fraction of her mind. The rest of her perception had turned inward, focused on this sudden rush of light-headedness, a buoyancy that she knew was more than just relief. So much more.

I love you. The words echoed in her mind and in her heart. It didn't matter that she had known Blake for only a few days. It didn't matter that she had thought the same thing about her feelings for Daryl Tubb mere weeks ago. This was something so vastly different, so complex and soul-deep, that she had no words to describe it.

It had to be love.

Real love. Not the lukewarm, confusing jumble of emotions that had characterized her relationship with Daryl.

Daryl?

She had barely given him a thought in hours. Was he still waiting for her? She glanced at her watch. It was after midnight. Surely he had left the roadhouse by now. Gone home to the apartment in Williamstown that she had never seen.

She was only dimly aware of the long minutes crawling by, of people coming and going, of the waiting room emptying until only the three of them remained. She closed her eyes and, unbelievably, dozed off until a bearded— and seemingly too young—man in surgical scrubs came to tell them that the surgery had gone just as her grandfather predicted. There had been no complications and no lasting damage done. Blake Weston was a very lucky man, considering he'd been shot with a slug calibrated to bring down a deer, the surgeon said, shaking his head. His recovery should be as uncomplicated as the surgery. He accepted Emma and her grandmother's thanks, shook hands with her grandfather and left the waiting room.

"I told you everything was going to be fine," Felix said with one of his rare, rusty smiles.

Emma smiled. "Everything," she repeated.

"It's going to be some time before you can see him. Why don't you come down to the cafeteria with your grandmother and me and have a cup of tea or some soup?"

"I'll stay here," she said, shaking her head. "I'm not hungry."

"We'll bring you back some broth," Martha said softly, but with as much conviction as one of Felix's commands would have held.

"Some soup would taste good," Emma admitted.

"Good. Soup it will be." Martha and Felix walked out of the room hand in hand and disappeared down the hall. Emma watched them go with a lump in her throat. That was what she wanted in life more than anything else. A relationship, a love affair that would last half a century and beyond. With Blake.

A movement in the doorway of the waiting area caught

her eye, and she turned her head to see Daryl standing there, snowflakes peppering the shoulders of his trench coat.

She'd forgotten all about him. About the meeting they were supposed to have. Even the reason for it.

It all came flooding back, and her heart, so light just seconds ago, felt like a stone in her chest.

"Daryl. What are you doing here?"

CHAPTER THIRTEEN

"GIVE ME SOME CREDIT, Emma. I came to make sure you were all right." Daryl looked relieved to see her, but his tone reflected hurt feelings.

"How did you know where to find me?"

"My parents," he said, as though speaking to a child. His tone grated on Emma's nerves, already rubbed raw by the trauma and anguish of the last hours. She should have told him from the beginning she found that particular habit annoying, instead of keeping quiet and hoping he'd grow to realize it himself. She opened her mouth to tell him so, but his next words forestalled her. "I should have known you wouldn't have stood me up if there wasn't a damned good reason." He crossed the room and took her in his arms before she could stop him. "Are you sure you're okay?"

His heart was beating like a drum in his chest, and she could feel the tremor in his hands as he hugged her tight. He had been worried about her. There was no faking a response like that. She was ashamed of herself for being suspicious that he might have been. Her anger melted away, replaced by a vague sort of sadness for what might have been. She remembered all the good times they'd shared in the months past, and there had been many of them. But that's all they'd been. Good times. Not the laying of a foundation for a life together. She had been in love with the idea of being in love, not with Daryl Tubb.

She should have admitted that to herself weeks ago when she first suspected his infidelity. Being willfully blind had cost her dearly. "I'm fine."

"What happened? Mom and Dad weren't too clear on the details. Philo and Phyllis called and told them you and Weston were shot in the hills below the old McGillicuddy place. I thought they must have misunderstood the report when it came over the emergency scanner."

She stepped out of his arms. He frowned but made no move to bring her back into his embrace. "Philo and Phyllis had it partly wrong. As you can see, I wasn't hurt at all."

"Thank God." Daryl reached out and touched the butterfly bandage her grandfather had insisted on applying to the cut on her cheek. "What's this?"

"It's nothing," Emma insisted. "A scratch. I didn't even need a stitch."

His touch was gentle, but it might well have been the touch of a stranger. "Tell me what the hell happened."

"We hiked into the hills, and someone took a shot at us. A poacher, I guess, because the surgeon said it was a deer slug that hit Blake." Her voice cracked a little but she steadied it with an almost physical effort of will. She wasn't going to break down in front of Daryl. She didn't want to be comforted by him. And that was the saddest thing of all. She didn't want to be comforted by the man she'd thought she wanted to spend every day of the rest of her life with.

Where she really wanted to be was in the arms of a man, still almost a stranger, who was fighting to recover only a few feet away. "He's going to be all right," she said so fiercely and with so much conviction that Daryl's eyes widened in surprise, then darkened with a dawning sense of understanding.

''That's good to hear,'' he said, but there was a bleakness in his voice that hadn't been there before. He sounded sincere, and once more Emma felt a twinge of remorse, but mostly she just wanted him to go away and leave her to her vigil.

''Why did you wait so long to come here if you were so worried about me, Daryl? We've been here for hours.'' She was so tired she could barely stand upright, but she reached deep inside herself and tapped into a last reserve of strength and clarity. She had intended to have the truth from Daryl about his affair with Blake's ex-lover tonight, and she meant to keep her promise to herself.

His sandy brows pulled together in a quick frown. ''You aren't going to make this easy for me, are you?''

''No. I think I've made everything too easy for you as long as we've been together.'' That, too, was her fault. She had never cared enough, even though she had tried to tell herself she did, and Daryl had picked up on those signals. He wasn't a bad man. Just a weak one. Perhaps someday he would find a woman he truly loved enough to be faithful to her. Emma wasn't that woman, and they both knew it in their hearts. But the words needed to be said aloud. The last frayed cords that bound them together, however tenuously, needed to be cut.

''Let's sit down. You look like you're going to collapse at my feet.''

''I'm not,'' she insisted, but she sat down anyway. As important as this conversation was, she found only half her thoughts were focused on it. The rest of her senses were concentrated on every sound, every door opening, every footfall in the corridor that might signal a nurse or doctor coming to give her news of Blake.

''I didn't hear what had happened up on the mountain

until nearly eleven. That's how long I waited for you to show up for our meeting.''

''I wondered if you would even come at all.''

His mouth tightened. He didn't like being put on the defensive. ''I didn't have much choice. Weston swore if I didn't get everything out in the open with you, he'd tell you everything.''

''Blake?'' She wasn't aware the two men had ever met face to face, except for that night at Blake's apartment.

''He tracked me down at the diner this morning.'' He glanced at the big round clock above her head. ''Well, I guess it was yesterday morning. And…made me an offer I couldn't refuse, shall we say.'' His gaze focused on the wall just past her left shoulder. A muscle jumped in his jaw. ''He's a damned hard man to refuse.''

''Were you going to tell me the truth?''

He looked directly at her. ''Yes,'' he said. ''I was.'' For a split second she wondered if he was lying to her once more. The fleeting thought must have shown in her expression.

''Give me that much credit, Emma. I was going to tell you everything about me and Heather. I…I was banking on your forgiveness and your love to give me a second chance.'' He reached out and took her hands between his. When she made a small effort to pull away, he tightened his grip a fraction, and she stopped struggling. He watched her closely for a moment, then sighed. ''I'm glad I didn't get any takers on that bet. I would have lost my money, wouldn't I?''

She nodded, tears stinging the backs of her eyes. ''Yes,'' she whispered. ''I can't love a man I can't trust.''

''She didn't mean anything to me, Emma, you know that,'' he said, his voice rising a little in desperation.

''I wish she did mean something to you, Daryl. It's an

even bigger betrayal of what I thought we had together that you were unfaithful to me with a woman you claim to care nothing about.''

Daryl winced. ''You make me sound like a randy kid who can't keep his pants zipped.''

''Isn't that the way you behaved?''

''It will never happen again, Emma. I'll swear that on a stack of Bibles. Give me another chance. I'll never look at another woman as long as I live.'' He leaned forward, his body rigid with tension.

''I can't, Daryl.'' An image of her grandparents walking hand in hand down the hall flashed into her consciousness. That's what she wanted from life. To still be holding hands with the man she loved in fifty years. She was like all the men and women who called her show asking for advice. She wanted to find her soul mate, her other half. When Daryl came along, she had tried to force him into the mold, and it had backfired on her.

''I thought you loved me.''

''I thought I did, too. But now I know I was wrong.'' She tugged free of his grip, and when he clasped his hands together between his knees, she covered them briefly with her own. ''I realize now that it wasn't love, Daryl. Not the kind of love my parents and grandparents have for each other. Not the kind of love that keeps a couple together for fifty years, day in and day out, through good times and bad, and still has them sneaking kisses behind the counter the way I've seen your parents do. That kind of love takes work. Hard work. And it can't be built on a foundation of lies and half truths.''

''You figured this all out in the last three days?''

''Some of it.''

''How much of it did you figure out because of Weston?''

She looked him straight in the eye. "Quite a bit. But your mother said a lot of the same things. She said your family stayed married. That they were in it for the long haul. We never had that kind of commitment. Admit it, Daryl."

"Weston's on the rebound from Heather, you know." That dart hit home, but she refused to let him know he'd scored a hit. *I love you.* The echo of Blake's pain-racked words filled her head. Perhaps he hadn't even been speaking to her, but to the phantom of his unfaithful lover. Emma shivered. She didn't want to consider that. But even if it were true, it didn't change anything between her and Daryl.

"This is about you and me. Not me and Blake. It's over between us, Daryl," she said as gently as she could. "You know that."

"It doesn't have to be. I know we'd have to start over from the beginning, but I love you, Emma."

"No, you don't, Daryl. Don't demean me or yourself by thinking you do. If you loved me, you wouldn't have betrayed that love as casually as you did."

There was no answer to that statement, and she could see it on his face when he realized it. "I'm sorry, Emma," he said quietly, once more taking her hands in his. "More sorry than you'll ever know."

She started to say that she was sorry, too. But the sound she'd been listening for, the whoosh of the heavy automatic doors leading to the surgery and recovery suites, forestalled her. She and Daryl were alone in the waiting room. The hallways were quiet and deserted. Surely whoever was coming through those doors was coming to take her to Blake. She stood up. From the corner of her eye she saw her grandparents making their way to the waiting room. Felix was carrying a foam container and a plastic spoon. Her soup.

The elderly couple quickened their steps, arriving in the waiting room just as a nurse in deep purple scrubs did. Martha and Felix exchanged a quick glance when they saw Daryl standing close to Emma, but like her, their attention was focused on the nurse.

"Ms. Hart?"

"Yes." Emma reached for her grandmother's hand. "How is he?"

"He's awake," the paunchy middle-aged man said with a grin that was tired but infectious. "He's asking for you. You can go in for a few minutes if you're quiet."

Emma didn't know what to do. She wanted to be with Blake so badly it was like a hunger inside her, but she could also see how tired her grandparents were. It was very late. They needed to be home, safe, in their beds. She hadn't thought about that until this very moment. Suddenly she was torn, unable to move. She glanced helplessly from her grandparents to the nurse's puzzled face. What should she do next?

Martha was gray with fatigue, and her grandfather was limping, his lumbago acting up from being out in the cold and rain. Why hadn't she noticed that before? But Blake was asking for her…

It was Daryl who read her thoughts and came to her rescue. The Daryl she'd thought he was when she first met him months before. With a ghost of the smile she had found so charming, he brushed her cheek with his lips and gave her a little push. "Go on, Emma," he said. "Go to him. Give me a chance to redeem myself a little. I'll see your grandparents get back to Cooper's Corner safe and sound."

BLAKE SAT on the side of the hospital bed, head bowed, breathing heavily. He hadn't expected it to be such a task just to shower and get dressed, even if all he was wearing was a pair of sweats and a flannel shirt that Clint had loaned him. Not much of a fashion statement, but there was no way he could get a pair of jeans on over the heavy surgical dressing on his side. He could use a pain pill, but he wasn't going to ask for one.

He'd spent the morning arguing with Emma and his doctor, neither of whom thought three days was long enough to be trapped in this pale blue cubicle of a room. But he'd had about all he could take of being poked and probed and prodded, and most of all, he was tired of the food.

If he ever saw another bowl of green gelatin in his life, it would be too soon.

So he'd called Clint Cooper at Twin Oaks and asked him to pack up his stuff. He could make it back to the city on his own if he had to. But he had other plans for transportation to New York.

"I see you're determined to go through with this." It was Emma standing in the doorway of his room, raindrops sparkling in her glorious auburn hair, her nose pink from the cold November air. What was left of Indian summer had been washed away by the rain the night he'd been shot. From the little slice of sky and parking lot he could see from the arrow slit of a window in his room, winter had arrived.

"I need to get back to the city. My parents are threatening to come up here from Florida and take care of me." Every word of that was truth. His parents were determined he needed their help, and it had taken all his persuasive skills to keep them in Kissimmee for the time being. "A steady diet of bean sprouts and tofu ought to set my recovery back another week or ten days. And Summer has already contacted an old classmate from med school who's practicing here to look in on me—''

"She's concerned about you."

"She's a pediatrician. So's this guy. He had Tasmanian Devil and Bugs Bunny on his tie. He offered me a lollipop to stick out my tongue.'' When Emma laughed, smoothing out the stress line that had developed between her softly arched eyebrows, he was glad he'd made the joke. There were dark shadows beneath her eyes from lack of sleep, and that was his fault, too.

"You've been acting pretty childishly this morning, signing yourself out of here when you can barely walk to the bathroom. Summer's friend probably figured you'd respond best to the same tactics he uses on his littler patients.''

"Very funny." He shifted his weight a little too quickly, and the stitch of pain in his side caught him off guard. He bit back a groan. Emma was beside him in a heartbeat.

"You'd better lie down."

"No. I'm not getting back in this bed. Help me over to the chair.''

"You're behaving worse than a sick child," she scolded, placing her hand beneath his elbow and taking most of his weight. He made it to the chair without becoming light-headed, an accomplishment, and lowered himself cautiously onto the hard seat. "How do you expect to look after yourself in New York, especially if you won't let your parents come up to help out?" she asked, stepping back and settling herself on the edge of the mattress. She'd barely touched him since he'd come out of the fog of anesthetic and pain pills. Before that, up on the mountain, she had been beside him every moment, and her touch had been soft and loving.

Perhaps he hadn't told her he loved her up there on the mountain, after all. Perhaps that had been as much of a dream as the nightmares that had haunted him since he'd been here. Dark figures with guns. Blazing, hate-filled eyes taking aim at his head. Old dreams of old enemies from ten years and half a world away, reinforced by the terror of that never-to-be-forgotten September morning in New York when the World Trade Center had come hurtling down around him.

"I'll be fine."

"You don't look fine."

"You're beginning to sound like your granddad."

"I—" That one scored a hit. She shut her mouth with a snap.

"I was hoping you'd offer me a ride back into the city."

Shock widened her eyes. "How did you know I was leaving Cooper's Corner early?"

"Your grandfather told me when he stopped by last evening." She hadn't wanted Blake to know she was going. He could see it in her face.

"I'm already packed and ready to go. It will mean over an hour delay to go to Cooper's Corner for your things."

"Clint's on his way with my stuff."

"Oh." She had hoped to put a wrench in his plans with that objection. She frowned a bit harder but seemed unable to think of any more excuses. "I suppose I can drop you at your building," she agreed reluctantly.

"Thanks." Step one of his objective had been successfully completed. On to step two. He had thought they could spend a day or two at Twin Oaks, but had changed his mind even before her grandfather had let slip that she'd checked out of the B and B the afternoon he'd been shot. Twin Oaks was where she'd come with Tubb, where they'd made love—possibly in the room he was renting. He didn't want her to be thinking of that. Someday they'd come back, when those memories had been replaced by ones they made together. They were better off in New York. On the drive they'd be alone together in her car. He'd have a clear head. He'd find out what was bothering her and make it right.

Her touch had been gentle and her voice soft and comforting those first hazy hours after his surgery, but then she'd withdrawn. She was still there every day, and sometimes in the night when he awoke, sweating and caught in the dream, but there'd been no passion, no fire in her touch. She might as well have been Summer looking after him. He hadn't had the strength or the clarity of mind to figure out why she'd withdrawn. He still wasn't sure what had happened, but he had a couple of theories, none of them comforting.

Had she thought twice about breaking her engagement? Had the Realtor Lothario managed to work his way out of the hole he'd dug himself into with his tomcat ways? Had she taken him back?

That was the first thing he intended to find out. And if she had, it was the first thing he intended to change.

"How will you get your truck back to the city?" she asked.

A knock sounded on the door frame before he could answer that Clint had business in the city the next week and had offered Blake a ride to Cooper's Corner when he returned home so he could repossess his truck. The man himself was standing in the hallway with Blake's carryall slung over his shoulder. At his side was a Massachusetts highway patrol lieutenant.

"Clint. Lieutenant Hunter." Emma smiled at them, but there were questions in her eyes.

"Hi, Emma."

"Hello, Ms. Hart."

"Blake, do you remember Lieutenant Hunter?"

"I think I do. You stopped by the morning after my surgery."

"That's right." He stepped into the room and handed Blake a hat. It was his old red baseball cap emblazoned with the Corps emblem. The one he'd been wearing when he was shot. Ash had bought it for him with his allowance money a dozen years ago when Blake went off to Saudi. He'd figured he would never see it again. "My men found it in the woods opposite the old McGillicuddy place. Were you wearing it that day?"

Blake gave a short nod. "It would have been pretty hard for the shooter to mistake me for a deer," he said. Or Emma, with the ends of Maureen's orange scarf trailing in the wind.

Hunter returned the nod. "We're going on a theory that it was a poacher. Doc says it was a clean wound, T&T, but it definitely came from a deer slug. Probably a twenty-gauge shotgun. The rain and snow pretty much took care of any physical evidence the shooter might have left behind. But there might be something you can tell us today that you weren't up to talking about before."

"I'm sorry I wasn't more help that night." His memories of the shooting and the day after were only bits and pieces of thoughts and sensations stuffed in the pockets of his mind like reminders written on scraps of paper.

"Do you feel like answering a few questions now?"

"I'll do my best. You caught me just in time. Emma's driving me back into the city this afternoon." She opened her mouth as if to make one more protest, then evidently decided it wasn't worth the effort.

Hunter's eyebrows rose a fraction of an inch but he didn't make any comment on Blake's leaving the hospital or the state. "Mr. Weston, can you give me any new details about the shooting? Emma's already told me what she remembers."

"I wish I could have been more help," she interrupted, leaning forward, both hands planted on the hard mattress. "I didn't see anything, really. The shooter was behind me. If Blake hadn't seen—"

"What did you see, Mr. Weston?"

"Not much." Blake turned his thoughts inward. "A shape, a glint of light on a gun barrel." Then his instincts had taken over. Instincts that were just rusty enough to make him a split second too slow. But at least Emma hadn't been hurt. Her grandfather had told him the hole in Maureen's coat had been close to the heart. As a matter of fact, the old man had ruminated, if you considered the slight difference in the size of the two women, the shot probably would have hit Maureen.

"The man in the car that passed the farm had a dark cap." Emma interrupted once more. "I couldn't see his face. The car windows were tinted. I know it might have been someone else altogether who shot at us, but he's the only person we saw up there."

"Do you remember what kind of car he was driving?"

"No, I'm sorry. I'm terrible with car models or years. It wasn't too big. Or too small." She closed her eyes, turning her vision inward, concentrating so fiercely that her brows drew together in a straight line. "It was light colored, pale gray, I think. Like a rental car, you know. Very, very ordinary." Emma opened her eyes and shrugged apologetically. "I'm sorry, that's all I can remember."

"It was a midsize. A Chevy Lumina," Blake said. "Late model. And it was pale gray, just as Emma remembers." He didn't add that he hadn't been paying attention to the driver of the car at the time, only to the woman standing so enticingly near.

"Can you give me any better description of the man driving the car?" Scott Hunter looked first to Emma and then to Blake. He caught the frown Blake couldn't quite keep from altering his expression. The old dream flickered behind his eyelids once more, just at the corner of his consciousness. "Mr. Weston?"

Blake shook his head. "Sorry," he said. Clint's hands had balled into fists.

"Are you sure there isn't something else you remember? Anything at all? My sister's life might depend on it." Clint moved to stand in front of the trooper. His face was tight, his jaw set in a hard, straight line. "I don't think the shooting was an accident. I think the gunman mistook Emma for Maureen. There was a man back in New York—" He broke off as though he had already said too much.

Felix's suggestion that Maureen might have been killed if she had been standing in Emma's place came to mind once more, and Blake knew that Clint Cooper had made the same connection, and obviously for a reason Blake knew nothing about. But he was right. Emma and Maureen were similar in height. They both had auburn hair, and Emma had been wearing Maureen's coat and scarf. From a distance they would be hard to tell apart, especially in the rain and gloom of a November twilight.

He caught Clint watching him through narrowed eyes. He felt the other man's anguish and the iron-hard determination to protect his sister from whatever it was in her past that might have followed her to Cooper's Corner. He held Clint's gaze for a long moment, but there was nothing he could say to relieve his anxiety.

"I'm sorry. The whole night's pretty hazy. Bits of sounds and pictures come and go." He lifted his shoulders in a shrug. "What I saw would never hold up in court. All the bad guys look alike to me. He might have been blond and blue-eyed. He might have been dark-haired. I'm sorry I can't tell you more."

"Thanks, Weston. When you feel up to it, I'll need a signed statement from you." The trooper settled his hat on his head.

"You're not going to pursue this?" Clint demanded of the other man.

"It's an open case. We'll follow up any leads we get," Lieutenant Hunter answered patiently.

"Damn it. Emma and Maureen could have been twins wearing that coat and scarf. You know damned well that was no poacher who took a potshot at Blake and Emma. I want Maureen protected, Hunter."

"I'm doing that. And don't underestimate your sister. She's one tough lady. She can take care of herself."

CHAPTER FOURTEEN

IT WAS DARK by the time they neared the city, the short November twilight giving way to a moonless night. Blake had been silent for a long time. Emma wondered what he was thinking about. They'd discussed the circumstances of the shooting, Clint's reaction in Blake's hospital room, and the conversation Emma had overhead between Maureen and Lieutenant Hunter. They had come to the conclusion that neither of them knew what the devil was going on, and probably wouldn't, unless the shooter was apprehended. Blake didn't seem to think that would happen anytime soon, and Emma reluctantly agreed. She also realized it would be a long time before she was comfortable walking in the hills again. Blake, however, didn't share her alarm. "You can't let the bad guys win, Emma," he had said, then settled back in the seat for a nap.

"I still can't get used to it looking so different," she said as the city skyline appeared before them, glittering against the dark night. "Were you here?" she asked. She didn't know if Braxton, Cartwright and Wheeler had had offices in the doomed twin towers. It was a high-profile company and a prestigious address like the World Trade Center would have almost been a given. How many friends and associates had Blake lost in the carnage? Had he been trapped in the masses of doomed souls trying to escape the flames and terror?

"I was there," he said. "I thought I'd seen a lot of terrible things in Kuwait and Somalia, but I was wrong. That day was the worst."

"Were your company's offices in the building?"

He shook his head. "No. B, C and W never left Wall Street. Not in twenty-nine. Not after Pearl Harbor. Not when they built the Twin Towers. It used to be a sore spot with most of the brokers and traders, even one or two of the partners. But no more."

But if he had been there, as he said, it meant he had moved toward the fallen buildings, not away from them.

"Most of our on-air personalities got caught outside the city," she said, keeping her eyes on the road so he wouldn't see the tears she still sometimes had trouble keeping back. "Armand and I—he's my producer—were in the studio getting ready to head off to a remote broadcast. We stayed on the air for twenty-seven hours."

"I remember," Blake said quietly. "I was at a triage center at Ground Zero. Somewhere WTKX was playing on a boom box. You did a good job."

"I just tried to keep it all going." He didn't say what he'd been doing at the triage station, and Emma didn't ask. He would tell her someday when the time was right.

There she was again, assuming they had a future. Repeating the same mistakes she'd made with Daryl.

"You kept people from panicking. You got them the best information you could find. I remember."

She didn't want to talk about what she had done. It was no more than what many others had done. "The radio station raised almost a million dollars in donations for the victims and the Red Cross," she said, channeling the subject in a slightly different direction. "I'm proud of that."

"You should be."

They fell silent again, as they had been for so many

miles. She turned her thoughts away from those bleak days. Life went on, and the city was moving forward. And she needed to move forward with it. Come Monday, she would begin negotiations on the syndication contract in earnest.

"Traffic's not bad at all this evening," she said as they neared the heart of the city. There was a steady stream of headlights outbound to the suburbs, though, as men and women headed home from work. "Are you hungry? Do you want to stop someplace for a bite to eat?"

He shook his head. "My housekeeper should have re-stocked the refrigerator when she cleaned yesterday. I'll find something. Don't worry."

"Okay." But she did worry. The doctor had been more than a little unhappy about Blake checking himself out of the hospital so early. But he hadn't asked her to stay and help him, and she wasn't going to volunteer.

He hadn't said or done anything since he'd regained his senses that indicated he remembered saying he loved her up there on the mountain.

Or had she only thought she'd heard the words?

She gave up on keeping a conversation going and con-centrated on her driving. Blake did the same, only break-ing the silence to give her directions to his building. "You can just pull up out front and drop me off," he told her. "The doorman can get my bag."

"Oh, no, you don't," she said. "Where's the entrance to your parking garage? I've got you this far. I'm going to make sure you get safely to your own bed."

"That's exactly where I want to be," he said, and something in the tone of his voice set off little shock waves of awareness so deep inside her that they echoed in her chest and belly like heartbeats.

His building was an Art Deco masterpiece close enough

to Central Park that the upper floors would have a good view. She bet the apartments had high ceilings and fireplaces and claw-footed bathtubs. It was the kind of building she'd love to call home.

If you married Blake it would be your home.

Love. Marriage. Only a week ago she'd connected Daryl's name to those words.

Now she was linking them with Blake.

She felt as though she'd walked through the looking glass. Everything was moving much too fast. But regardless of the warning bells inside her head, her body still thrummed with desire for the man in the seat beside her.

Only desire, not love? How could she tell? Would she ever completely trust her feelings again? Would she always have these doubts? It was an unwelcome thought and it circled to her fears that it would carry over into her work. Then where would she be? Alone and out of a job.

Emma's mind was still racing when she pulled into the entrance to the underground garage and then the empty parking space Blake indicated. Thankfully it was within a few yards of the elevator. She turned off the engine, and silence filled her little car. He unfolded his long legs from the cramped front seat and used the armrest, and then the roof of the car to lever himself upright.

"You couldn't wait thirty seconds for me to help you," she scolded as she hauled his duffel out of her trunk, letting her perfectly justified annoyance at his stubbornness push her uncertainties and sexual frustration into a tiny, dimly lit corner of her mind.

"I'm fine."

"Sure," she said. "You're ready to run a marathon. Can you make it to the elevator or should I call nine-one-one here and now?"

When the elevator doors slid open on Blake's floor, he

motioned to the left, preceding her into the carpeted hall-way. He had a corner apartment, it seemed. The view would be spectacular. When he dug in the pocket of his sweats for his key, Emma kept her eyes averted, but it did no good. Immediately she was transported to the lean-to, could feel again the heaviness of his sex along the edge of her hand as she searched for his penknife. The desire and longing she'd suppressed for an entire five minutes came surging back, and her pulse rate kicked up several beats. The key turned easily in the lock, and he swung the heavy, six-paneled door open into a wood-floored foyer. The room beyond glowed softly in the reflection of the lights of Central Park shining through two tall, sheer-covered windows.

Blake walked slowly into the living room. He rested both hands on the back of a huge leather couch and bowed his head. Emma let his bag slide off her shoulder, kicking the door closed. Blake never even flinched at the sound as it thudded shut behind her.

As Emma watched, uncertain what to do next, he moved around the couch and lowered himself stiffly onto it. The uncertainty of his movements released her from her hesitation. Before he could protest, she stooped to lift his feet onto the cushions and untied his shoes so he could toe them off. They landed on the soft woven carpeting with two substantial thuds. "Thanks," he said with a rue-ful twist of his lips. "I never realized it was such a damned long walk up from the garage."

"You ought to be in bed."

The smile faded from his mouth. "This will do fine."

She grabbed a throw pillow and positioned it behind his head. Glancing around for something to use as a blan-ket, she got her first good look at the room. It did have high, corniced ceilings and a fireplace along one wall. The colors were rich and warm, shades of brown and mellow ivory with touches of gold and copper. The furniture was substantial, supple leather and dark wood. A man's room. If Heather had wanted to change things in Blake's life, she hadn't gotten as far as his living room. Heather again. She had to get the woman out of her mind.

"I'll get you a blanket." She stood, hesitating. Getting a blanket would mean going into his bedroom. She could feel heat creeping from her belly to her breasts. No, not his bedroom. Not yet. "Or a throw, maybe? Yes, a throw. Do you have one lying about?"

Blake grabbed her wrist. Regardless of lingering weakness and fatigue, his grip was strong and sure. "There's one right here, at the end of the couch."

"Oh." She looked where he was pointing. The throw was mere inches from her hand. Cashmere, soft as down. "If it was a snake it would have bitten me." The saying was one of Martha's favorites, and she blurted it out without thinking. Emma felt the heat rise even higher, into her cheeks.

"It's okay, Emma. I don't need a blanket. I just need to catch my breath. You don't have to stick around and wait on me hand and foot."

"I'm not waiting on you hand and foot. I just want to make sure you're comfortable before I leave." His touch was making her anything but comfortable. She searched frantically for something to do that would remove her from his immediate vicinity before she threw herself on the couch beside him. "Are you hungry? Where's the kitchen? You said the housekeeper would have stocked the refrigerator. I'll make you something to eat."

He didn't loose his hold on her wrist. "I don't want anything to eat."

"Well, I do. It's been hours since lunchtime." She gave her hand a tug, and he released her. "Where—"

He pointed toward the wall where the fireplace stood flanked by two doorways. "Door to the right. Down the hall." Emma fled.

The kitchen had been updated recently. The appliances were stainless steel, the granite countertops and tiled floor in the same shades of earth tones as the living room. There was a small alcove with a polished wood table and chairs whose bay window opened onto a balcony and another spectacular view of the park. She opened the restaurant-size refrigerator and found a number of covered plastic dishes. One of them contained a rich, aromatic vegetable soup, and Emma's stomach rumbled when its scent reached her nostrils. Blake's housekeeper was obviously a treasure.

In five minutes she had the soup simmering on the stove and at least a little bit of her composure back. She couldn't find tea bags, and it was too late for coffee, so she settled for glasses of bottled water. There was, however, a wonderful crusty loaf of multigrain bread and what looked like homemade jam in the refrigerator. She added spoons and napkins to the bowls of soup and loaded everything on a tray.

Emma stepped back and surveyed her handiwork, then swiped her damp palms down the legs of her slacks. She couldn't hide out in Blake's kitchen forever. He was hungry and needed nourishment. A quick mental image of cooking for him every night in this kitchen streaked through her mind. She'd never had fantasies like that before—except that day in the old McGillicuddy farm kitchen. It was almost as unsettling as the dreams of sex with him that tantalized her in the wee small hours of the night.

She returned to the living room and placed the tray on a table between the windows. "It's soup," she said, turning to find him asleep, his head resting on one hand propped on the back of the couch. The pain lines had smoothed out, but a slight frown between his brows told her he was still uncomfortable.

What should she do? Wake him? Leave him to rest? Go home before she found herself on her knees, brushing a stray, stubborn wave of dark hair off his forehead? Bending forward to kiss him? Lying beside him to keep him safe and warm, as she'd tried so hard to do those terrifying hours on the mountain?

No. She had to be honest with herself. This time she didn't want to lie beside Blake to protect him, but to love him.

A lamp on a table beside the couch was shining directly on his face. He frowned a little harder in his sleep, as though annoyed by the glare. She had taken a step or two forward without realizing it. Her last thought, making love with Blake, set off warning bells. A ringing in her ears that would do justice to a four-alarm blaze. But she ignored the inner clamor and crossed the remaining expanse of carpet. She turned off the light, and soft shadows closed in around them. Then she did what her heart bid, not what her mind ordered, and sank to her knees beside the couch. She reached out and laid her hand gently on the side of his face. His skin was cool to the touch, a little rough. He probably needed to shave twice a day. Another intimate detail she wanted to become familiar with.

"Blake," she whispered. She couldn't have spoken louder if she wanted to. Her throat was constricted with nerves and longing, a paralyzing combination. "Blake."

His eyes opened, more brown than green-gold in the half light. He stared through her for a long moment, then seemed to come to himself. He smiled. "You're still here."

A smile, nothing more. But Emma was grateful she was sitting down. Her knees would have been too weak to hold her upright otherwise. "I'm still here. I wouldn't leave without telling you. I made you some soup."

"I don't want any soup," he said.

"What do you want?" she asked, no more able to stop the words than she could fly away.

"You. Making love to you is all I've wanted to do since almost the moment I first laid eyes on you."

Emma's heart fluttered in her chest. But that had only been seven days ago. *Too soon, too soon.* The inner warnings screeched. *Slow down. Wait. Don't leap before you look, the way you did with Daryl.*

"That's what you want, too, isn't it?"

Once more the words jumped unbidden to her lips. "God help me, yes."

His hand closed on her upper arm. He urged her closer until she was sitting beside him on the couch. She braced her arm above him, settling her weight gingerly, careful not to cause him more pain. He continued to watch her, leaning against the pillows. His grip didn't lessen. When he raised his head, she bent hers to meet him more than halfway, and her eyes closed reflexively. The siren shriek of warning was silenced as her brain shut down. She was nothing but a shivering mass of need and desire. She was lost and she didn't care. All she could see were bright colored pinpoints of light, and then darkness, as his mouth found hers.

He tasted of the same need, the same desire she was experiencing. Her mouth opened to the urgency of that need, the inevitability of that mutual desire. Resting her palms lightly on his shoulders, she kissed him. Beneath her fingers she felt the beat of his heart, felt her own accelerate as blood rushed through her veins to pool in the very center of her. She bent forward until her breasts brushed the fabric of his shirt, longing to stretch out beside him and have him take her in his arms.

As though reading her mind, Blake shifted his weight, sliding his hands beneath her sweater, cupping her breasts. Her nipples hardened at his touch, and she sucked in her breath on a moan. Blake skimmed the sweater over her head and strung a chain of kisses along her neck and throat to the swell of her breasts above her bra. He lifted his head, leaving her aching for more. She wanted his mouth on her nipples, his hand between her thighs. Instinctively, she arched toward him.

He fumbled with the clasp behind her back but gave up with a frustrated growl. Emma reached behind her and undid it, letting the wisp of cotton and lace fall beside her sweater. He covered her breasts with his hands and once more lifted his head to claim her lips. After that there was no turning back. Emma unbuttoned his shirt without breaking the kiss. She let her fingers curl into the crisp hair on his chest, felt the rock solidness of bone and muscles beneath her palms.

Kneeling by the couch, she slipped her hands under the waistband of Blake's sweatpants, uncovering the dressing over his wound. He lifted his hips, and she pushed the sweats down and off, then stood to kick off her shoes and wiggle out of her jeans. She stretched out beside him, feeling slightly decadent and wholly feminine. She had never done anything like this before, lie naked on a butter-soft leather couch with a man she *loved*. No, she wouldn't try to analyze the rightness, the utter conviction of that thought. She would only feel.

She trailed her fingers over the flat plane of his stomach, mesmerized by the stark whiteness of the gauze bandage against the darkness of his skin. Then she let her fingers wander lower until she closed her hand around the solidness of his sex.

"Emma, damn it. I don't have any way to protect you if we go any further." His voice was a low, feral growl, and she turned toward him, her hand still wrapped tight around him.

"It's all right," she whispered. "I'm on the pill." She didn't want to think about birth control, or second thoughts, or even think at all. She only wanted to feel, to explore, but he was too impatient for that. He urged her upward until she straddled him, then he pulled her down, taking first one, then the other swollen nipple between his teeth, teasing, arousing until she splayed her hands along his head and brought his mouth to her lips.

His tongue invaded her without preamble, and the sensations he produced demanded repetition in an even more intimate manner. She slid down, letting her breasts brush against his chest, until she felt him at the most intimate of openings and took him deep inside.

He gasped and surged upward, completing the union. Emma met him thrust for thrust, taking the initiative, setting the pace, because she knew the movement must cause him as much pain as pleasure. Time ceased to have meaning for her. She was no longer herself, a being alone, apart, separate. She was a part of him, a melding of bodies and minds and hearts. Arching her back, she took all of him inside her. Then she lowered her head, sought his mouth once more with her own. That final joining sent a ripple of pleasure arcing through her. She climaxed around him. Her release gave him his own, and he shuddered within and without.

Emma laid her head on Blake's shoulder, dazed and

disoriented, retaining only enough sense to keep from resting her full weight on his injured side. She had never responded to lovemaking quite that way before. They were still joined, and she didn't want to break the connection. She felt him lift his hand and smooth it over her hair, his breathing beginning to slow and even out.

Slowly she relaxed, coming back to herself. She was so tired, so sated, she could barely hold her eyes open. "Wow," she mumbled against his throat.

"Wow, yourself," he whispered in her ear with a chuckle.

"That was pretty spectacular."

"Yeah, and I'm only operating on half my cylinders."

She attempted to sit up, her hand going instinctively to touch the bandage on his left side. "I don't think I could live through a full-scale demonstration."

"Me, either." He groaned, though she had barely touched him.

"Did I hurt you?"

"No," he said. "It was just a twinge. Lie down."

"We can't stay here all night." She was beginning to regain her senses and her inhibitions. She couldn't sleep naked on his couch. She needed to get dressed and go home. All her old doubts and fears came crowding back, released from the temporary prison her desire for Blake had exiled them to.

Blake held her still. "You don't have to stay all night. But don't go for a little while, please."

She could no more refuse him than she could pull down the moon. "For a little while," she said, stifling a yawn. She was so tired, not even her doubts about the wisdom of what she had just done could keep her awake. There would be plenty of time for regrets in the morning, but not now. Not with Blake holding her in his arms.

He pulled the cashmere throw over both of them and shifted his weight to find a more comfortable position. Emma snuggled into the curve of his body and wrapped her arms around his neck. She kissed him very softly.

Blake turned his head to kiss her. "I love you, Emma," he whispered against her hair, but she was already fast asleep.

DAMN HIS TIMING. Blake shifted position once more to relieve the incessant ache in his side. He needed a pain pill to get to sleep, and he needed to stretch out in his own bed. But he wasn't about to move an inch from where he was. In the first place, his bedroom and bathroom were still filled with reminders of Heather. It didn't make one damned bit of difference to him if he saw her toothbrush by the sink or her lingerie in the wardrobe, but it sure as hell would make a difference to Emma.

On the other hand, if he woke her now, she'd probably hightail it out of his apartment as though she'd been shot from a gun, and he wouldn't have to worry about her seeing Heather's abandoned belongings. He didn't like either scenario. Almost any amount of pain was worth keeping Emma right where she was. In his arms. He'd make everything right in the morning. And then they would make love again. And again.

God, he had never come like that before. He'd thought for a moment he'd burst a blood vessel, or at least a few stitches. Making love to Emma was just as fantastic as he'd dreamed it would be. The mind boggled at what it would be like when he could pull his own weight in the business. He smiled, but the smile soon gave way to a frown.

There he was, thinking with his balls, not his brain. Definitely not his heart. She hadn't been ready for this, not really. Even the fact that she was on the pill had played into the equation. He hadn't had to worry about protecting her, he'd only had to feel, and that meant taking what he wanted most in the world. Big mistake.

She was too tired and on edge, unsure of what was between them. He'd known that all week, but he couldn't get his pain- and drug-fogged mind to come up with the right plan of action. He had the horrible suspicion that if he'd told her he loved her, as he had up on the mountain, as he'd tried to moments before, she would have nodded, patted his hand and called the nurse to come and give him another pain shot.

But surely after what had just happened between them, she wouldn't react that way. Not if she was awake and rational when he told her what was in his heart.

He loved her. He wanted to spend the rest of his life with her.

But it would be to his disadvantage to forget she'd been badly hurt by an unfaithful lover—made leery by a false case of love at first sight. She wasn't going to be that easily convinced. Her edginess and wary demeanor all the days he'd been in the hospital proved that.

Hell, he didn't even know for sure if she'd sent Tubb packing for good, although he'd bet his last dollar she had. Emma would never give herself to one man if she still felt obligated to another. He held on to that certainty as a tidal wave of fatigue broke over him, sending his thoughts whirling into the void. He clung to the last one he could remember.

Tonight, in the darkness she'd been his, heart and soul.

Tomorrow, in the light of day, he hoped and prayed it would be the same.

CHAPTER FIFTEEN

IT WAS VERY EARLY when Emma awakened. Blake was still asleep, his forehead wrinkled in a frown. He had held her through the night, though it must have been uncomfortable for him. She wiggled out from under the throw, careful not to wake him before she could find her clothes.

She didn't want him to see her naked this morning. She didn't want to make love to him again, not until she could straighten out all the conflicting arguments in her mind. Last night she must have been a little crazy. With love, or merely with lust? Had there really been fantasies dancing in her head of home and hearth and babies? Had Blake told her once more he loved her as she dropped off to sleep, or had she only dreamed it? The doubts were back full force with the dawn, and her stomach roiled with the force of her uncertainty.

The room was still in shadow. She groped around on the floor and found her sweater. Her bra was nowhere to be seen. Holding the sweater in front of her, she looked up to find Blake's eyes on her. "Oh," she said, feeling as dense as the word she had uttered. "I didn't want to wake you."

"Why not? So you could leave without talking about what happened last night?" He sat up, the throw falling to his waist.

Emma rocked back on her heels, clutching the sweater to her like a shield. "No. Of course not." But she felt her face flame. That's precisely what she'd hoped to be able to do. She needed time to herself to sort things out. She couldn't think straight with Blake naked beside her. "I need my clothes." With a shaking hand she pushed her hair back. "I...I can't find my bra."

"It's here," he said, pulling it out from behind a cushion. She snatched it from his hand, refusing to meet his eyes.

"Is there somewhere I can dress?" She wasn't going to crouch there, eyes downcast like a harem girl. She lifted her chin defiantly. She had to be strong. She had to do what was right for her.

"The guest bathroom is the second door on the left down the hall."

He had guessed how badly she wanted to shower, to wash the scent of their lovemaking off her skin. Maybe that's what was making her so dizzy and confused, that constant reminder of how it felt to be in his arms, to have him deep inside her, to be joined so completely. Yes, a shower would restore her sanity.

She looked over her shoulder. If she was as strong as she wanted to be, she'd get up and walk across the room just as she was, but that only brought to mind a vision of Heather coming naked into this very room to meet Daryl.

"Hand me Clint's sweats, and you can have the throw," Blake said, swinging his legs gingerly over the side of the couch.

She grabbed the much-washed cotton pants and handed them over, averting her eyes as he pulled them on. The throw dropped in her lap. She wrapped it around herself, snatched up her panties and slacks and rose awkwardly to her feet. She was stiff and a little sore in unaccustomed places, and she felt her color heighten as she hurried across the room, away from the man who had turned her world upside down in less than a week. He didn't try to stop her.

The guest bathroom was small and old-fashioned, with a pedestal sink and the claw-foot tub she'd imagined. It had a black and white tile floor in tiny hexagon shapes, which had to be original to the building. She wondered if Blake's bathroom had the same kind of high-sided tub, then began to worry about him getting in and out of it with his limited mobility. What if he slipped and fell?

Emma hurried through her shower, goaded by visions of Blake unconscious on the bathroom floor. There were a comb and brush on a shelf above the sink, and several toothbrushes, still in packaging, in the mirrored vanity. She made use of all three and pulled on her clothes. She was beginning to feel a little more in control, but she was still worried about Blake's condition. She opened the door and stuck her head into the hallway. She could hear water running in the room next door. The bathrooms were evidently back to back. She would knock and ask if he was okay. She might be in control, but when she'd made certain he was all right, she was going to turn tail and run.

She had her hand raised to knock when he spoke from behind her. "I'm not in there."

She spun so quickly she had to grab the door frame to steady herself. "I heard water running. I wanted to make sure you were all right." Clint's old pants rode low on his hips and clung to him like a second skin. She wasn't going to let his near nakedness throw her. Wasn't going to reach out and run her fingers over the line of his collarbone or let her lips follow the path her fingers were itching to explore.

"I had to go into the kitchen to get this."

This was a roll of plastic film, the stuff you put on top of leftovers and casserole dishes, the better to see how disgusting they'd become when you dug them out of the refrigerator two weeks later. "Why do you need that?"

"Can't get the dressing wet."

"Oh, of course."

"There's juice and bagels in the kitchen. And there's coffee if you want it. No tea, I'm afraid."

She shook her head. "I'm fine."

"You should be starving. We never got around to eating the soup you fixed last night." His hand was shaking as he fumbled with the ends of the wrap, trying to pull it off the roll without wrinkling it.

"Here, let me do that." It gave her an excuse to touch him one more time. She took the roll of film and smoothed a piece over the dressing. A dark bruise spread out below it, testimony to the damage done to flesh and muscle. He sucked in his breath at her touch, and his sex stirred and hardened beneath the thin cotton sweats. Emma forced herself not to notice. "Am I hurting you?"

He pulled her into his arms. "Emma, don't be so obtuse. You know I want you. You want me, too."

She ignored him, ignored the clamor of her senses, the very real evidence of the truth of his words. Instead she stuck to her Florence Nightingale impersonation. "There. That should keep it dry. Should I tape it, do you think? Just to be sure? Do you have any bandage tape in the bathroom?" She was babbling and she knew it. She pushed open the bathroom door. As an escape route it left a lot to be desired, but she was desperate to get away from the tantalizing heat and hardness of him.

Opening the door was a mistake. The room was twice as big as the guest bath, and the claw-foot tub had been replaced with a huge whirlpool bath. A glass-walled walk-in shower sent billows of steam toward the high ceiling.

It was warm and inviting and Emma felt shivers up and down her spine.

Evidence of more than one person making use of the room was everywhere. Blake's toiletries resided on a glass shelf above the commode, but more feminine touches were visible here and there. Bottles of scent and bath gels in a rainbow of colors, sponges and makeup brushes in a basket near the sink. Another comb and brush sat beside his aftershave, but they weren't brand new, placed there by a thoughtful host for the use of a guest. These were Heather's things. Heather's silvery blond hair caught in the bristles. Heather's silk robe on a hook by the shower.

"Emma, come back here," Blake ordered. He was standing in the doorway, his face a dark, unreadable mask. She could see him clearly reflected in the large mirrored cabinet above the twin sinks. That's where she would find the tape, she thought, clinging to her errand of mercy and the tatters of her composure with all her might. She knew she would find even more intimate details of his life with Heather once she opened that door, but she couldn't stop herself.

"Tape. Do you keep tape in here? Even adhesive bandages would do if you don't stay in the shower for a long time."

She saw him moving toward her, hand outstretched as she swung open the cabinet door. There wasn't any tape, or even many objects on the shelf. Two toothbrushes, two brands of toothpaste, antacid and first aid cream. And a container of birth-control pills.

Heather's birth-control pills.

She slammed the door shut, rattling the glass. She felt as though she'd been kicked in the stomach. *Too soon. Too soon.* Why couldn't she have taken her own advice?

Blake reached out and grabbed her arm, spinning her

to face him. "I love you, Emma." He didn't sound con-flicted. He sounded as sure and certain as he always did. He sounded as if he meant it.

But it didn't help. She searched his face. He wasn't himself. He was pale and haggard, and the pain lines were back, deeper than ever. "Blake, don't. You don't know what you're saying."

"I know exactly what I'm saying. I'm not half-conscious. I'm not half-zonked on pain meds. I love you."

"And barely a week ago you found the woman you thought you loved, naked with the man I thought I wanted to spend the rest of my life with. Listen to how crazy that sounds. You haven't even had time to move her birth control pills out of your medicine cabinet." *One week.* Had it truly been only that long? It seemed half a lifetime. She felt herself spinning out of control. Even though she'd thought she'd fallen in love with Daryl at first sight, she hadn't considered sleeping with him for weeks after that. Now she could barely take two breaths without remem-bering what it felt like to be in Blake's arms. *One week.* She was losing her mind. She had to leave, to get away, or she was going to start crying. Then Blake would gentle his grip and take her in his arms, and she would be lost all over again.

His jaw tensed, and his hold was anything but gentle. She bit her lip to keep from crying out in pain. "Okay, you've got me there. But I didn't love Heather. Not the way I should have. Finding her with Tubb only brought a quick end to a relationship that was already dead. You've got to believe me, Emma."

"Okay. Maybe you didn't love her. But you tried to make yourself believe you did. What proof do I have that your heart isn't pulling the same trick on you with me?"

"I love you." This time his tone was implacable. His

green-gold eyes held hers with the same strength as his hands on her arms. "I love you. And you love me."

She couldn't be as sure as he was. She had to get away from this clawing need for him that warred with her doubts until she could sort through all her conflicting emotions. "No," she said. "I don't know that at all."

BLAKE DIDN'T TRY to follow Emma when she broke from his arms and ran blindly down the hallway, but it took every last ounce of his remaining strength to keep from doing just that.

This wasn't the hill he wanted to die on. He knew damned well he could bring her back to him, maybe even talk her out of enough of her doubts to get her to lie beside him on his big empty bed. But he wasn't going to risk the happiness of the next fifty years of his life on one more incredible session of lovemaking.

Emma was spooked. And she probably had every right to be. Hell, how many sane, intelligent women would believe what he'd just told her? It was too soon. She loved him. He wouldn't let any of the doubts that were so obviously tormenting her get a foothold in his thoughts. It didn't make any difference that they'd met each other at just about the worst moment in both their lives. What had happened was love at first sight, and sooner or later she was going to have to admit it to herself.

Emma, marshmallow-soft, romantic at heart, who had talked herself into believing that a fast-cooling case of the hots for a loser like Tubb was the real McCoy, was going to have to admit she'd fooled herself.

But what they'd found together was the real McCoy.

Love at first sight.

Love for the rest of his life.

And hers.

But he couldn't bully her into accepting that love any more than he could force her to stay with him today.

He wasn't going to storm the beach and get himself blown out of the water.

Besides, he was just too damned weak to follow her to her apartment, lugging a couple dozen roses and ten pounds of candy, and throw himself on his knees and beg her to marry him.

This was going to be a long campaign. And he was going to have to be at his best to win it. Food. Rest. Then recon. He didn't even know where Emma lived, or her phone number. But he would get them both. He'd start with her granddad. The old devil dog was shrewd and protective, but Blake would talk him around. He didn't have any choice. By the time the weekend was over, he'd be ready to go on the offensive.

Blake caught sight of himself in the mirror. He wouldn't be surprised if the grim, determined look on his face hadn't helped scare Emma off. If it hadn't, hearing some of his thoughts of the last five minutes spoken aloud would have. It was funny how you returned to your roots when the going got tough.

He didn't mean the values his gentle, make-love-not-war parents had tried to drum into his head, but the tenets of his stint in the Corps. He was ready to go to war with Emma's doubts. And he intended to win.

"OKAY. I've had it," Armand said, closing the door to the studio very deliberately behind him. "This is the third night in a row you've let this Blake guy hang out there to twist in the wind. I wouldn't have put him on the board if I didn't think he'd be a good call."

Emma had known this was coming, but she still dreaded telling Armand why she had no intention of taking calls from any guy named Blake, even if he was some perfectly innocent computer programmer and not one inactive Marine trying to get onto her show—and into her head.

"I just ran out of time," she lied.

"Three nights in a row?"

"All right. I have a bad feeling about this guy. I don't want to talk to him tonight or any other night."

Armand leaned forward, hands planted firmly on the console. "Are you telling me you don't trust my judgment in screening callers anymore?"

"Of course not."

"Well, you'd never know it from the way you've been acting. Three shows and hardly two dozen calls with any substance to them. How long do you think your audience is going to sit still while you read self-help book reviews and take instant polls on designing a memorial to singles across the country? And where the hell did you come up with the harebrained idea of starting a single by choice support group? You're supposed to be the guru of couples, for God's sake. Are you getting cold feet? Are you trying to sabotage the syndication deal?"

"I want the syndication deal as much as you do."

"You sure don't act like it."

He stomped over to the refrigerator and pulled out a bottle of beer. It had been in there for months, maybe even since the station Christmas party the year before. It was a measure of Armand's agitation that he went looking for it at all. After popping the top, he took a swig, then settled his hip against the console, crossed his arms and fixed her with a penetrating stare. "I want to know what the hell is going on with you. And I want to know it now. It's my future you're trying to flush down the tubes as much as yours."

Lord, this was all she needed. An argument with her best friend and partner. She was going to have to break down and tell him the truth. He was already upset enough over her arbitrary decision to postpone negotiations on the syndication deal for a week without trying to make up any more evasive, half-baked excuses for her behavior.

Emma looked at her hands. They were shaking. She hadn't been sleeping well, and it showed. "I've lost it," she said, glad at last to get the words out into the open. "I'm not taking calls because I don't know what to say to people who want my advice on solving problems with their love lives when mine is an absolute, unmitigated disaster." Horrified, she felt tears run down her cheeks, and ten seconds later a forlorn little sob seeped between her lips. "And I especially don't want to take any calls from Blake—because I don't care how many hundreds of guys there might be in this city with that name, he's the one I'm in love with."

"Jesus, Mary and Joseph," Armand said reverently. "You lost me way back there." He pulled up a chair and swiveled hers to face him. "You're in love? What happened to old Daryl? Not that I'm sorry to see him go. And if you're in love with this out-of-the-blue guy named Blake, why won't you talk to him?"

"Because it can't be love so soon after Daryl and Heather. Not real love. Can it?" She couldn't help asking the question, because, dear heaven, she wanted the answer to be yes. You didn't hurt this bad if it wasn't real love, did you? No wonder some of her callers sounded as if they were in true physical pain. Heartache. There ought to be some kind of pill you could take, a cure-all like her grandfather's hangover elixir.

"You're in love with a guy you met just over a week ago and that you won't talk to?"

"I'm Emma Hart. Queen of Late-Night Talk. The woman with all the answers about your love life." The tears were coming harder. "I'm nothing but a fake and a phony. I can't do this job anymore. How can I tell other people how to live their lives when mine is such a mess?"

CHAPTER SIXTEEN

BLAKE SLID into the booth of the neighborhood pub that was housed in the street-level corner of his building. He was still stiff and sore, but the dizziness and most of the weakness of shock and blood loss were gone. That was good, because he was going to need all his wits about him tonight.

In less than ten minutes he was supposed to meet with Emma's producer, Armand Williams, and he had the suspicion that if it didn't go well, his battle plan for getting Emma back was going up in smoke. And he might end up with a split lip and a black eye, to boot.

Williams hadn't sounded too friendly and he was more than a little protective of Emma—to the same degree as a mother grizzly bear for her cub. Blake wasn't surprised Emma inspired that kind of loyalty in her friends. It had also been evident from the man's first words over the phone that Blake's routine of calling Emma's show every night wasn't going to fly much longer, either. He'd listened every night this week, and she was stumbling badly. And that was his fault, too. Maybe he'd played it wrong that first night back in the city. Maybe he should have gone after her right away and kept her with him until she'd come to her senses and admitted she loved him as much as he loved her.

But it was too late for what ifs now.

He'd made it past Williams's screening process three

nights running. He should have known the other man would be suspicious when Emma refused to take his call every time. Tonight Emma's producer had called him by name, rattled off his address and threatened to inform the cops Blake was stalking his boss if Blake didn't tell him just what the hell he was up to. Blake didn't waste the time or energy trying to feed Emma's producer some line of bull about old high school friendships or practical jokes. He told Williams the truth.

The other man had agreed to meet him at the pub after Emma's show without telling her, but his cooperation was grudging, to say the least. Blake was obviously going to have to do some fast thinking and fast talking to get Williams on his side. The waitress stopped by, interrupting his internal strategy session. She was dressed in an off-the-shoulder frilly white blouse and full, dark green skirt. The bar's theme was an Irish pub complete with dartboards, leaded glass and dark paneling. Thankfully the jukebox was playing good old rock and roll instead of treacly Irish folk songs. Blake ordered coffee. He could use a beer, but he needed his wits about him.

He leaned his head against the high padded back of the booth and watched the door. Exactly five minutes later a tall, coffee-skinned man with a battle-scarred face and a nose that had been broken more than once walked into the bar, gave the half dozen patrons one quick glance and headed straight for Blake's booth.

"Weston?" he asked without preamble.

Blake attempted to stand, but the other man waved him to his seat. He didn't make any effort to shake hands but slid into the booth, opposite Blake. He also didn't waste any time getting to the point.

"All right. I'm here. Now you've got precisely fifteen minutes to convince me why I should go behind Emma's back to help you get to her? Or better yet, why I shouldn't drag you out the back of this place into the alley and beat the hell out of you for making her cry."

"I'm surprised you're giving me fifteen minutes," Blake said, refusing to rise to the other man's bait.

Williams's expression didn't change. "Let's just say I'm feeling generous."

Blake nodded. "Fair enough. I love Emma and I want her back."

"Want her back? Hell, as far as I know, you've never had her. How the hell can you say you're in love with her? You've known her just over a week. And from what she told me, you were in the hospital half-dead for three of those days."

So she had told Williams about him. He didn't know if that was good or bad. Williams had said he'd made her cry. Blake hoped it was from longing, not out of frustration and fear. He pushed the niggling doubts out of his mind.

"I didn't say it made sense." Blake leaned forward until their noses almost touched. Williams was two or three inches taller, but Blake figured he outweighed him by twenty pounds. The other man never moved a muscle. "But it's the truth. And what's more, if she wasn't so screwed up from her time with that bastard Tubb, she'd know she loved me, too."

"I can't argue with you there. Tubb was a real loser," Emma's producer said grudgingly.

"We agree on something."

"We also agree Emma is one special lady."

"Special enough that I want to spend the rest of my life with her."

Armand's eyes were hard, and his gaze bored holes through Blake's skull. Blake didn't flinch. The other man put his palms on the edge of the table and leaned back slightly. "Okay. I believe you. But don't think it's because one look at you convinced me you're Emma's soul mate. I've spent the last twenty-four hours checking you out. If Emma's grandfather—"

"You talked to Emma's grandfather?"

"Damned straight, I did. First person I called. He said he thought you'd be damned good for Emma. Said she sent Tubb packing the night you got shot up there in the wilds of the Berkshires." For the first time, a hint of ordinary human curiosity colored Armand's low baritone. "No shit, Sherlock. Someone shot you?"

Blake gave a curt nod, then smiled. He couldn't help himself. Emma's granddad had vouched for him.

"What's so funny?" Williams took offense at the smile and balled one big hand into a fist on the table between them. "Don't seem to me that someone taking you for a deer and drilling a hole through you is anything to laugh about."

"The old devil dog vouched for me?"

"Devil dog? Emma's grandfather. Yeah."

"Well, I'll be damned. He's the first person I called to track down Emma's phone number and address when I got back to town. He refused to give them to me. He told me to do my own legwork. If I wanted to marry his granddaughter, he said, I was going to have to do my own heavy lifting to get her." It had taken his secretary at B, C and W about three hours to find the information he needed. He would have done it himself, if he could have gotten to the office.

"If you have her home phone and address, how come you've been calling the show? Why didn't you just go to her apartment, camp out on her doorstep, get down on your hands and knees and beg her to marry you?"

"Because I've been listening to her show. She's not taking any more calls than she has to. She's lost her nerve. She's afraid she's lost her insight, right?"

"She's the best there is. But she's running scared. I've talked until I'm blue in the face, but she won't listen."

"That's as much my fault as it is Tubb's. I came along at just the wrong damned moment." Blake caught the other man's quick frown. "The wrong moment for her peace of mind. The rightest damned moment of my life."

"Ain't life a bitch." Armand uncurled his fist and signaled the waitress for a beer.

He leaned against the dark pine wainscoting, and a slow, almost feral smile curled his lips. Blake decided Armand Williams was a man he definitely didn't want to cross. But he would be a hell of a man to have at your back in a fight. The waitress appeared with the beer in record time. Williams picked up the bottle and clicked the base of it against Blake's coffee cup. The smile turned genuine.

"Okay, you've convinced me. I'm going to stick my neck way out on this. You're going to get your shot at talking Rapunzel down out of her tower. And you're going to get the chance to do it on her show. I want you killing two birds with one stone, Weston. You win the fair lady, and you get her talking again. Take it or leave it. It's my only offer."

Blake held out his hand. "One chance is all I need."

EMMA STARED at the console, her fingers hovering over the familiar levers and switches as though she was afraid they had suddenly become electrified and would shock her to death if she touched them. She slid her damp palms down the sides of her slacks, then adjusted her headset.

Armand was watching her from the producer's booth, frowning at her ill-concealed show of nerves.

"You're on in ten," he said into her earphones. The sound of her theme music came up as he used hand signals to count down the remaining few seconds until she was on the air. Emma wished time would stand still. She wished she was anywhere but where she was. She—

"Hello, New York," she said, amazed her voice sounded normal. "This is Emma Hart, and you're listening to *'Night Talk'* on WTKX, the voice of Extreme Talk Radio in the city that never sleeps. We've got a great guest for you tonight. He's Barry Fitzhugh, the author of *Dating Rules in the New Millennium.* He'll be taking calls after the interview, so have your questions ready. We'll be right back after this quick commercial break."

Emma figured she could get through the first hour of the show without fielding any calls on her own. Most self-help authors were more than ready to pontificate for hours on their theories, which let her off the hook. She doubted Blake Weston would try to get through to talk with Barry Fitzhugh.

Armand hadn't been quite the sympathetic sounding board she'd hoped he would be the night before when she'd finally sniffled her way through all the twists and turns of her whirlwind romance with Blake Weston. He'd told her she might be right, that she couldn't be in love with a man she'd known for such a short time. But she sure hadn't been this upset breaking up with Daryl Tubb. If she wanted his two cents worth, he went on, this affair must be pretty damned serious. She was risking both their careers trying to run away from it.

She knew he was right. And she was going to do something about it. Tonight. Or as soon as she could get Blake's phone number and make arrangements to talk to him. She couldn't show up at his apartment unannounced. She wasn't that brave. It had to be someplace neutral, someplace where they could try to hammer out a plan for a cautious, low-key relationship that would give her the time and distance to figure out her true feelings. A flash of the two of them in the lean-to, the terror in her heart as she held him close and prayed he wouldn't die, caught her unaware. That wasn't love, she reminded herself sternly. And neither was the explosive, unplanned sex on his couch.

No more thoughts like that. Take it slow. One step at a time. That was the best way to get her equilibrium back, to be sure her heart wasn't leading her into another emotional dead end. Tomorrow she would call him, even though she would have to ask Armand for the show's call-in logs to get his number. There, see, another argument in favor of taking it very, very slow. How could you be in love with a man whose phone number you didn't even know?

"We're back in sixty seconds." Armand said into her headphones. "And brace yourself. Your author interview just called and canceled. You've got a twenty-minute segment to fill."

"Oh, crap. What should I do?" she asked, her chest tightening in sudden panic.

"Take the damned calls." Armand ground the words out. He wasn't going to be any help. "That's what you get paid for. That's what your audience wants to hear."

"But—"

"Thirty seconds," he said heartlessly. "Here's the first batch up. Do your stuff."

What stuff? Emma thought helplessly. She didn't have any stuff. Not any longer.

She focused on the computer screen just to her left,

which held the name and a brief description of the callers on each line. All seven lines were lit. All seven lines carried the same name! She blinked, then rubbed her eyes. She couldn't believe what she was seeing. A terrible suspicion jumped into her mind. "Fitzhugh didn't cancel. You dumped him, didn't you?" Her voice rose in panic. "I can't do this."

"It's every man for himself tonight, boss," Armand said with a grin that was absolutely fiendish. "I've got a wife with expensive tastes, and two kids to put through college. I want this settled before we go into the syndication negotiations. Pick whichever line you want. You're still gonna get him. Ten. Nine. Eight." His fingers flashed the last five seconds in silence.

She was trapped. No way out. Instinct and habit took over when the green light on her console blinked on. "We're back," she said, and swallowed hard to keep the nerves in her stomach from jumping into her throat and strangling her. "We've got a few technical problems here tonight and lost our connection to our guest. We'll have to try to get Barry Fitzhugh back another evening. In the meantime, let's go to the phones." Which line should she take? It didn't matter. Armand had seen to that. She stabbed the toggle and wished it was Armand's heart. "Blake. You're on 'Night Talk.' This is Emma Hart. What can I do for you tonight?"

"Thanks for taking my call, Emma."

Her heart pounded in her chest, and she had to make herself take a breath. The sound of his voice was almost her undoing. She had never reacted that way to Daryl's voice. She nodded, then scolded herself for the futility of the gesture on radio. It was time she pulled herself together. After all, she was the granddaughter of a man who had fought at Chosin Reservoir. She was the granddaughter of a woman who had traveled halfway around the world to make the soldiers' lives a tiny bit easier. She could take a phone call from a man who had turned her life upside down in a matter of days. "You're welcome, Blake. What's your problem?"

"I fell in love at first sight with a woman who's afraid to trust her instincts when it comes to loving me back."

"Maybe she doesn't say she loves you back because she just doesn't know what real love is." She had worried over that possibility night and day, so it popped out before she could censor the thought.

"Maybe that's part of the problem. She doesn't trust her own instincts even though they're right on the money about everything else." *He loved her.* Emma felt a little smile curve her mouth, then told herself to stop being so easily distracted. This was F. Blake Weston talking, the Cartwright, Braxton and Wheeler golden boy, the Wall Street shark. A man with a mission. He wanted her, and he intended to have her. Love as a power trip was as old as mankind.

"A lot of people don't believe in love at first sight. Especially if they've come off a bad whirlwind relationship in the past." She forgot about Armand and the engineer in the booth. She forgot about the tens of thousands of listeners sharing this conversation with her and Blake.

"That's part of the problem," he admitted. "For both of us. It's made her skittish. I just need to know what advice you'd give me to help her see past the walls she's put up around her heart."

"You've already told her you loved her?"

"More than once."

"And you were sincere?"

"Yes, Emma Martha," he said, his voice calm with

rock solid conviction. "I would have spoken those words to you if it took my last breath to do it."

Emma closed her eyes to hold back the tears. How could she have been so blind? He was still a stranger in many ways, but at last she admitted to herself that she knew Blake Weston well enough to believe what he said. She was there with him in the lean-to once more, could hear the same conviction in his voice. He had been facing death on that mountain, and he had told her what was in his heart.

She had to summon the courage to listen to hers. "Blake." The faint telltale click in her earphones was as loud as a thunderclap. "Blake?"

Dead air.

He was gone. She'd waited a pulse beat too long to reply. The screen in front of her blinked empty for a moment, then reappeared with a dozen new names flashed for her attention, none of them was Blake. "Armand, get him back," she said into the open mike. She didn't care who was listening.

Her eyes flew to the glass partition that separated her from her producer and engineer. Armand lifted his shoulders in a shrug. "That'll take a minute, boss. Why don't you answer another call while I'm working on it."

Answer another call. She couldn't do that. She had to find Blake. Nothing else mattered. The screen continued to blink. She didn't want to talk to these people. Armand could do it.

She lifted her hands to pull off the headphones that tethered her to the console. Armand was watching her with a tight, set look on his face. The engineer beside him was frankly panicked. She thought of the others who depended on her for their jobs, the listeners whose loyalty she depended on for her own. She couldn't just walk away, even if it meant losing the man she so stupidly refused to admit she loved.

Squaring her shoulders, she punched the toggle. "Okay, folks." She hit the cough button that momentarily closed her mike, then cleared her throat. She was a professional; she was going to act like one whether or not she was going to pieces inside, because it was the right thing to do. Her fingers curled into fists and her nails bit into her palms, but her voice came out steady and clear. "There you have it. Your host has a real love-life dilemma of her own. Love at first sight? Is it real or is it chemistry? And if she follows up on it, is she going to live happily ever after or regret it until her dying day? Let's hear your opinions. David on line one. What have you got to say?"

"Wow! This is heavy. I don't really know what to say. I was going to call to ask you what you think of a date who orders the most expensive meal in the restaurant and then leaves most of it on her plate and won't ask for a doggie bag. I work hard for my money. I mean, is it really crass to tell the waiter you want to take it home?"

Emma smiled, using the back of her hand to wipe away her tears. "That is a problem. If the date's going well, I'd say leave the chateaubriand on the plate and look like a real player. If it's not and you don't care if you impress her or not, hey, that's a great piece of beef going to waste."

"Yeah, I kinda thought the same thing. She was a real witch, so I brought the steak home. But I'll remember what you said. It's a good rule of thumb. And, Emma, can I say something else?"

"Sure, David. Fire away."

"I guess I do believe in love at first sight. It's never happened to me, but my mom and dad only knew each other five days before they ran off to Vegas and got married. They've been together for thirty-five years.''

''Thanks, David. That's good to hear. And let me know when you find a girl that either cleans her plate, or suggests you share the leftovers in the morning. Leah, you're on *'Night Talk with Emma Hart.'* It says here you think love at first sight is the most romantic thing that can happen to two human beings. Do you want to expand on that a little?''

''Hi, Emma. Longtime listener. First-time caller. I think that Blake guy, whoever he is, has the sexiest voice I've ever heard....'' Emma let the woman talk, paying her only the slightest attention. The next two calls were a little easier. She had her groove back. By the third, the tears had dried on her face and her hands were no longer trembling, but she was still trembling deep inside with the need to reconnect with Blake.

''Okay, guys. Dion, Ruby and Javier. You're up next, right after the break. This is Emma Hart and you're listening to *'Night Talk'* on WTKX.''

She switched her mike to a secure channel and keyed Armand. ''Is he on the line?'' she asked.

''Nope,'' Armand replied. Emma's heart fell. He wasn't going to call back. She'd lost him, and it was no one's fault but her own.

''Keep trying.'' She may have been her own worst enemy in the past, but now that she'd come to her senses, she wasn't going to give up without a fight. ''I have to talk to him.''

''No problem.'' Armand grinned.

''What? I thought you said you couldn't get him back.''

''Didn't have to, he's right behind you.'' She felt the brush of air across her neck and shoulders as the door to her studio swung open on silent hinges.

Blake was standing there, leaning on a cane. He was dressed all in black, his free hand thrust deep into the pocket of his trench coat. There were still deep grooves carved from nose to chin, but beyond that and the cane, he looked completely recovered from his wound.

"We were cut off," she said, reaching up to pull the headset off.

"You've got two minutes, thirty seconds till we're back," Armand warned, his voice growing faint as she discarded the apparatus and rose from her seat. "Don't waste it."

"I won't," she answered aloud.

"You won't what?" There was a hint of a smile along the edges of his lips, but otherwise Blake didn't make a move toward her.

"I won't waste the two minutes and fifteen seconds we have until the break is over." She took a step toward him. "I thought you'd cut me out of your life when you hung up." There was a distinct quiver in her voice, but she didn't try to cover it up.

"No," he said. "It was just tough love. I wanted you to get back to your show. I knew what you were going to say. I didn't need to hear it right then."

"You're very sure of yourself."

"No," he said. "It was the hardest thing I've ever done."

Emma flew into his arms. "I love you. I should have told you that days ago, but I was afraid. I'm not afraid anymore."

His arms came around her, and he held her so tightly she could scarcely breathe. "I know. I could tell from the way you handled your callers. You're back on track, Emma."

She pressed herself against him, smiling with the rightness of it. "I'd rather stay right here."

"We're down to a minute and a half, and then you're back on the air." His head swooped down, and he covered his mouth with hers. The kiss was quick and deep, soul-shattering and over much too fast. "We'll take it as slow as you want from now on, Emma. Long courtship. Long engagement. Long, long marriage."

"Oh, no, you don't. Now that you've got me, we're going to make this legal ASAP." She looked at him, raised her hand to touch his cheek. He would have kissed her again, but she put her hand on his chest to hold him back. "We've only got a minute left. We've got a million things to work out. What about the McGillicuddy place? Your getting back to your roots? What about the syndication deal?"

"Yes to the McGillicuddy place. I don't give a damn if they elect Tubb mayor of Cooper's Corner. I want that place. I think you do, too. Yes to getting back to my roots. Yes to the syndication deal. Did you think I'd ask you to give it up?"

"I— No. But—" How could they make it all work? She didn't know, but suddenly, excitingly, she wanted to try.

"Some day we'll leave the city. I want to raise my kids where there are trees and grass and creeks to play in. All four of them," he said, smoothing her hair behind her ear.

"All four of them?"

He nodded. "Three boys and a girl."

"Thirty seconds," Armand hollered from the door of the engineering booth.

"Okay. Four. Radio is one career you can adapt to pregnancy." She could see all of them playing in the meadow behind the old farm. The boys would look like

Blake. And her little daughter, she would look like Blake, too. But first things first. Babies would come later. She could see something else in that vision of the future. In the restored barn on their farm, a state-of-the-art broadcast studio. If she was going into this syndication deal, she was going to ride it all the way to the top. Limbaugh had his own studio. So did Imus and Dr. Laura. In five years she would write her own ticket.

She looked at Blake with shining eyes, and he smiled at her. "You can write your own ticket in seven or eight years," he said, reading her mind with no trouble at all, with one exception.

"Five years," she said. "That's all it's going to take." Hours ago she had been too conflicted to decide between whole wheat or rye with her ham sandwich. Now she was settling her career, her future, her entire life in a matter of moments. She was either crazy or truly, irrevocably in love.

"My mistake." He touched her lips to his. "Five years it will be. Then I'll retire to the life of a gentleman farmer, and you can support our substantial brood." He was suddenly serious, his hands tightening almost painfully on her arms. "I love you, Emma Martha. I think I fell in love with you the moment I first saw you. I love you today. I'll love you tomorrow. I'll love you until the day I die and beyond."

"I was a little slower on the uptake," she confessed, feeling the sting of tears behind her eyelids and blinking them back. She wouldn't cry. She was too happy to cry. "But once I make up my mind, there's no changing it. I love you, Blake. Today. Tomorrow. Forever."

"Fifteen seconds," Armand yelled, slamming open the door to his booth.

"Back to work, woman," Blake ordered, spinning her

into her seat. She picked up the headset and slipped it on just as her theme music faded into silence. She felt Blake's hands on her shoulders as he stood silently behind her chair. Reaching up, she covered his hand with her own. She would never be afraid to listen to her heart again. She would never doubt her ability again. She would never doubt love again.

With a flip of the switch, she sent her voice out over the airwaves. "We're back. This is *'Night Talk'* on WTKX. Tonight we're talking about love at first sight. Is it myth? Or is it magic? How many of you have experienced the phenomenon? Did it last? I know what I think about that, but let's hear what you all have to say. C'mon, Manhattan, light up those lines." She turned her head and smiled into Blake's eyes, leaving no doubt that her next words were for him. "This is Emma Hart. Let's take on the night together."

EPILOGUE

Thanksgiving

IT HAD STARTED to snow sometime in the last hour, Maureen observed as she lighted the candles in the deep window recesses of the dining room at Twin Oaks. Not enough on the ground yet to warrant a sleigh ride, but it was still easy enough to envision a Currier and Ives moment, with the church steeple just visible beyond the humpbacked bridge and the hills smoky-gray in the fast falling twilight.

She wondered if Grace Penrose had noticed. Of course, it was over a month before the village Christmas Festival got underway, but as far as the festival organizer was concerned, it was never too early to start snowing. Grace was turning pages for Beth Young as she played the piano in the gathering room. Maureen decided not to disturb the performance. She'd let Grace discover for herself that it was snowing when she called the assembled group in to dinner.

She lingered for a moment, watching the people gathered around the blazing fireplace. Her father was talking animatedly to the couple from Boston who were staying at Twin Oaks because their son was in the military and unable to get back to the States. They hadn't wanted to spend the holiday alone in their empty house, they'd explained, and they didn't want to go to an impersonal hotel.

A friend had suggested Twin Oaks was just what they were looking for. It was exactly the kind of referral that Maureen wanted for the B and B, a place homey enough that people were comfortable spending an important family holiday there.

Her father, bouncing Randi on his knee while Robin hung on to his arm, was laughing at something the gentleman from Boston had said. Justin Cooper looked well, Maureen decided with satisfaction. His new job teaching in an English language school in France had been good for him. She missed him being nearby, but she was happy that he was finding a new life and a new career for himself. Maureen still missed her mother terribly, they all did, but life went on, and the pain grew a little less each day.

Folding her arms beneath her breasts, Maureen turned to survey the dining room. It looked just as picture perfect as the New England landscape. Copper and gold mums and red daisies nestled in crystal vases flanked by lighted tapers. A huge centerpiece of gourds and Indian corn, nuts and apples, topped by a pineapple, anchored the great mahogany table where Clint would carve the turkey.

The sideboard was already groaning under the weight of half a dozen pumpkin and mincemeat pies, molded salads and homemade nut bread. A separate table had been designated for the hot dishes. Clint had hollowed the biggest pumpkin from the garden, saved from Keegan's marauding jack-o'-lantern raid a month earlier, and had turned it into a punch bowl with the help of a plastic liner. The aroma of mulled cider mingling with the myriad other good smells emanating from the kitchen made her stomach growl. She glanced at her wristwatch.

"We'll eat at three," Clint had told her. "I'll call you when I need help bringing dishes to the sideboard. Until then, go mingle. Just keep me informed of the football scores.''

It was two-thirty. All the guests had arrived except Ed Taylor, their neighbor, and Martha and Felix Dorn. But the doctor and his wife would be along shortly. Blake Weston and Emma had left to pick them up an hour ago. A flicker of movement caught Maureen's attention. She leaned forward to look out the window, instinctively keeping out of sight of whoever was outside. Her heart rate had accelerated to an unacceptable level, and she took a couple of deep breaths to settle it. She'd been jumpy since the night Blake Weston had been shot on the mountain. Her cop's instinct told her it hadn't been an accident, even though there'd been no evidence to the contrary so far.

A familiar rail-thin figure was coming up the walkway, stooped shoulders hunched against the cold. Maureen threw open the big door. ''Ed. Happy Thanksgiving! You didn't walk, did you? Why didn't you call? Someone would have come by to give you a ride.''

''Happy Thanksgiving, Maureen. I didn't need a ride. Isn't more than half a mile or so from my place. Sure smells good in here.''

''Dinner will be ready in half an hour or so. Why don't you go warm up by the fire,'' Maureen said, taking his threadbare canvas coat and old felt fedora from his skeletal hands. He'd lost weight over the fall and looked more frail than she'd ever seen him. But she knew how proud he was. He wouldn't welcome any inquiries about how he was taking care of himself these days. She'd leave that task to Felix Dorn. The best help she and Clint could give their neighbor was to keep buying his chickens, something she had every intention of doing. And she'd make sure he had a ride home later in the evening, too. She didn't want him trudging to his farm in the dark.

A car was coming up the drive, and a few minutes later Martha and Felix arrived at the door, accompanied by Blake and Emma. "We haven't kept you from serving dinner, have we?" Martha asked anxiously as Blake took her coat to hang on the brass rack inside the gathering room.

"Clint's resting the turkey. We'll eat in fifteen or twenty minutes."

"We got to talking about wedding plans and lost track of the time," Martha explained, unconsciously rubbing her arthritic hands to ease the ache from being out in the cold.

"You lost track of the time," Felix grumbled. "I didn't. I'm starved half to death."

"A Christmas wedding in Florida. Doesn't that sound lovely?" his wife continued, paying her spouse no heed whatsoever.

"It does," Maureen agreed.

"Very small and very simple," Emma said. "That's the only way I can get Granddad and Blake's parents to even come." Emma helped her grandfather stash his gloves in the pockets of his coat.

"Martha and I are going along to Costa Rica to put a crimp in the honeymoon," Felix said in his usual bad-tempered growl.

"Oh, Felix. We're doing no such thing."

Emma laughed and shooed her grandfather toward the fireplace, where the others were gathering in anticipation of being called to the feast. "Granddad and Nana are going to visit my parents at the consulate in San José. Blake and I are planning to spend a few days in a jungle retreat my parents have visited and enjoyed before. Monkeys come right up to the veranda of your cottage, and there are dolphins swimming in the bay."

"Sounds wonderful."

"It does. It will be the last chance for a vacation I have for a while. The new syndicated version of my show debuts the first week of January."

"I'm looking forward to being able to pick you up on one of the local stations," Maureen said, and meant it.

"I'm looking forward to the new concept. It'll still be cutting edge, but I want to move past the sex-in-the-city format and take on a few more topics. Kind of life-after-sex-in-the-city."

"No more shop talk," Blake interrupted. "Go back to talking about the honeymoon trip. Emma's father found a poison dart frog in their bathroom sink at this place one morning."

"It wasn't a poison frog," she said, wrapping her hand around his arm and giving it a little shake. Blake smiled at her. He seemed completely recovered from the gunshot wound that had nearly taken his life only weeks before. Emma and Blake had accepted Maureen's reluctance to talk about her former life, even though they suspected the shooting might have had something to do with it. It was a sign of true friendship, to Maureen's way of thinking, and she hoped someday she would be able to tell them everything.

"But it was a very big frog."

"Tyskita's a wonderful place." Emma turned her attention to Maureen. "It's going to seem even more wonderful tomorrow morning if I wake up and there's a foot of snow on the ground." She shivered. "It's getting really cold out there."

"I'll make sure you have an extra blanket for tonight," Maureen said automatically. Both Blake and Emma were staying at Twin Oaks, even though Emma's grandparents had protested it would be the last time they would have Emma to themselves.

Blake put his arms around his fiancée and gave her a little hug. "I don't think that will be necessary, Maureen. I'll make sure she stays toasty warm."

Emma turned in his arms and gave him a quick kiss on the cheek. "Shh, don't let Granddad hear you say that. He thinks we have separate rooms."

They walked off hand in hand, Emma's diamond engagement ring sparking fire in the candlelight. If Maureen had had any doubt about the depth of their commitment after such a whirlwind courtship, it had been dispelled over the last few days they had been at Twin Oaks. Blake and Emma were in love. Period. End of discussion. Maureen had no trouble at all envisioning their fiftieth wedding anniversary party here in this very room.

She turned to find her brother watching the exchange from the kitchen doorway. "I must say they do look made for each other. To tell you the truth, I never did see Emma as being right for Daryl Tubb."

"Neither did I. Maybe he'll find the right woman now that he's taken himself off to Boston." Philo and Phyllis had been full of the news of Burt and Lori's youngest turning the Williamstown office of Berkshire Realty over to his manager and moving to Boston. Brokenhearted, they'd hinted, over losing Emma.

"Yeah, maybe." Clint didn't sound convinced. He'd heard the same stories Maureen had about Daryl's numerous lady friends since they'd moved to Cooper's Corner.

Keegan came wandering through the dining room, casting a critical eye over the sideboard and taking a baby carrot from the relish tray. "I'm starving," he said. "When are we going to eat?"

"Ten minutes—as soon as I get rid of this apron and put on my tie," Clint told him. "Wash your hands," he added. "And stay out of the dill dip." The phone in the kitchen started ringing.

"I'll get that," Maureen offered, waving Clint toward the family quarters so he could change. "It might be the Weatherbys' son. He was going to try to call from overseas. Twin Oaks," she said, picking up the receiver. "This is Maureen."

"Mo. Good to hear your voice. It's me, Frank Quigg. Happy Thanksgiving." Maureen pictured her bluff ex-boss at the NYPD, in his trademark rumpled suit and ugly tie. Frank seemed to have a million of them, each more ghastly than the one before.

"Happy Thanksgiving, Frank." A cold shiver went up and down her spine. It had nothing to do with the weather outside. She hadn't heard from Frank in weeks. Why was he calling now? She turned to face the oven, staring unseeingly at the huge, golden-brown bird surrounded by roasted onions and carrots. A tiny corner of her mind wondered where Clint had come across the correspondingly huge china platter it was resting on. It looked big enough to shelter under in a rainstorm.

"How's everything been going up there?" Frank's gravelly voice carried into the kitchen. From the corner of her eye she saw Clint come into the big room, his shirt collar upturned as he struggled with the knot of his tie.

"Who is it?" he mouthed, tossing his jacket across the back of a chair, the better to do battle with his neckwear.

She covered the receiver with her hand. "Frank Quigg."

Clint's brows drew together in a frown. "What does he want?"

"We're fine, Frank," she said into the receiver, ignoring Clint's demand. "But something must not be all right there, or you wouldn't be calling on a holiday."

"Well, yeah. There might be something wrong. I won't sugar-coat this. Owen Nevil's missed his last couple of parole meetings."

"And you only found out today?"

"I'm sorry, Mo. Someone screwed up big time here. It's just a fluke that I came in to the office and saw the report before someone filed it away. Seems Nevil's regular parole officer went on maternity leave early. No one told the replacement I was to be informed if Nevil so much as put a toe wrong. Damn, Mo. I hate like hell to have let you down like this."

Two weeks. Owen Nevil, the brother of the man who had sworn to see her dead, had been on the loose for at least two weeks. As a detective with the NYPD, Maureen had worked on Carl Nevil's case, and her testimony had helped place the murderer behind bars. She'd come to Twin Oaks to start a new life—a safe life—for her twin daughters, but she was worried that the Nevil brothers had found out where she was. The cold shiver of dread came back, magnified a hundred times.

"You've completely lost track of him?"

"'Fraid so. About three weeks ago he took off for a day or two, but he showed up for one more meeting. Then, pfft. Gone. Damn it, Mo. I don't know what to tell you to do next."

"It's okay, Frank. This was out of your control."

"I don't like things that are out of my control. I'll get someone tracking down leads first thing in the morning," he continued. "Just as soon as I'm done giving my people a good chewing out. I've already contacted the Massachusetts highway patrol. I'll get word out to your county sheriff's department, too. I'm sorry as hell to spoil your Thanksgiving, Mo. But I thought you'd want to know.''

"Thanks for the heads-up, Frank.''

"Watch your back, detective.''

"I will. Goodbye, Frank.''

"What's up?'' Clint demanded.

"Owen Nevil's disappeared. Someone broke the line of communication and didn't let Frank know he'd skipped town. He's been gone at least two weeks. Maybe longer.''

Clint's brows snapped together. "Maybe longer?''

"He disappeared for a day or two three weeks ago.''

"That would have been about the time that Blake Weston was shot.'' Clint had given up trying to tie his tie. He yanked it off and leaned both hands on the back of a chair. "Are you thinking what I'm thinking?''

Maureen couldn't help herself. Her eyes went to the hook where she'd always hung her sage green coat. "That Emma Hart and I look enough alike from a distance we might be mistaken for each other?''

"Damned right, you could.''

"The thought's crossed my mind more than once.''

"Mine, too.'' Clint lunged for the phone. "I'm calling Scott Hunter.''

Maureen reached out and stopped him from punching in the highway patrol lieutenant's number. "No. This is Scott and Laurel's first Thanksgiving together. There's nothing he can do tonight, anyway.''

"First thing tomorrow morning, then. You think it could have been Nevil who shot Blake Weston, don't you?''

"Yes.'' She couldn't hide her fears from Clint. She didn't want to.

"Me, too. I've got a permanent crick in my neck from looking over my shoulder all the time.''

"Just because you're paranoid doesn't mean someone isn't following you," she said as lightly as she could. She felt the corded muscles in his arm relax slightly. She picked up his tie and slipped it around his neck, knotting it the way she used to when he was a little boy getting ready for Sunday school. "I'm a big girl, Clint. I was a cop. A good one. I can take care of myself."

"You don't have eyes in the back of your head."

"That's what you're here for, bro. To watch my back."

"So what do we do next?" She took his jacket off the back of the chair and held it so he could slip his arms into the sleeves.

"You're going to pick up that incredibly delicious-looking turkey and carry it into the dining room, and I'm going to put on my best innkeeper's smile and say to our guests, "'Ladies and gentlemen, dinner is served.'"

Welcome to Twin Oaks—the new B and B in Cooper's Corner. Some come for pleasure, others for passion—and one to set things straight...

COOPER'S CORNER, *a new Harlequin continuity series, continues in November 2002 with MY CHRISTMAS COWBOY by Kate Hoffmann*

Bah humbug! That's what single mom Grace Penrose felt about Christmas this year. Grace was in charge of the annual Cooper's Corner Christmas Festival, and so far there was no snow, moths had eaten the pageant costumes and the sleigh-ride horses had just been sold to Montana rancher Tucker McCabe.

Here's a preview!

CHAPTER ONE

TUCK CAREFULLY FOLDED the bill of sale and slipped it into the breast pocket of his canvas jacket. "I have to hit the road," he muttered. "I've got to be in Pennsylvania by nightfall."

All hope drained from her expression and she reluctantly nodded. "I—I suppose you have a wife waiting for you at home. Big plans for the holiday."

"Nope," he replied as he jogged down the steps and headed to the barn. "No wife. But I do have plans." Plans to find himself a woman. But he couldn't say that out loud.

"Why do you even want these horses? You haven't even looked at them."

"My friend at Tufts has, and he says they're a good buy. And I've been looking for some harness-broke stock for a while."

She was beside him in an instant, her fingers clutched around his arm. He stopped and only then realized the effect of such an innocent touch. God, he really did need a woman! "Let me make you another offer I don't think you'll be able to refuse," she said.

He stared down at her. Tuck wasn't sure what it was about Grace Penrose that he found so appealing, whether it was her guileless beauty or her unabashed pluck, but he suspected once she turned those huge doe eyes on any man, he'd have a hard time refusing. Hell, why not listen to her offer? He didn't have any place to be. Pennsylvania could wait. And that warm, willing woman would be there when he needed her—hell, she might be here in… Massachusetts? "All right," he muttered. "I guess my plans could wait. Let's hear it."

"I can offer you the picture-perfect New England holiday experience," Grace said. "You'll enjoy Christmas here, in Cooper's Corner. I get you a room at our very popular bed-and-breakfast, the Twin Oaks Inn. It's a lovely place. I'll pay for the feed for your horses."

"What about my kids?" he asked.

"Kids?"

"I have nine kids in the trailer. They have to be fed, too."

Grace's eyes went wide. "You—you let children ride in a smelly old horse trailer?"

The look of sheer horror on her face was enough to make the misunderstanding worthwhile. "Yeah, come on." He took her hand and pulled her along after him. "I want to introduce you. After all, you'll be spending a lot of time together in the next few weeks. And they do love to eat."

She tagged along after him, and when they reached the trailer he unhitched the door and swung it open. Tuck hopped inside and held out his hand. Grace reluctantly took it, then followed him into the dark interior of the trailer. When they reached the front, Tuck leaned over a rope barrier. "These are my kids," he said.

Grace pasted a smile on her face and stepped up beside him. Her smile faded. "These are goats," she said.

"Kids. Young goats are called kids."

"I—I thought— I mean, when you said 'kids,' I assumed you meant—"

"I know what you assumed," he said. "No wife, no plans and no children, either."

She studied the goats for a long moment. "All right, nine goats and four horses. Silas has already agreed that you can keep them in his barn until the festival is over. So that solves one problem. I think I can get Dave over at the feed store to donate food for the animals. Do we have a deal?"

"Not so fast," Tuck said, enjoying the barter a little too much. "We've decided how to feed my animals. What about me?"

Grace blinked. "You?"

"Who's going to feed me? If I'm correct, a bed-and-breakfast only provides breakfast. I'll need lunch and dinner."

"Well, I suppose I could give you a small stipend for your meals. There's a nice little café in town where you could—"

"Naw. I'm not much for eating out. How are you in the kitchen?"

"What?"

"I'm pretty much a meat-and-potatoes kind of guy. Nothin' too fancy. I like my lunch at noon and dinner at five. In between, I can fend for myself."

Grace gasped. "You expect me to cook for you?"

Tuck watched the expression of horror return to her face. She was so easy to tease, and so pretty to look at. Grace Penrose probably appeared quite plain to the casual observer. But looks could be deceiving. A man had to look closer—to the perfect complexion and the wide, sensual mouth. To eyes that mirrored her every emotion and to a voice that could make a man go crazy with lust just listening to it. To a body not fashionably thin, but feminine, with curves in all the right places.

Not that he was looking, Tuck told himself. Grace was definitely not the kind of woman he usually associated with, the kind of woman who wore her desire on the outside. She wasn't the kind of woman a guy just seduced, then dumped. Grace Penrose was the kind of woman that a guy—a nice guy—might marry.

Tuck swallowed hard. "And I expect some help caring for the horses and the goats. If my horses are going to appear in public, they're going to have to look good. And that takes work. Hard work."

She thought about the deal for a long moment, then nodded. "All right. It's a deal."

Tuck smiled. Maybe this wouldn't be such a bad holiday season after all. It would be like a little vacation, a stay in a picturesque New England town with all his needs catered to by a pretty woman. He glanced down at the hand she offered, and he took her fingers in his, wondering at the warmth that seeped up his arm at her touch. "Deal," he murmured. He let his grasp linger for a moment before he dropped her hand. "Now, why don't you and I get my goats unloaded, then we'll take my stuff over to this bed-and-breakfast place."

Grace pushed her glasses up the bridge of her nose, then nodded, watching the goats warily. "Do goats bite?"

Tuck chuckled. She was quite a woman, this Grace Penrose. And he was looking forward to knowing her a little better.

COOPER'S CORNER

FREE Bathroom Accessories
With proofs of purchase
from Cooper's Corner titles.

YES! Please send me my FREE bathroom accessory without cost or obligation, except for shipping and handling.

<u>In U.S., mail to:</u>
COOPER'S CORNER
P.O. Box 9047
Buffalo, NY
14269-9047

<u>In CANADA, mail to:</u>
COOPER'S CORNER
P.O. Box 613
Fort Erie, ON
L2A 5X3

Name (PLEASE PRINT)

Address   Apt. #

City   State/Prov.   Zip/Postal Code

Enclosed are three (3) proofs of purchase from three (3) different Cooper's Corner titles and $1.50 shipping and handling, for the first item, $0.50 for each additional item selected.

Please specify which item(s) you would like to receive:

❑   Liquid Soap Dispenser
❑   Soap Dish
❑   Toothbrush Holder
❑   Drinking Cup

COOPER'S
CORNER
ONE PROOF
OF PURCHASE
CCPOP

093 KJJ DNC4   © 2002 Harlequin Enterprises Limited   CCPOP

International bestselling author

SANDRA MARTON

invites you to attend the

WEDDING *of the* YEAR

Glitz and glamour prevail in this volume
containing a trio of stories in which
three couples meet at a
high society wedding—and
soon find themselves
walking down the aisle!

Look for it in November 2002.

If you enjoyed what you just read,
then we've got an offer you can't resist!

Take 2
bestselling novels FREE!
Plus get a FREE surprise gift!

Welcome to Twin Oaks—
the new B and B in Cooper's Corner.
Some come for pleasure, others for passion—
and one to set things straight...

C O O P E R ' S   C O R N E R

If you missed the first two books in the
Cooper's Corner series, here's your
chance to order your copies today!